What's Left Unsaid

What's Left Unsaid

Deborah Stone

Matador
9 Priory Business Park,
Wistow Road, Kibworth Beauchamp,
Leicestershire, LE8 0RX
Tel: 0116 279 2299
Email: books@troubador.co.uk
Web: www.troubador.co.uk/matador
Twitter: @matadorbooks

ISBN 978 1789014 921

British Library Cataloguing in Publication Data.
A catalogue record for this book is available from the British Library.

Printed on FSC accredited paper
Printed and bound in Great Britain by 4edge Limited
Typeset in 11pt Aldine by Troubador Publishing Ltd, Leicester, UK

Matador is an imprint of Troubador Publishing Ltd

To my father

Living a lie will mess you up
Gilbert Baker

Part One

Joe

If Annie had just been honest with me, we might have avoided much of the ugliness which followed…but she wasn't and we didn't. I sometimes wonder if I should blame myself. After all, throughout my life, I prided myself on being a great reader of souls. Yet it appears that I missed all the signs. Or did I simply choose the path of least resistance? I have so much time on my hands now to contemplate my possible past motivations; a task which I recognise is ultimately futile. The truth is that I accepted what the fates threw at me. Annie and I created a set of armour plating to hide behind as we forged through our lives, colliding with others in our path, damaging them.

Sasha

I heard a strange scratching sound as I reached the top of the stairs leading to my attic office. I glanced around before taking another step, but I could see nothing in the hallway. I edged towards the door, floorboards creaking underneath my feet, my heart picking up speed. Walking slowly towards my desk, I saw one of my files lying open, weighted down with a pair of scissors. I picked them up and glancing around, I crept over to the window and rattled it. It was tightly shut.

'Boo!'

I jumped, dropping the scissors to the floor. The tea I was holding leapt in a perfect arc into my handbag. 'Jesus, Zac! You frightened the life out of me. What the hell are you doing hiding behind the door? Damn.' I grabbed a wad of tissues from the box on the filing cabinet and swabbed my phone, pressing the home button to check it was still functioning. 'I didn't realise you'd be back so early today.'

'I just thought I'd surprise you,' Zac answered. 'I had an unexpected free period.' His face looked slightly flushed and he was still wearing his football kit, his long legs caked in dried mud. There were streaks of dirt on his cheeks and neck, as though he had made a poor attempt at army camouflage.

'You almost gave me a bloody heart attack, you idiot! What are you doing up here anyway?'

'I was just looking for some sticky tape to fix the cover on my book.'

'You've got some on your desk in your bedroom. If you tidied up a bit, you might even find it. But before you do that, can you go and shower? You're dropping mud all over my floor. How many times have I asked you to take your filthy kit off before walking dirt all over the house?'

'Christ, you're in a bad mood. Hello to you too.' Zac lurched towards the doorway. He was so tall now that he needed to duck slightly as he crossed over the threshold. He hurdled down the stairs two at a time, flecks of soil bouncing off him as he went.

I could feel a headache wrestling to emerge from between my temples. I sighed and closed the opened file, placing it back on the left-hand side of my desk in its correct colour-coded position. I didn't know what Zac had been doing in my office. It was bad enough that he could never put away anything that he'd used, but especially so when he moved stuff in my personal space. It was a great source of irritation to someone like me, whose debilitating OCD required all things to be in all the right places at all times.

I bent down to retrieve the scissors and replace them in my drawer, but they would not close together and the blades seemed to be blunted. What the hell had

Zac been up to? It was then I noticed that the metal around the lock of the centre drawer of my treasured antique desk was scratched. Clutching the scissors, I bolted downstairs to Zac's room, banging on the door. There was no answer, no doubt because he had already plugged in his wretched earphones. One day, he would have to have them surgically removed. Wrenching open the bedroom door, I stormed up behind him and yanked them out.

'Get off, will you, Mum. You'll break them!' Zac barked, grabbing his earphones back.

'Never mind your damned earphones, Zac,' I shouted, waving the scissors in front of him. 'What about my bloody desk? It's scratched to hell. And you must have used these scissors. They're totally bent out of shape.'

'A bit like you,' Zac retorted.

'Excuse me? What did you just say? Look, Zac, I don't know what you were doing in my office, but what I do know is that my desk is badly damaged.' I waved the scissors at him like a deranged psychopath on day release. 'I've had that desk for years and it'll cost a fortune to fix. And you've got no business in my drawer. It's private. How would you like it if I poked around in your stuff?'

'I didn't bloody touch it, OK? What would I want in your mangy drawer anyway? Are you actually accusing me of burgling your desk? You're so lame.' He turned away from me and slumped face down on the bed, pulling a pillow over his head.

'How many times have I asked you to show some respect for other people's property?'

Zac snorted, lobbing the pillow at me, which narrowly missed. 'I'll show you respect when you show some to me.'

'Excuse me?'

'You know what I mean.'

'Zac, what on earth are you talking about? First, you frighten the life out of me, and then you get defensive the moment I ask you a question. I really don't have the time, or frankly, the energy, for your nonsense today. And somehow this conversation seems to have turned from me asking you what the hell you've been doing in my office, to you accusing me of something, which is what, exactly?'

'Why don't you tell me?' Zac glowered at me, unblinking.

'You're not making any sense, Zac and you know I don't enjoy riddles, so spit it out.'

'Ooh, that's a good one,' he replied, sitting up and staring straight at me as though I were now his sworn enemy. 'You do like riddles, as it turns out, so why don't you spit it out? What are you hiding up there that's so important anyway?'

A flush of heat tore around my body and I could feel sweat trickling down my back and seeping underneath my bra. Unbidden tears pricked my eyes and for a moment, I couldn't answer him. Zac lay on his unmade bed, prone and half camouflaged in a pile of dirty washing, wiring himself back into his iPod.

'Zac,' I shouted, pulling an ear bud out of his head yet again, 'in future, just stay out of my damned office, will you!' He just stared at me, unblinking, defiant. 'Right, I'll speak to your father about your behaviour later. Right now, I need to feed Stanley, reply to a snotty email from my wretched new client, and decide what to cook for dinner.'

'Just get out of my room. You're totally pathetic.'

It must have been a combination of the magic words 'feed Stanley' and 'dinner', because at that precise moment, Stanley arrived behind me – even though, technically, he wasn't allowed upstairs – tail wagging, brown eyes wet with hunger. With every movement, he signalled imminent starvation. He was, after all, a golden retriever. 'OK, Stanley, let's go. Kibble awaits.' As I turned to leave Zac's room, my toe caught a glass of chocolate milk – it had clearly been left on the floor for several days – sending globules of foul smelling liquid all over the cream carpet. Well, it was a stupid choice of colour for a teenaged boy's floor, but anyway. Stanley waited expectantly at the top of the stairs. 'Christ, that's all I need. What the hell was that doing there? Zac, get up and fetch me a towel, will you?'

Naturally, Zac couldn't hear, because he'd stuffed his earphones back into his lugholes yet again and was too busy staring at some inanity on Twitter to notice that anything was amiss. The chocolate concoction was soaking rapidly into the cream carpet, so I bolted downstairs for a couple of towels, stopping to wet them in the bathroom. Running the tap, I glanced up at myself in the mirror. Deep, dark shadows underscored my eyes and my mascara had flaked. I hoped I hadn't looked like this in my meeting. The client must have thought she was conversing with a zombie, or at the very least, someone who'd had a traumatic experience on the way to see her. I reassured myself with the well-known fact that bathroom lighting is never flattering, but these days, I wasn't too sure which light was. What I really wanted was to be able to wander around in soft focus, like older actresses in films. Living life through a filter would improve so many things. I wrung the towels out and headed back to tackle the carpet. Sinking to my knees, I scrubbed away for several minutes, with Stanley standing over me watching, head cocked to one side like a benign inspector. I got the worst of it out and when I stood up, my knees complained of being locked in one position for too long.

It was then that I noticed the mess under Zac's desk. There were books, football magazines, balls of paper, empty ink cartridges, tangled headphones, various assorted wires and pieces of Blutak – anthills of detritus. 'Zac, Zac!' I shouted, yanking the perennial earphone out of the left side of his head, attempting to reconnect him with reality.

'What now?' Zac scowled.

'Stop being rude, Zac. Please. Look at all this mess underneath your desk. Find a bin bag and get rid of some of this rubbish, will you? I don't know how you can work in such a dump.'

'It's my room and I can keep it how I want. I'm seventeen years old, not five. Stop telling me what to do.' Zac kicked his legs down hard onto the bed like a toddler having a tantrum. Filthy laundry bounced underneath him, emitting unpleasant odours of teenage boy.

'And it's my house, so sort it out. I'm going downstairs to make dinner and when you're in a better mood, perhaps we can talk about what you were really doing upstairs when I came in.'

Zac rolled onto his side away from me. 'When *I'm* in a better mood? Jesus!'

I ignored him. 'Come on, Stanley. It's definitely time for kibble now.' I wheeled around and Stanley took his cue, leading the way out of the door, tail wafting. He turned his head to make sure that, this time, I was following him towards his bowl. Zac slammed the door shut behind us. I reminded myself to buy some new scissors and maybe to think about fitting a lock on my office door.

Joe

I'm not sure I agree with Kant. He asserted that people only lie out of selfishness to get what they want, and for that reason, one should never lie under any circumstance. But surely there are occasions – many occasions, in fact – when it is preferable not to tell the truth, or at least to fudge it, bend it, or possibly deny its very existence. Childhood is built upon a bed of lies – Father Christmas, the Tooth Fairy, the Bogeyman. Yet we do not all grow up to be corrupt individuals, bereft of any understanding of right and wrong. We lie to protect our children, to shelter them from emotional harm. Can you honestly tell me that you have never told a little white lie to save the feelings of others? I know I can't. The question is, in hindsight, was it the correct thing to do?

Annie

I think I might have said the wrong thing to Zac. I'm sitting here in the conservatory, chatting to him and we're watching the sparrows eat the breadcrumbs, which Zac has spread out for them on the garden table. They nibble at them in short, sharp bursts, glancing around in case some larger bird might arrive to spoil their feast. He's a good boy, Zac, coming to see his Grandma every so often. I make him a cheese sandwich and give him milk to drink and he tells me about his day and I tell him about mine. I don't have a great deal to say, but fortunately Zac does. He's a very chatty boy. He explains what he gets up to at school and what he's studying, although I usually forget what he's told me five minutes later. He's very handsome, rather like his Grandad. He reminds me very much of Joe, only he's much taller. He's got the same thick dark hair, deep brown eyes and a smile which warms your insides. When he walks in, I think, Joe is back. Hi, Joe, I don't remember you being so tall and how much younger you look. You look younger than you did when we first met. Then Zac says, 'Hello Grandma' and I realise it's not Joe. How I miss Joe.

I'm showing Zac one of my old photo albums with ancient pictures of Joe and me with all our celebrity friends back in the day. My stereo is belting out 'Downtown' by Petula Clark. I do love Petula. She's so neat and tidy, you know, elegant. I met her once, but I can't remember where. 'Look, Zac, this is Jackie Lamarr, one of the most famous actresses in the Sixties. She was in that thriller with – you know – what's his name? I can't quite remember. Never mind. Look at her fabulous fox fur and those diamond earrings. Not hers, mind you. Always rented. She never had a penny to her name. Terrible gambler, you know. And this is Billy Burns, who read the BBC News, in the days when all the newsreaders looked smart and spoke properly. Not like today when you can't understand half of them.' Zac smiles, but I don't think he can remember any of these people. Before his time, I suppose.

Then I show him some pictures of Joe in his heyday. Joe has a photograph taken with every guest he invites onto his show – he insists on it – and we take many more photos later, at the after-show parties. Joe parades up and down with his dark hair slicked back, wearing the smart navy blue suit with a slight sheen to it and a thin red tie with his matching handkerchief peeping out of the top of his jacket pocket. I show Zac pictures of me as well. In one of my favourites, I'm wearing a shimmering silver floor length evening gown. He tells me how stunning I look. A real glamour puss, he calls me. I feel my cheeks redden.

In another album there are photos of Zac's mum, Sasha, pouting at the camera. Such a vain little girl, always posing. There are hundreds of photos of Sasha and Joe together. Joe adores her. They are inseparable. Well, they were, Zac reminds me. He tells me how much Sasha misses Joe. She doesn't miss him as much as I do, I tell him. A child can never miss their parent as much as a wife misses her husband. How many times have I told her that? She is so self-indulgent. Zac tells me how he wishes that he could remember his Grandad. I show Zac photos of Sasha and Jeremy. Zac laughs at the clothes his mum and dad are wearing with their high shoulder pads and enormous glasses. He is shocked to see that Jeremy has a full head of shaggy brown hair.

I show Zac some of his baby photos. 'Here's you, Zac, with your Grandad Joe. You were such a beautiful baby.' He picks up the photo of a bare baby lying face down on his plastic changing mat, smiling up at the camera. Joe is standing next to him with an air of uncertainty, as if he's frightened that the baby is about to do something which he can't handle. Zac turns the picture over and frowns.

'Grandma, this date says 1996. I was born in 1998.'

'Oh, that's the other one,' I say.

'The other one?' Zac is staring at me oddly and pulling at his fringe, rolling his hair into tight twists. 'What other one?'

I stop. I think I've got a bit confused. I know there's something I've muddled up here. Something I'm not supposed to say. I fiddle with the buttons on my cardigan. One of them is coming loose, but I can't sew it back on any more. My hands won't work the thread. 'I don't mean the other one. I mean you, love.'

'But I wasn't born until 1998. This says 96.'

I need the toilet and start to get up, using the arm of the chair to heave myself forwards.

'Oh, I don't know, Zac. You know Grandma's stupid. I probably wrote down the wrong date. Now fetch me my stick, would you?' He's staring at me, but I inch past him, reaching for the wall to steady myself.

Zac leaves just after I shuffle back to my chair. I know I've said the wrong thing. I must remember to tell Sasha. I'll ring her later, when I've had a short rest. I settle down in my chair, using my hands to wrench my knees onto the poof, before pulling the blanket over them. That's better. I reach for the TV remote. The racing is on. The horses are so handsome. I'll just watch the races for a bit. Just for a moment, until I get my breath back.

Joe

I am watching her age. When I passed on, she was only in her sixties; elegant, willowy, still a head turner. She is shrunken now, desiccated. Inch by inch, she concertinas in on herself, her back bent into a permanent question mark. We speak regularly, of course. She asks me how much longer it will be before we can resume our life together, sitting side by side, sipping whisky with a little water and ruminating on our day? I cannot answer her. I can only observe her wilting, shedding herself, leaf by leaf. I want to tell her that when she does arrive, life will be different, infinitely improved. Past deeds and dirty secrets will no longer haunt her. She will wear her red stiletto heels once again and swish her pleated skirt as she glides along. I will be there to hold her hand.

Sasha

I'd started to dread it, the after school pick up. That probably made me a terrible mother, but something was going on with Zac. I just didn't know what. He'd been acting oddly ever since the desk incident. I wished there was a notification, an email or text, something, which parents received to say, 'Warning. This is the last day you will spend with your gorgeous child before they become stroppy and completely uncommunicative, if not downright strange and bloody awkward.' If there was, we could not only steel ourselves for the onslaught which can – if you're really unlucky – last for several years, but also savour those last moments of sweetness, spontaneous kisses, hand holding and I-love-yous. Whoever invents that particular app will become a billionaire.

I waited at the bus stop, hovering on a double yellow line next to the betting shop, with its trickle of unsavoury characters wandering unsteadily across its threshold, while keeping an eye out for over-zealous traffic wardens, who seemed to be able to issue a ticket before you could get the car back into first gear. The school bus finally crawled up to the stop and the doors folded open, ejecting a cornucopia of boys of differing shapes and sizes. The younger ones emerged weary, but happy, uniforms intact, blazers on, balancing their school bags and instruments as they looked around for their pick up, smiles on their faces. The older ones tumbled out looking as though there had been an attack en route, or at the very least, a small skirmish, with untucked ink-stained shirts, ties loose or missing and bags unzipped and overflowing. Hairstyles ranged from barely there to birds' nests. They chatted and hit each other, before sauntering off in different directions, as if they didn't have a care in the world. At the back of the bus, I could see Zac, his dark hair flopping over his eyes and his head scraping the roof. He nodded to Tim, who had been his friend since they started in Year Seven and with whom he now shared the title of King of the Bus, which meant absolutely nothing, except that they were the two most senior boys on that route and crucially, they got to sit on the back seat.

Zac spied me waiting in the car and walked over unsmiling. My chest tightened. I unlocked the passenger door and Zac opened it, slinging his bag onto the back seat before folding himself into the front.

'Hi, sweetheart, how was your day?' I smiled, hoping he would be in a better mood than of late.

'Fine,' Zac intoned, looking studiously out of the window.

'That's good. And how was football?'

'Fine.'

'And did you win?'

'No,' he muttered.

'Oh, I'm sorry to hear that. Well, never mind. There's always Saturday.'

Zac turned towards me sharply. 'Never mind? You just don't get it, do you? You can't say never mind when you lose. You have to care. You don't care about anything, do you?'

My neck felt hot. Here we go. 'Well, you know I don't really understand football, Zac, but I'm genuinely sorry that you lost. I'm not sure what else I can say, but I have made lamb chops for tea and your favourite chocolate cake, you know, the one with the gooey middle, so that might cheer you up.' When Zac was little, he used to call this cake *chocolate cake with chocolate spurting out of it*. If only restaurants used such perfect descriptors of their wares.

Zac rolled his eyes. 'I had a burger before I got on the bus and I'm not hungry. Anyway, I need to work when I get in.' He wound the window down and a blast of icy air assaulted my left cheek. I held my breath. I often found this more effective than counting to ten, as more often than not, I didn't reach ten. 'Well, maybe you can eat again with Dad and me later?'

'Oh, he's home tonight, is he? Good of him to put in an appearance.'

I could feel Zac's hard stare on the side of my face, and I whipped my head around to face him as we pulled up at the traffic lights. 'What's that supposed to mean? You know how hard your father works.' I was trying hard not to raise my voice, but I squeaked slightly with the effort.

'Everyone works hard, but they still get back in the evening to see their wife and kids. He's literally never home. He can't be in the office 24/7. How do you know where he actually is?'

'I don't know where he is every minute of every day, but he doesn't know where I am all day either. When you're married to someone, you have to trust them, and we wouldn't want to live in each other's pockets anyway. You're being ridiculous, Zac. What's got into you recently?'

We turned into our road and onto the drive, gravel crunching angrily beneath the car. I turned off the ignition and grabbed for my handbag, which was tucked by Zac's feet. He lifted it up and thrust it towards me, spilling the contents all over the dash. I really ought to get a bag which zips up.

'You've got no idea, have you? Or are you just not interested, like the football?' He got out of the car, striding off to open the front door, which he promptly slammed shut before I could follow him.

'Zac! Come back here! I won't have you slamming doors in my face! Zac! You've dropped all my stuff all over the car. Come back and clean it up!' I felt around on the floor and under the seat to retrieve my things and then banged the door knocker and rang the bell, but Zac didn't come to let me in. I fumbled around in my bag for my keys, which I seemed to have lost. They were probably still under the seat of the car. I could see Stanley smiling at me from the hallway, welcoming me home and wondering why I wasn't coming in.

Jeremy returned late as he did so often and dinner was burnt. I never understood why it was so difficult to pick up a phone, or email, or text, or message to say, 'I'm delayed. Please hold dinner,' yet somehow there was always time to read trivial Twitter updates on some footballer's latest gaff. Jeremy sat opposite me at the kitchen table, chewing his leathern chicken and picking at the wilted asparagus amidst the smell of gently smoking oven, while flicking through the newspaper. 'Where's Zac?' he asked without looking up, his mouth slightly open and full of food.

'Upstairs. I don't know what's got into him at the moment, Jeremy. I think maybe you should have a chat with him. I think he's missing not having you around so much.'

Jeremy glanced up at me over the rims of his glasses, raising his bushy salt and pepper monobrow slightly before returning to survey the unappetising contents of his plate. 'I'm not sure I follow, Sasha. I'm never here that much, so why does he suddenly mind?' He washed his mouthful down with a large slug of red wine.

'I suppose because you're his Dad and as he gets older, he'd prefer a bit of male company, instead of having to chat solely to his dear old mother every day. Maybe there are things he'd like to talk to you about that he feels he can't discuss with me. You know, men's talk. I read this really interesting book recently about how teenage boys need their father more than their mother at this age, as well as an external male mentor. Maybe we need to think about who might be a good mentor for Zac?' I leant across to touch Jeremy's hand, but he pulled it away in favour of the remote control.

'He never discusses anything with me, Sash,' Jeremy murmured, staring at the television screen as it flickered into life. 'You know that, so why would he start now? He's probably just being a teenager.'

'Look, please try to talk to him before we go to bed. I'm genuinely worried about him. Maybe there's something going on at school that he won't tell me about. Otherwise, you're away until Friday. I'm sure he'd appreciate it.'

Jeremy scowled as he flicked through the Sky channels. 'It's incredible, isn't it? We now have a million channels and yet, there's still nothing to watch on any of them. Look, I'll try to talk to Zac later, but I can't just bring it up out of nowhere. It has to be the right time.'

It has to be the right time. That's what Jeremy said whenever I asked him specifically to speak to Zac. And funnily enough, there was never a right time and they never talked…except about the football, when practically any time was a good time.

'Oh and I meant to tell you, I'm away over the weekend now. I've got a problem with the big case in New York. I'll be back on Tuesday.' Jeremy's eyes did not leave the screen as he addressed me.

'But that's the third weekend in a row that you've not been here and I've got theatre tickets for us on Saturday. You know, the new play at the Haymarket, which I spent ages queuing for online. Can't you get back for it?'

Jeremy stared at me over his glasses, which hovered halfway up his aquiline nose. 'Sorry Sasha, but I really can't. Why not ask a girlfriend to go with you. Or maybe Zac might go?'

I looked at him in disbelief. 'Seriously? Zac come with me to see a play? About Arab/Israeli politics in the 1970s? Have you been listening at all?'

At that moment, Zac lurched into the kitchen and headed for the biscuit tin. Lifting the lid, he extracted a large handful of chocolate digestives and then turned to leave again without speaking. Stanley woke with a start, hitting his head on the underside of the table in his rush to follow Zac in order to hoover up any potential offerings or crumbs. Before Zac and Stanley reached the bottom of the stairs, Jeremy called out to him. 'Hi, Zac. Good day at school? Stanley, not upstairs!'

'Fine,' Zac replied, continuing to head back to his room. Stanley hovered at the bottom, one paw on the first step, waiting for Jeremy to look away. Jeremy did not allow Stanley upstairs and to all intents and purposes, had no knowledge that he ever disobeyed him.

'I'm away now until Tuesday, so be nice to your mother', Jeremy called.

'You too,' Zac replied.

And that was the end of their man-to-man chat.

Joe

The young love to test the old. Day by day, they snap the tiny threads which bond you to them. Most days, you don't even notice, but sometimes, it really hurts. Maybe just for an hour, or for a day, or maybe for a little longer. The process is painful for both. The young feel frustrated, trapped inside their bodies and their lives, which are changing, but out of their control. The old have been in control, yet now find this harder to maintain. The soft, loving pliable creatures they have been nurturing since birth become prickly. Alternately needy and then not at all, they are simmering cauldrons, whose bubbles erupt without warning. It's impossible to keep your balance.

Annie

Joe and I are having a few people over for dinner this evening. I've been working hard with the chef all day to manage the menu. Louis is very French and extremely precious about his food. I find negotiating with him quite exhausting. We have finally compromised and agreed that we will serve a cheese soufflé, followed by salmon tartare, after which we will have beef wellington, with cauliflower gratin, and then a chocolate tart with crème anglaise, followed by cheese and petit fours. My housekeeper has assisted me with the table settings. The crystal glitters in the candlelight and the central flower arrangement of red roses and baby's breath looks spectacular. I've sampled all the wines we are due to serve – the Chablis, the Merlot and the Sauternes – I'm particularly partial to the Sauternes, but it comes in such small bottles that once I've had a few sips before the guests arrive, it's almost gone, and I have to ask the housekeeper to open another one.

It's the best of everything tonight for Ambassador So and So – I forget his name, but Joe will give me the usual last minute briefing and tell me who's who and what to and what not to mention, although I'll never remember it all – and the ambassador's excruciatingly dull wife is coming, as well as Joe's current producer and her other half. I think they're living in sin. She's a pretty little blonde thing – all giggles and cleavage – and I'm not too keen on the way she bats her eyelids at Joe. I have placed her at the end of the table near me to keep her out of harm's way. For some reason, Sasha is invited as well. Joe insisted, but to be honest, it's a school night and I don't think it's necessary to have her at the table. What can a naïve sixteen-year-old possibly contribute to adult conversation? But Joe tells me that it is all part of her education on life and the world in general. It's ridiculous, if you ask me, but no one ever does.

The hairdresser has been and gone and now I'm putting the finishing touches to my makeup. I don't like looking in the mirror so much these days. I suppose I look presentable, but I hate the feathering of wrinkles around my mouth and the network of fine lines around my eyes. My foundation tends to settle in the cracks after an hour or so, like grouting between tiles. I look at Sasha with her perfect complexion and I marvel that I looked like that not so long ago. It's alright for men. They seem to get better looking with age, well, those of them who keep in shape and don't develop a paunch, or go bald. Joe's lucky in that respect. He has a full head of hair, which he dyes black these days – although that is a trade secret – and he has kept the weight off, despite the number of dinners he has to go to every week. I think he just burns it off with all his nervous energy. It's not as if he ever does any exercise. On the contrary, I have to work at it. I've just bought one of those machines, which is like a conveyor belt. You put it around your thighs, switch it on and then it vibrates like crazy. It's supposed to take pounds off you, but so far, it's just made the tops of my legs rather red and itchy. I'm wearing a short Chanel sheath dress tonight. It's gold with a gorgeous shimmer to it and I've chosen some matching shoes from my favourite shop in Bond Street. At least I won't need a bag, as we are hosting at home, which is one less thing to worry about.

'Darling, you're not wearing *that*, surely?' Sasha walks in, literally five minutes before the guests are due to arrive, and, as usual, she is inappropriately dressed. She is wearing a plain black woollen skirt, which is far too short and a checked shirt, like she's going out shopping during the day or something. I'd rather she had stayed in her school uniform.

'What's wrong with it?' Sasha asks me.

'Pretty much everything. I put an outfit out on your bed for you to wear. Didn't you see it?'

'I saw it.'

'Well? Go on then. Go and put it on.' I sigh and reach over for my wine glass from the side table.

'I don't like that dress. It's got a Peter Pan collar and it's too tight across my chest. I can barely breathe in it and it makes me look about twelve,' Sasha grumbles.

'Well, the outfit you're wearing now makes you look about fifty, my dear. Now, off you go.'

At that moment, Joe bustles in, loosening his tie and undoing his shirt buttons as he goes.

'Christ, I'm so late. The traffic was murder. Are we all set? You look lovely, darling,' he says, giving me a peck on the cheek as he whizzes past, 'and so do you, Sasha. How lucky am I to have two such gorgeous girls.' Joe sails out of the living room and I hear him tackling the stairs, two at a time, up to his dressing room to don a clean shirt and tie.

'Pour me a whisky, please darling,' he calls down from the bannister.

'See, Daddy says I look nice, so I'm fine as I am,' says Sasha, smiling at me.

'What the hell does your father know about fashion? Now, I'm not asking you, Sasha, I'm telling you. Go and put on that other dress, quickly, before they get here.'

The doorbell rings.

'I'll go,' says Sasha brightly and she trips off to open the front door. I can hear her greeting our guests as if she's the lady of the house. I top up my wine and wait, glass in hand, for my darling daughter to bring them through to the lounge. 'Ambassador, what a pleasure,' I say as the portly American waddles over the threshold with his dumpy wife in tow. 'I see you've met my daughter Sasha.'

The ambassador is short and squat and wears one of those odd leather buckle fastenings at his neck as if he's just emerged from a John Wayne film. His wife is even more of a dwarf and sports a dowdy tweed dress and flat pumps. She barely smiles as she comes in. I suspect she wants to be here as much as I want to host her.

'I sure have, Mrs Stein and if you don't mind my saying, she's a real beauty. You're going to have a mighty big problem when all the boys come a calling, my dear, which they surely will.'

Sasha smiles demurely. I turn sharply and advance on the cocktail cabinet by the window, which overlooks the park. It's twilight now, but there are a few hearty people out and about, wrapped up in thick scarves and hats, taking an evening stroll with their dogs.

'Now what can I get you both to drink? Ambassador? Madam Ambassador? Joe will be right down. I'm afraid he got stuck at the studio.'

'I'll have a whisky and soda, please Mrs Stein, or may I call you Annie?'

I begin to pour the whisky into a heavy crystal tumbler. We bought them because they reminded us of the ones we drank from at the Dorchester, when Joe and I had our first elicit weekend away together. The ambassador flumps down into one of our regency style sofas with all the grace of a basking walrus and pats the cushion next to him.

'Now Sasha, my dear, you come over here and tell me what you're up to these days, and what your plans are after you finish up at school. Are you fixing on going to university in England, or do you fancy one of our fine American schools? I'm sure I could pull a few strings if you do.'

I knock over the whisky bottle by accident and a few drops splatter onto my dress leaving dark marks.

'If you'll just excuse me a moment,' I say as I rush from the room, but no one seems to notice me leave.

Joe

The lines on our faces, the scars we acquire, are like the rings which form around the trunks of trees. They signal our age, our experience and our wisdom. We should not fear the marks of time. Youth is over-rated, peppered with red faces, gauche moments, unfulfilled longings and disappointed desires. We long for age when we are young and yet, we pine for youth when we are older. Blink and you might miss the exact moment, the split second, when we are truly satisfied.

Sasha

Zac's suggestion that we produce a family film made me feel nauseous, yet I didn't want to take the wind out of his sails, given how prickly he'd been of late. Inexplicably, over the last twenty-four hours, Zac had transmuted from grumpy as hell to Mr Congeniality. I couldn't quite work out why – but whatever the reason, I would take it. Zac's proposed family movie was to be based on our lives: mine, Mum's and Jeremy's. Zac reminded me of the many times I'd said how much I had regretted not recording my father's life before he died, but, let's face it, Joe Stein was well-known, a bone fide celebrity. There was something you could say about him – a great deal, in fact. What did I have to say about myself which wasn't either deathly dull, or which I preferred simply not to remember? And my mother. I dreaded to think what inadvertent slip or barbed commentary might be captured on film from her vitriolic lips.

Zac and I were lolling about at the kitchen table. I had my umpteenth mug of tea in front of me and the one chocolate digestive left on the plate, which Zac had not yet devoured, was beckoning to me. Zac had graduated to erasing the fruit bowl. Stanley was hovering in between the two of us, trying to decide who might be more generous. Zac was waiting for me to reply, smiling that smile of his, where his mouth stayed closed, but his lip lifted slightly on the right-hand side, his gorgeous smirk-smile. He slouched on one of the tall-backed leatherette kitchen chairs, his long slim body bending in a perfect curve, punching the keys of his smart phone with the lightning speed, which only comes from being born into the digital age and knowing how to use both thumbs, rather than all fingers. He reassured me that there was nothing to fear.

'Oh, come on Mum. Lighten up. It's just a cosy chat with a friendly woman, who films you whilst you talk. My friend just used her to make a film for his Dad's fiftieth and it was awesome.' Zac squinted at his screen, while his fingers repeatedly brushed his dark fringe backwards. I'd told him more times than I can count that he'd go bald if he didn't stop pulling at it. I frowned into my mug of tea, watching the brown liquid circle and eddy. Tendrils of steam rose up and stroked my chin. 'Everyone is supposed to have an interesting story to tell. It's just that they don't realise it, apparently.' Zac went on.

'Well, of course they would say that. I've worked in advertising long enough to know how to overegg a concept.' This was such nonsense. 'And how are you going to pay for this film, Zac?'

'Well, obviously I can't afford to pay for it at the moment, but it would be a present for you and Dad in the end. So I was thinking that you and Dad could pay for it now and then one day, when I'm rich and famous, I'll pay you back.'

I suspected we would pay for making a film like this in more ways than one. 'Look, Zac, it's a lovely idea – it really is – but I'm not sure I have the time, I'm certain your father doesn't, and Grandma gets so muddled these days. It might never happen and then we will have wasted quite of bit of money. Making a film like this can't be cheap.' My willpower crumbled and I reached for the lonely chocolate digestive.

'Oh Mum, chill and don't be such a spoilsport. It won't cost that much and I will definitely pay you back, won't I, Stanley?'

Stanley bowed and licked Zac's hand.

I got up from my chair and stuck my head into the fridge to cool down my peri-menopausal head, as well as to inspect its contents. It turned out there were none. It was merely a chilly carcass as usual and I'd have to go to the supermarket again. 'What do you fancy for dinner?' Maybe a change of subject, especially to that of food, might make this film business go away.

'What is there?' Zac was always hungry. His thin frame belied his food intake. His body used it to grow ever upwards, like Jack's beanstalk.

'Well, not a lot. I might have some pasta in the freezer. Do you fancy that?' I asked, hoping he would acquiesce and save me a trip to the shops. Zac lifted the lid of the biscuit tin and took another handful of chocolate digestives. He proceeded to eat the stack all at once. Stanley, supposedly at that moment lying dead to the world on the kitchen floor, was at Zac's side in less than a second, hoping his brother would share the odd morsel, or at least drop some significant crumbs. He was in luck. Zac threw him a piece of biscuit and Stanley caught it in mid-air before it even hit the floor. He stared lovingly at Zac with his dark brown retriever eyes, imparting to the world that he was still, and always would be, starving.

'I had pasta yesterday and the day before. Look, back to this film thing, will you ring Grandma and ask her if she'll do it?'

'Absolutely not. Firstly, we haven't even said we will do the film and secondly, if I ask her, she'll never say yes. When has she ever accepted any suggestion from me? It's your idea and if you ask her, she'll find it harder to refuse. But there are still no guarantees, so don't get your hopes up…and don't call her until we've discussed it with your father.' I kept my fingers crossed that Jeremy would object vehemently and kill the whole idea off, while I donned my coat to head out to the shops. And my mother was obstreperous about – well – just about everything. Hopefully she would put a stop to this charming, yet impractical exercise, even if Jeremy didn't.

I struggled over the threshold, laden with over-stuffed shopping bags. The handle broke on one of my supposed bags for life and fruit tumbled all over the wooden hall floor. Stanley emerged sleepily from his bed in the kitchen and headed over to sniff the fallen food. 'Leave, Stanley. Good dog. Zac! Can you come and give me a hand?' After calling him several times, Zac finally ambled down the stairs in a way which suggested a total lack of urgency. I felt my jaw clench, as I fought with myself not to lose my temper. 'Today, please!' I hissed. He relieved me of a couple of bags, leaving me to scramble on the floor to gather the wayward apples and lemons. Stanley helped out by licking my face. 'It's fruit, Stanley, you silly dog. You don't like fruit.' Stanley gazed at me steadily, suggesting that I was probably wrong in my assumption. He followed me, tail wagging furiously, as I carried the last of the food into the kitchen.

'So, I called Grandma,' Zac said, picking up one of the stray apples and biting into it with the total confidence of youthful teeth. 'And she said OK.'

'Do you think you should have washed that first?' I asked, lobbing the rest of the fruit into the kitchen sink and switching on the tap. Then I realised what Zac had just said.

'You did what? Jesus, Zac, I specifically told you not to call her until we'd had had a chance to chat with Dad. What didn't you understand about don't call your grandmother?'

Zac put his head down and took another bite of his apple.

'And did Grandma really say yes? Did she know exactly what she was saying yes to? You know how confused she gets,' I asked, starting to load the fridge. I never required help with packing the fridge, as I was most particular about what went on which shelf, and no one else ever got it quite right, no matter how often I explained the basic rules. The same principle applied to stacking the dishwasher. Zac jumped his backside onto the kitchen side and l looked at me, happy to watch the master at work.

'Well, I think so. She did ask me the same questions a couple of times, but I think she got the general gist. I said I'd let her know when the woman is going to come to see her.'

'You said what?' I ran a pan under the tap to boil the peas for dinner. 'Bugger!' I jumped back, having soaked my shirt from turning the cold tap too high. 'Damn this bloody tap! I keep asking your father to fix it, but he's never bloody here.'

Zac giggled and I snapped at him to set the table. 'I'll do it in a minute. Here, Stanley.' Zac leant down and handed the apple core to Stanley. It disappeared in seconds and Stanley stared up at Zac, hoping that another one might miraculously appear.

'Please don't feed him apple cores, Zac. It can't do him any good.'

'You're fine, aren't you, Stanley?' Stanley answered in the affirmative by extending a deep bow to Zac, who jumped down from the kitchen side with the effortless athleticism of youth and patted Stanley on the head, before running upstairs.

'Table!' I screamed after him.

'I'll do it in a minute. By the way, I called the woman – her name's Sarah– and she's going to pop in to see you next week. I checked your calendar and it looked like you were working from home next Tuesday afternoon, so I said that would be fine.'

'You did what? Christ Almighty, Zac, call her back right now and cancel. I mean it.'

Zac sloped out of the kitchen without replying.

'Did you hear me?'

I finished setting the table, just as Jeremy walked through the front door. I wandered into the hall to say hello. He looked rather crumpled, his tie loosened around his neck and his suit jacket slung carelessly over one shoulder. He threw his keys onto the rickety table by the front door, as Stanley rushed past me with his favourite toy in his mouth, a large stuffed penguin called, imaginatively, Penguin. This offering to Jeremy instantly instigated a tug of war, which Stanley won, because Jeremy conceded. Stanley trotted off happily with Penguin in his mouth, to place him triumphantly back in his bed.

I'd spent a long time trying to persuade Jeremy that getting a dog was a good idea, only to be countered with lucid, logical and learned arguments about how we would never find the time to walk him, the prohibitive cost of insurance and vet bills and the vexed question of who would look after the dog when we went away. Jeremy was finally swayed when we went on holiday to Portugal and the house we rented came with its own stray, with whom we all fell in love. We named him Whisky after our evening tipple. We fed and watered him for two weeks and he lay in the shade while we baked around the pool. Jeremy was equally smitten and caved in about a dog of our own as soon as we returned home. Six weeks later, we brought Stanley home, a platinum blonde bombshell of a retriever, who became the centre of our universe. Now I don't think there is any doubt that, of all the people in the house, Jeremy loves Stanley the best. Even after the worst day ever at the office, Stanley was the most effective stress reliever you could wish for.

Stanley was now upside down, having his tummy tickled. 'So how was your day?' I asked Jeremy, as I watched fur drift upwards in great wafting clouds, which fell back down to earth to land on Jeremy's dark suit trousers.

'Oh, terrible, as usual. This case is dragging on interminably and the client is impossible. Stanley, I'm going upstairs to get changed. Sasha, where's the Velcro roller?' I handed it to him and he wandered up the stairs, dabbing at his legs with the sticky tape. He didn't ask me how my day had been, but then he rarely did. I'd got used to it, but it still angered me. I worked from home, ran the house, helped Zac with his homework, walked the dog. My day was my day and I suppose it was nothing at all to get excited about, yet sometimes, it would just be nice to be asked anyway. 'Let's get dinner ready, shall we, Stanley?' I fished a frying pan out of the drawer and placed it on the hob, clicking on the gas. I hunted for the steak, which I'd only just stowed in the fridge. When I returned to the hob, Stanley had positioned himself by the counter top, so that I had to lean forwards over his body to fry the steaks. 'Zac! Call your father. Dinner's ready.' Jeremy hated it when I bellowed up and down the stairs, but how else were we to communicate? Most of the time, my voice went unheard regardless, either due to selective deafness, or to the perennial use of headphones. Jeremy ambled downstairs, followed by Zac, and I served up the steak with some peas and boiled potatoes.

'So, have you told Dad that he's going to be a film star?' asked Zac.

Jeremy raised an eyebrow. In his faded T-shirt, sweatpants and five o'clock shadow, he didn't look much like George Clooney, but I lived in hope. I glowered at Zac, willing him to be silent.

Zac ignored me and, stuffing an enormous piece of steak into his mouth, he continued. 'Oh yeah, Dad, so, I've organised this really cool thing, right, where a woman is going to interview Grandma, and you, and Mum and then, she'll edit a film about your lives for me to watch in future years when you're dead.'

'How utterly charming, Zac. Hopefully, that won't be imminently.' Jeremy turned to me, fixing me with a hard stare, as though he were in court about to savage one of his witnesses. 'Sasha, I assume this is just a little joke?'

I stared at my plate and played with my peas.

'No, not at all. It's going to be really good,' Zac interjected. 'Grandma has already said she'll do it.' Zac shovelled forkfuls of food into his mouth at breakneck speed as he spoke, as if he was competing in a time trial and the plate might be snatched away from him when the whistle blew.

'Well, if your Grandmother has acquiesced to speak, we'll all be in for a real treat, won't we?' Jeremy grimaced at me and then turned to address his son. 'Look, Zac, this not going to be really good. There's nothing for us as a family to say and I, for one, don't have the time, or indeed, the slightest inclination to participate. So, I'm sorry to tell you that it's not going to happen at all.'

That was Jeremy all over. An aggressive argument and case closed, m'lud. Zac's eyes slid downwards to examine the stains on his serviette.

I turned to Jeremy and refilled his wine glass, which normally served to lighten his mood. 'Surely you can see that it might be nice to have a film as a memento, and it's lovely that Zac's arranged it for us, isn't it, darling?' I tried to wink at Jeremy. He ignored me. 'Maybe you and I can discuss this later – in private – and get back to Zac afterwards?'

'I don't think we should discuss our family life in private, or in public, and certainly not on film. There was quite enough of that when your father was alive and I would have thought you, of all people, Sasha, might acknowledge that. Think about it for a second. You want to do this? Really?'

I felt my colour rising and I stuttered in response. I found it impossible to argue with Jeremy and it made me angry. 'Well it's probably just a general chat, not warts and all, Jeremy.'

Zac was staring at the two of us, waiting, his food demolished. Jeremy removed his glasses, rubbing his hands up and down his face. He replaced his glasses and stood up from the table, taking his wine glass with him. He turned to address me, ignoring Zac. 'Your choice,

Sash, but I'm sure as hell not tempting any skeletons to walk, so you can count me out.' Jeremy picked up his newspaper and stomped into the study.

'What was all that about?' asked Zac. 'What skeletons?'

'I have no idea what he's talking about, Zac, but if he wants to be awkward, then let him. He's probably tired, that's all. You know how he gets. Maybe it wasn't the best time to tell him. It's my fault. I'll see if I can talk him round.'

'He's being so unfair, Mum. It's my last year at home, and then I'm going to be away travelling for ages, and then I'm going to uni. I may not get another chance to do this.'

Why did Jeremy have to be so bloody-minded, so tactless, when Zac was only trying to do something kind for us as a family? And Zac was right. Our lives would change soon – far too soon for my liking. 'Sod it. I tell you what, Zac. I will do the film for you, and so will Grandma, and it'll be lovely, alright?' I collected the plates from the table and planted a kiss on the top of Zac's head as I went past him to drop them in the sink. Zac shrugged and loped off to his room with his earphones already back in place, cocooned in a world where reality rarely reared its head. I wished I could join him there.

I scrapped the remains of my food into Stanley's bowl and he bounded over. His metal dog tag clinked against the side of the bowl, as he licked and chewed until his bowl sparkled. I cleared up the rest of the table, wiped it with a damp cloth and put the dishwasher on. I could hear Jeremy watching TV in the lounge, no doubt with another large glass of red in hand. I teetered on the threshold, watching the lights from the screen flicker on the pale painted wall, before turning to head upstairs to put on the washing. I knew that if we spoke now, we would have a terrible row and I was simply too exhausted.

Joe

Film creates schizophrenics. On screen, I was everybody's friend. I entered their homes most evenings, introducing them to an array of famous faces. I was confident, witty and handsome. I was suave, debonair and everywhere. But when I walked off set, I switched back to my other self, the one without all the fame and glamour. Like Cinderella's coach, much of the time I was also a pumpkin.

Annie

I had it in my hand a moment ago and now I've lost it. It's a letter, or a note, or something. I can't quite remember. I wrote it down when she called me, so I wouldn't forget, and now I can't find it. I've looked everywhere – by the bed, in the bathroom, by the kitchen sink, next to the phone. The problem is, I'm not sure what I'm looking for, but I know that it's on a piece of paper and that it's something I need. Bugger. The phone is ringing. Where is the phone? 'Hang on! Hang on! I can't move that quickly.' It keeps on with its infernal ringing. 'Wait! I'm almost there!' I reach my chair in the lounge and lower myself carefully. I pick up the receiver. 'Hello? Hello? Who is it?' Silence. There's no one there. I sit, my chest heaving, and I blow my nose in my handkerchief. It's a proper hankie, with a red rosebud embroidered on the corner. I don't like paper tissues. They are so, oh, what's the word? You know. The phone rings and I jump. I fumble for the receiver and drop it onto my lap, before managing to get it to my ear. 'Hello?'

'Hi Mummy, it's me, Sasha. I've been trying to call you all morning.'

'Well, I've been here and the phone hasn't rung. Are you sure you called me?'

'Yes, positive, and I left you a message each time. You must check your machine when the light is flashing. Anyway, how are you?'

'Yes, fine, you?'

'Yes, not bad. Rushing around. I've just walked Stanley and he's filthy. We got absolutely soaked today.'

She's always rushing around, apparently, but I'm never sure what she's actually doing. Too busy to come to see me every day, that's for sure. 'I don't think it's rained here. But I've not been out, so I don't know. I'll go and have a look.' I put the phone back onto the receiver and struggle out of my chair. I hold onto the back of it and reach my other hand onto the wall to steady myself. I look towards the window, but the curtains are closed, so I can't see out. I wonder what time it is. The phone rings. 'Hang on! Wait!' I yell at the phone, but it keeps calling incessantly. I shuffle back into my chair and pick up the phone. 'Hello?'

'Hello, Mummy. It's Sasha. You put the phone down.'

'I wasn't on the phone. It must have been someone else.'

'I was speaking to you just now. Remember? I told you how I'd been for a walk with Stanley and we got wet?'

'Well, I don't see how. It's not raining here.' I twist in my chair to look out of the window, but the curtains are closed. 'What time is it?'

'It's eleven-thirty. Listen, Mummy, I was calling to remind you that the lady is coming on Friday to do the film.'

'What film?'

'You know, the one Zac's arranged. He spoke to you about it. There is a lady coming to talk to you about your life and she's going to interview you on camera.'

'Well why on earth didn't you tell me before? I've got my housecoat on and I've not brushed my hair.'

'I did tell you. I reminded you yesterday. But don't worry. She's not coming until Friday. I'll remind you again before that.'

'Well, you don't need to remind me again. I'm perfectly capable of remembering, thank you very much. But I haven't made any sandwiches. I think I need to go to the shops.'

'You don't need sandwiches and she's not coming until Friday. I'm sure she will be happy with just a cup of tea, or a glass of water. Don't worry. She seems very nice, and she just wants to have an initial chat.'

'A chat about what?'

'About you.'

'Me? What does she want to know about me?' I can hear pots clattering in the background. 'Sasha, what are you doing?'

'I'm unloading the dishwasher. So don't forget. Write it down. Sarah. Interview, two o'clock, Friday.'

'Stop telling me what to do, Lady Muck! I'm not an idiot.' I slam the phone down.

I take a piece of paper and hover over it with my pen. My hand is shaking slightly as I write. This is a lovely notepad, with a blue penguin in the top right-hand corner. So who is Sarah? I've written down Sarah, but I don't know anyone called Sarah. I rip the piece of paper into two, and then two again and drop the pieces into the bin by my feet. I haul myself out of my chair and lean on the back of it while I move over to the sideboard. I pull out the drawer and extract a half empty bottle of wine. I'll just unscrew the cap and have a quick sip. Yes, that's better. I think I'll go and lie down on the bed for a bit and rest my eyes. I should go to bed now anyway, given the time, and I've already closed the curtains.

Joe

Doing your homework is crucial. Know your subject, research your interviewee, plan meticulously, write a detailed script. Only then can you gain their confidence, draw them out and peep behind the façade. Without it, the shutters stay closed.

Sasha

The doorbell trilled and Stanley bounded over. He stood up with his front paws on the heavy brown oak door and looked through the glass. The woman on the other side leapt back in surprise. 'Come on, Stanley, get down. Let's open the door.' Stanley returned to all four feet and I worked my way around his wagging body. 'Hello, Sarah? Do come in. Are you alright with dogs? This is Stanley.'

'Hello, Stanley.' Sarah bent down and stroked Stanley behind his ears, who rolled over for a tummy tickle, blocking the whole of the porch.

'OK, Stanley, enough. Let Sarah come into the house, please.' Stanley looked crestfallen, but bounded back up and into the house ahead of our guest. 'I'm so sorry, he has no manners. Do come in.'

Sarah laughed as she walked into the hall. She was an attractive, petite, blond woman wearing blue jeans, a white shirt, a short denim jacket and a gregarious smile. She was carrying a video camera and a couple of large bags, so we couldn't shake hands. 'It's lovely to meet you. I've heard so much about you from Zac.'

'That sounds ominous, I must say!' Sarah giggled,

as I ushered her into the kitchen, relieving her of one of her bags as we walked. I asked her what she'd like to drink.

'Coffee would be lovely. Oh, I love your house. What a great kitchen.' She put her other bag and the camera down on the floor and Stanley had a good sniff to make sure they weren't edible. 'Oh, and what a terrific garden. Such gorgeous flowers.' She sounded like an over-zealous estate agent. My kitchen was not great. In fact, it was rather small. The table and its four matching, rather uncomfortable, chairs were placed right in the centre and the rest of the kitchen ran around the walls, so that if you were in there with another person, and they were sitting at the table, you couldn't access the fridge, or some of the cupboards. Stanley took up the remaining floor space.

'I can't take the credit for the flowers, I'm afraid, or indeed, tell you what they are. We have a wonderful gardener, who keeps it flourishing. Of course, it looks better in the sunshine, like today.' I gazed out of the window and took an unusual moment to appreciate the daffodils basking in the spring sunshine. 'Would you like to sit here, or on the comfy chairs in the lounge? There might be a bit more room in there. It's a shame it's only March, or we could sit outside.' I hovered with my own mug of tea and a plate of chocolate chip muffins I'd made the night before.

'I'm fine, here, honestly,' Sarah replied with a smile. 'If we sit here at the kitchen table, I can scribble notes as we go.'

'OK, if you're sure. The chairs are not that hospitable to your rear end after more than half an hour, I'm afraid.' I retrieved a large dinner mat and placed it under her notepad. The table had a glass top and scratched easily. I spent my whole life polishing it and cursing the day I hadn't bought a granite one. I made a mug of coffee for Sarah and tea for myself – I can't stand coffee, not even in cake, never could – and then sat opposite her, lacing my fingers together to steady them. 'Muffin? I made them fresh this morning,' I asked, proffering the plate piled with more cakes than a family of five could manage, never mind two women who were supposed to be having a meeting about being on film. Doesn't the camera add several kilos?

'How lovely, thank you.' Sarah took the smallest muffin in the stack and placed it on the side plate I'd given her. I handed her a napkin and a cake fork. Stanley also thought the muffins looked appetizing and positioned himself strategically at Sarah's feet, just in case she didn't want to eat the whole thing. I pulled at the skin on the back of my hands, watching it pucker and wrinkle.

'So, today I just wanted to have a chat about the way I usually go about the interview process. I brought the camera to take a bit of footage of the room where we might film, so I can judge the light.' Sarah smiled warmly and tucked a stray blonde hair behind her ear. 'I want to talk generally about you, your husband and your mother, and then I can come up with a series of questions to ask, when we actually film. There are no right or wrong answers and the conversation can flow in any direction you choose.'

'I'm not sure that my husband will have any time to take part, I'm afraid, so you might have to plan to proceed without him, for the time being at least. He travels a great deal, you see.'

'Not to worry. I'm sure, if he has a free moment at a weekend or something, I can see him then and edit it in. If not, it's no problem at all.' Sarah smiled shyly and forked some cake into her mouth. 'Mmm, this is delicious. Did you make them yourself? You are clever. I can't bake at all,' she muttered while chewing.

'Oh, they're easy, really.' I paused. 'Look, Sarah, I must admit to you that I'm a little nervous about the whole film thing. I'm not sure I've got much of interest to say, and it might all be a little dull. And when you get to talk to Zac's grandmother, she might be, well, somewhat confused.'

'Please don't worry at all. I'm used to interviewing older people, and it's often fascinating how much they do have to say once they get going. Reminiscing is often much easier for them than remembering what they ate for breakfast, or did they day before, so I'm sure she will be fine. If you can give me a little background before I meet her, then that would be very helpful.'

My mother. It was hard to know where to begin. My own view of my mother was very different to that of the casual observer, who knew her as the glamorous widow of one of broadcasting's greats. Sarah would meet the authorised version, neat and elegant, wearing a matching twinset and pearls, garnished with mountainous trays of sandwiches and cakes, and almost certainly, a glass of white wine, whatever time of day Sarah happened to meet with her. Annie would be charm personified, regaling Sarah with the whirlwind life she led as my father's consort, meeting, greeting and socialising with celebrities from all walks of life. She would play queen bee. Well, that was fine by me. She tended to reserve her real vitriol for when she and I were alone. It was rarely unleashed in public. 'I think the main thing with my mother is to get her talking about her life with my father. They had a quite remarkable time together. I'm sure you might be familiar with him? He was quite well known.'

'Yes, absolutely. I grew up watching his interviews on television and to be honest, I have always aspired, and frankly failed, to be even a smidgeon as good as he was. You must have had a fascinating childhood, meeting all those celebs!' Sarah tucked her hair back behind her ear and sipped her coffee, her eyes searching me expectantly over the rim of her mug.

'Truthfully, I used to get quite bored at times, which might sound ridiculous, or even slightly blasé, but I used to long for an evening when just the three of us would have dinner alone together, rather than having to entertain some famous actress or politician. When my parents had visitors, they used to pat me on the head and then forget I was there. Yet I always had to stay at the table until the bitter end. I was their mascot, I suppose.'

Sarah nodded, making a small note in her book and then returned to sipping her coffee.

'My parents were both rather larger than life, so I stayed in the background. Don't get me wrong, it was an amazing childhood in some ways, but a little like living within one of those reality TV shows.'

'I'm sure it must have had its moments. So, if it's OK, we will talk a little about your childhood and then, I thought we could also chat about how you met your own husband and highlight some of your own adventures together. Does that sound OK?'

Adventures together. Had Jeremy and I had many adventures? We'd been together for twenty-five years, most of which had shot by in a blur of routine, but I guess that's what life is like; day to day mundanity punctuated with the odd neon highlight. Yet I had found this rather a relief, after a childhood spent leaping from spotlight after spotlight, rarely punctuated by any kind of shadow. I had spent the first part of my life wishing for dullness and the second half mired in it. Or perhaps that was rather unfair. 'Yes, that sounds perfect,' I answered brightly. 'And we must include Stanley, of course. After all, he's the most important member of the family. Can I tempt you with another muffin?' Stanley stood to attention, his brown eyes fixed firmly on the plate in anticipation. 'Not you!' I laughed.

'Oh, I'd better not, delicious as they are, or I'll have to waddle out of here!'

Stanley stared at me without blinking and I found him a crumb off my plate.

Joe

I wonder what they will both say about our lives together. What will they embellish and what will they delete? What lies will be told deliberately and what misinformation will be imparted due to lack of knowledge of the real facts. We like to believe that we are honest and open with our loved ones, but I kept secrets from Annie and she kept secrets from me. We both lied to Sasha and she to us. Human nature. It's often for the best. Truth can shatter trust and destroy lives. Truth can kill.

Annie

The doorbell is ringing and my mind rushes to answer it, but my body refuses to keep pace. The bell rings again. 'Coming.' My legs shuffle forwards an inch with the aid of my stick. 'Hold on, I'm nearly there.' I'm sweating as I open the door. A woman with a lovely smile is standing there.

'Hello, Mrs Stein, I'm Sarah. Sarah Hardy. I'm here to have a chat with you. I think Zac mentioned me to you?' Her eyebrows shoot up at the end of her sentence, in time with her voice.

'Zac? Zac?' I know Zac's name.

'Your grandson, Zac. He has asked me to make a film about you and your daughter.' The lady has a lovely smile.

'Zac. Yes. Zac. The film. Yes. Do come in. And what's your name?'

'Sarah. Sarah Hardy.'

'Like Laurel and Hardy, in the pictures?'

'Yes, precisely.' The lady's laugh tinkles.

'Do come in. Would you like a cup of tea or a coffee? Or maybe you'd prefer a glass of wine?' I shuffle backwards and the lady follows me. My stick leads us through into the lounge. I steady myself by holding on to the wall, and then to the armchair. I tend to walk on my heels these days. I used to be able to put my feet flat on the floor, but now they are gnarled and curl up at the end, like those ornate embroidered Arabian slippers that Joe and I bought in Turkey once.

'Tea would be lovely, but why don't you let me help you?'

'No, not at all,' I say, but the lady puts her bags and camera down by the sofa in the lounge and follows me into the kitchen anyway. It's not too far to travel anywhere now that I live in a bungalow. I couldn't manage the stairs in our old house anymore.

'Ah, I see you've got it all ready,' the lady remarks, pointing to a tray laden with two cups and saucers, two wine glasses and some sandwiches and biscuits. I stare at the tray. Did I set the tray? I can't remember, but I suppose I must have. The kettle boils and the lady pours the hot water into the teapot. 'Let me take that through for you.' She is a little presumptuous, I must say. I'm not an invalid. She lifts the tray and takes it through to the lounge, placing it down on the coffee table in the centre of the room. I hope she doesn't knock over any of my ornaments. People can be so clumsy, slapdash, I find. I shuffle behind slowly. I can't place her name. I get to my chair and lower myself down using the armrests. 'Would you mind passing the bottle of white wine from the fridge. I thought we'd have a glass together.'

'Not for me, thank you. I'm driving and if I drink this early in the day, I'll fall asleep! Tea will be fine.'

She's going to be dull, this one, I can tell. 'In that case, please help yourself to tea. Do have a sandwich and some cake.'

'Thank you. Your daughter gave me cake as well. You obviously like fattening people up in your family!'

I'm sure Sasha wouldn't have gone to any trouble. 'Would you mind getting the wine for me, please? I'll have a small glass while we chat, even if you won't join me.' The lady goes into the kitchen and brings back the wine. She pours a very small amount into a glass for me. 'Ooh, don't be too stingy! Give me a proper glass.' She shoots me an odd look, but fills the glass up a bit more.

'Here you go.' She sits down on the sofa opposite me. 'Now, I spoke to Sasha last week and…'

'You know Sasha?' I fidget in my chair, trying to settle my back into a comfortable position.

'Yes, I met her last week. She is charming, and you really do look quite alike.'

I pat my hair. 'Do we? Maybe. I never thought we looked that alike personally, I'm blonde and she's dark and to be truthful, she's quite vain, fussy.'

'Well, I think you're very striking in person, just like in all your photos. You're a very good-looking family.' The lady pushes her blond hair out of her eyes.

'Would you like a glass of wine?' I enquire.

'Oh, no thank you, really. The tea's perfect.' The lady giggles and her eyes crinkle at the edges. I doubt she'll age well.

'Do you mind filling mine up a little?'

'No, not at all,' the lady says, although she gives me another funny look as she gets up and takes my glass from me. I start to feel a little steadier as she hands it back to me. The blonde woman sits down again. 'If it's OK with you, I thought we could start today by talking a little bit about your childhood, and if you don't mind, I'm going to set up the camera and record our chat.'

My wine glass wobbles in my hand and I look down as the cold clear liquid slops onto my lap. I dab at it with my handkerchief. A dark stain appears on my skirt. 'What would you like to know about my childhood? Really there's very little to say. My life didn't really get interesting until I met Joe.'

'Ah, yes, your husband. What an interesting life you must have had together.' The lady smiles at me and nibbles a sandwich. I wish she'd use a plate. The crumbs will go everywhere. She clearly has no manners.

'Indeed we did. We were always busy going to functions, parties. We travelled a great deal. We were very lucky.' I sip my wine. It feels warm as it goes down. The woman is fiddling with her equipment and she sets up a light which shines into my eyes. I blink.

'Right, camera's ready. So let's give this a go, shall we. Annie Stein, take 1.'

I stare at the blonde lady and she smiles back.

'So Annie, if I can call you that, can you tell me a little about your childhood, where you were born, who your parents were, where you lived?'

I sip my wine. 'Well, I was born in Manchester in an area called Wythenshawe. You may have heard of it?'

The lady shakes her head. 'Well, never mind. It's not that exciting as a place. My father, Jim, was a cooper. Do you know what that is?' The lady shakes her head again. What do they teach people these days? 'A cooper makes barrels. My father made them by hand at the yard. His father had been a cooper, as had his father before him. It went back generations, as a family trade. I'm not sure they have them any longer – coopers I mean, not barrels. They are probably all made by machine now. I used to visit my father sometimes after school –his name was Jim, by the way – and I fed sugar to the big shire horses who pulled the carts. They were beautiful creatures, with eyes you could drown in. I used to feed them lumps of sugar off the palm of my hand. It used to tickle. Dad was good with horses too, but he was always a bit wary, because a horse had killed his own father, my grandfather. He stood behind a horse and something frightened the animal. It kicked backwards and its hoof smashed into my grandfather's jaw. He died in agony several weeks later. My father saw it happen and I don't think the image ever left him. No, I don't think it ever really did.' The blonde lady gasps at my story and I pause, watching my gentle father in his yard.

He is a smart man, tall with round glasses which fall forward from the top of his nose whenever he leans down. He spends hours every day pushing them back into place. He wears a brown overall over his waistcoat and trousers and sports a brown tweed flat cap on his balding head. Every so often, he removes the fob watch from his waistcoat to see what the time is. At clocking off time, he's always nips to the pub for a few pints before wandering home, much to my mother's annoyance.

'What was your father like?' asks the lady with the camera.

'Oh, he is a lovely man. Very amusing, too. He's always trying to make me laugh. He fashions stick men out of pipe cleaners and makes up funny stories about them. He spends hours trying to cheer me up, especially after…'

'After what?' The lady with the blonde hair is leaning towards me, smiling.

'After what? Oh, after nothing, really. I've forgotten what I was saying.'

'You were saying that your father used to spend hours trying to cheer you up, especially after something. Did something happen?'

I am feeling a little cold and I pull my handkerchief from my sleeve to blow my nose. How does she know that something happened? No one knows, except my mum and dad and they're long dead. 'I don't know what you're talking about!' She's a nosy cow.

'Please, Mrs Stein, don't worry. Tell me about your mother. What was she like?' The blonde lady tucks her hair behind her ear. She ought to get it cut.

'My mother was a practical woman. She worked in a munitions factory during the war, when I was evacuated. She just got on with things, she had to. No fuss and nonsense in those days. She used to get cross with Dad when he messed about. He was a real joker, but she had too much to do, you see, and she was very house proud. She worked all day and then she came home, and washed, and ironed, and scrubbed. Her hands were often chapped and bleeding from working that mangle. She used to scrub me the same way, until I shone like a new penny.'

My mother stands by the tin bath in the kitchen, pinny on over her day dress with the faded red flowers and her auburn hair tied back in a neat ponytail, flaying my face hard with a flannel, as if she is trying to peel the skin off it. Cleanliness is next to godliness, she tells me every day. Don't be a dirty girl in any way; with your clothes, your hair, or with your body, especially with men. Don't be dirty, don't ever be a dirty girl.'

'Where were you evacuated to?' The lady sips her tea and takes a piece of cake. She has a large appetite for a thin little thing, I'll say that for her.

'How do you know I was evacuated?' I shuffle in my seat. I need the toilet, but it will take too long to go.

'You mentioned it just now. You said your mother worked in a munitions factory when you were evacuated.' The lady speaks with her mouth open and I can see the cake inside.

'Ah, yes, I was evacuated. I was sent to Carnforth. I was only five at the time, and my mother took me to Victoria Station in Manchester. She never told me where we were going. She just took me there and the next thing I knew, I had a label round my neck and I was on a train.'

'Come on, come on, Annie, we're going to miss this bloomin' train. Come on! Move!' My mother's cold breath hangs in the air as she drags me through the station, clasping my tiny hand with a crablike grip. I struggle to keep pace, weighed down by my gas mask, which is clamped to my chest like an alien creature. It bounces into my chin as I run along. In my left hand, I clutch a small paper parcel tied up with string. 'Come on,' shouts my mother, tugging my arm so violently that I stumble and almost fall. I am overwhelmed by the noise, by the smoke and by the vast crowds of people, all of whom seemed to be running in different directions, banging into me. Gaggles of soldiers, all khaki legs and rifles, stub out cigarette butts under big black boots, swearing loudly as we pass by. Engines scream, fogging the air with steam, while station guards pierce it with their whistles. I want to block my ears with my hands, but I can't, what with one arm being dragged off my wrist by my mother and the other struggling to stop my gas mask from head-butting me and giving me a bloody nose. Suddenly we stop, forcing me to crash into the back of my mother's legs and I earn another scolding. I look up to see a ruddy faced woman sitting at a table, with a long typed list in front of her.

'Morning,' pants my mother, exhausted from rushing through the heaving station. 'I'd like to …'

'Name,' barks the woman.

'Mrs Brewer,' answers my mother meekly.

'Not you, madam. The child,' the scary woman says, peering menacingly at me over her horn-rimmed glasses. I shrink back behind my mother's skirts.

'Ah, yes, sorry. Annie. Annie Brewer.'

'Right, Annie, Annie Brewer, let's have a look.'

The woman runs her pen down the lists in front of her, continually repeating my name like a shopping list. 'Annie Brewer, Annie Brewer, Annie Brewer, Annie…ah, here we are. She's on the 11.05 to Carnforth. Platform 9.' She pulls out a large luggage label and writes in large capitals:

ANNIE BREWER, AGED 5.
EVACUATION. CARNFORTH.

'Put this on her coat, tied very tightly, mind. We don't want to lose her now, do we? Go immediately to Platform 9. Next!' With that, the woman turns her broad behind on us and starts to label another breathing parcel.

I start to cry and my mother stops, pulling me to one side behind a white stone pillar. She kneels down, right in the middle of the chaos in the station, and knots the label to my coat lapel with the attached string. I watch my mother as she bites her lip and I notice a thin trickle of blood at the corner of her mouth, where her lips are most chapped. 'Mummy,' I venture.

'Yes, darling.'

'Mummy, why have I got to wear this label? I don't like it and anyway, I know what my name is. I *am* five. And where are we going?' My mother stares at me, tears trickling slowly down her cheeks. I feel afraid. Mummy never cries. 'Mummy, why are you crying?' My mother pulls her handkerchief out from her coat pocket and dabs at her eyes.

'I'm not crying, sweetie. It's just the smoke from the trains making my eyes water, that's all. Listen, darling, you'll have to wear this label, so that we don't lose you in such a big crowd of people, what with all the soldiers and other people and that, going away for special holidays. You're going to Carnforth, where there are sheep, and pigs, and horses, and chickens and lots and lots of grass, just for a bit mind, until we've sorted out old Mr Hitler, and then you can come home again.'

'So where will we stay, Mummy?' I ask, my eyes brightening, as I picture my own menagerie of farmyard animals that Mummy and I can play with every day.

'Well, I can't come with you, you see, love. Mummy has to work to help us win the war, so you'll go and stay with a lovely family, who'll look after you, just until I can pick you up again.' My mother fiddles with the label on my coat.

I stare at her, drinking in her words, and then I begin to wail so loudly that even the soldiers in the station turned to stare. 'I'm not going! I'm not going without you, Mummy! I'm not going! I'm not going!' I wrap my arms around my mother's legs and hold on as tight as I can. My mother scowls, then scoops me up and shakes me fiercely. 'Now, give o'er and listen to me, young lady. I don't have a choice in the matter and you'll do as you're damn well told, understood?'

The train journey passes in a blur of jolting terror. A frazzled female volunteer, who struggles to cope with the crowd on the platform, asks the station master to help me onto the train. He has a large red nose and smells slightly funny, a little like Daddy when he has been out to the pub with his friends and Mummy tells him off. The train is old and creaking. There is a narrow corridor just inside the train, which smells vaguely of stale wee. Off the corridor, there are separate carriages with chipped wooden doors and red, fraying banquette seats on each side, every one crammed with children. The station master places me in one of these carriages in a seat by the window and pats me on the head as he leaves. The seats are stained with the remnants of old sandwiches, and there are holes all over the place from cigarettes stubbed out on the upholstery rather than on the floor. The floor is also covered with butts and the carriage smells stale and musty. There are several other older children already in my carriage, all of whom seem to be very happy and extremely excited about their trip. I watch them quietly, as they rip open their ration boxes and eat the chocolate inside, licking their fingers as they finish. They toss the wrappers onto the floor to mingle with the used cigarettes. There are twin boys with matching knitted Fair Isle tank tops over grey shorts, revealing scabbed knees above long socks, which droop to their ankles. They smile at me slyly as they thump each other. One suddenly hits the other hard and gives him a dead leg. He lies on the dirty floor moaning. I flinch, in case he decides to hit me next. Three sisters gabble quietly together in the other corner, nibbling on their sandwiches. They drop crumbs all over their pinafores. My mother would call them dirty girls. Other children bang our carriage door open, and then pull it shut again, making me jump with every clang. No one speaks to me and I sit alone, holding my own parcel as tightly as I can and looking down at the floor. I need the toilet, but I don't know where it is, so I sit jiggling my legs up and down to make the feeling go away.

'I need the toilet. I'm sorry,' I say to the smiling lady. I fumble for my stick and she rises to help me up.

'Please don't worry, Annie. Take all time you need.'

I stagger slowly down to my bathroom. I wonder if she noticed that I'd dozed off a little. I sit down on the toilet.

I wish I knew how much longer I am going to be on this train. There is a clock on the wall, but I don't know how to tell the time. My mother is teaching me, but we hadn't got very far with it yet. I twist my hair into tight balls. This is the very first time I have ever been out alone and I don't really like it. Normally, Mum screams at me to stop if I walk unaccompanied so far as the front gate. I can't seem to stop my body from shaking, quite separately from the train, and tears stream down my cheeks for the duration of the long, long journey. Everyone else in the carriage still ignores me. Occasionally, I pull out a photograph from my pinafore pocket, which my mother put there just before she left me on the platform, and I stare at it for a long while. I give the picture a little kiss, before returning it to the pocket in my gingham pinafore.

'See here, Annie. There's a photograph of me and you from our trip to Blackpool last year. Give it a kiss every night and think of Mummy. I'll see you very soon.'

I wonder at the image of myself and Mum on the pier, smiling into the camera, 99s dripping down our hands and raspberry sauce smearing our lips. I remember how good it tasted and how sticky my hands were. 'Do you remember the donkey we saw, Mummy?' I ask, glancing up, but my mother is nowhere to be seen.

I feel slightly dizzy as the carriage begins to sway less. All the other children push past me to have a first glimpse of their new temporary home through the window, forcing me back into my seat. One of the twins hits my knee and it hurts, but I bite my lip to stop myself from shouting out. 'Blimey,' exclaims one of the twins, 'there's nothin' here, 'cept a 'ut and an 'orse!'

A guard opens the train doors and the other children pile out. Cold air floods into the stuffy train, causing me to shiver more violently. I shuffle off my seat until my legs reach the floor, patting my photograph to check it is safely in my pocket. I walk to the door, holding my parcel tightly to my chest, my gas mask still around my neck. I wander into the corridor and follow the rest of the children to the main door, where they all jump down and run off along the platform. I feel scared as I look down. It is a long way and far too far for me to jump. I start to cry, thinking that I might be left alone on the train now that it's empty.

'Annie. Mrs Stein? Are you alright in there?'

I jump, pulling up my pants and straightening my

skirt. 'I'm fine. Just doing a little tinkle. I'm coming right out.'

The lady with the nice smile is outside the door, and she helps me back to my chair. 'Shall I put the kettle on again and make a fresh pot of tea?' she asks me, pushing her hair back behind her hair.

'No thank you, but I'll have a top up of my wine, please.' I close my eyes a moment.

'Now, who've we got here then?' I look up to see an older lady with smiley eyes. She wears a tweed coat and a red cloche hat, from which clumps of grey fuzzy hair are succeeding in their bid to escape. She reaches out to read my label. 'Ah, little Annie Brewer, is it? And how are you today?'

I half-open my mouth, but only air escapes. I don't know what to do. My mother and father tell me never to talk to strangers.

'Ah, don't worry, cherub, it's all a bit daunting, isn't it? Don't you worry yourself, lovely. My name is Mrs Mortimer, but you can call me Auntie Val. Is that alright with you?'

I nod, staring at Aunty Val.

'Righty ho then, let's go,' warbles Aunty Val in a singsong voice, and with that, she scoops me up and lifts me off the train and out of the station, which is now empty, save for an enormous poster advertising Pears Soap to keep your skin looking soft. I wonder whether the pretty girl with curls on the poster has been sent away by her mother like me. Aunty Val carries me, which was just as well, as I am so exhausted that I could not put one foot in front of the other, even if I wanted to. Val strides briskly down the street by the station towards a small house, which turns out to be the village hall. The other children run on far ahead, desperately letting off steam after being cooped up for so long.

The village hall is even louder than Victoria Station. Groups of boys and girls, all sporting large labels on their clothes, sit on the floor, while a few noisy ones run about pretending to be fighter bombers. They knock into the tables, making the adults very cross. There is a large trestle table, upon which are a few dry sandwiches and jugs of water. Some of the children grab handfuls of the sandwiches and are being told off. Don't they know there was a war on? The adults sit around another wooden table, some dressed in city style hats and coats, whilst others look much scruffier and very muddy. Auntie Val settles me on a chair near the other children and disappears. Where has she gone? Why do people keep disappearing? I begin to shake again.

'Order! Order! Ladies and Gentlemen, boys and girls, do settle down, or we shall never get through this process before dark.' The noise in the room just gets louder and the woman who shouted at everyone looks dismayed. Then, putting two fingers to her mouth, she produces the loudest wolf whistle I have ever heard. The din stops immediately. 'Excellent. *Thank you* all for your attention. Now, let me introduce myself to those of you who don't know me. I am Mrs Prendergast and I am in charge of evacuee distribution.' She speaks very loudly, like a megaphone. 'Now, by my calculation, we have forty-five children to settle into new homes today and we have thirty-one possible options, so let's get on with the auction. As you know, we must all pull together at this difficult time, and I thank you all for your generosity in taking in these poor children. Do remember that you have the added incentive of an extra 10s 6d per week for taking in one child, and even more if you take multiples, not forgetting the extra rations you'll be eligible for, so it's not all bad. Now, you children, here are some rules for your stay in Carnforth. You must respect your new homes and the people who are giving them over to you. You must be good, speak *only* when spoken to and help with chores as and when you are asked to do so. I do not need to remind you that there is a war on and we must all do our level best. You are here to be safe, but remember, at all times, that it is at our expense.' Mrs Prendergast sighs deeply and peers into the assembled crowd through her thick bottle-top spectacles. 'Right, children, I would like you all to line up against that wall and then, Ladies and Gentleman, I would like you to go along the line and pick out those parcels which most appeal. Each one is clearly labelled. Good luck!'

There is a great deal of shoving and pushing as all the children move to line up against the wall. 'Get off! Watch your bleedin' elbows, Ow.' I stay frozen, unable to move, until an older girl pulls me up roughly by the hand and places me in the line next to her. My mouth and nose are caked with thick snot, but I haven't got a handkerchief and it's dirty to wipe it on your sleeve.

Mrs Prendergast resettles her glasses. 'When you have chosen the ones you want, just let me know who you're taking for my records. Now come on, children. We don't have all day. Stand up and look sharp while you're at it!'

Everyone quietens down. I stand in the line, swamped by bigger children on either side, who jostle me.

'I'll take these two scalliwags, as they'll be useful in the fields and with the milkin', Mrs Prendergast,' announces a large woman in a patterned headscarf and a large red face.

'Right you are, Mrs Bostock. Hopefully you can tame them!' She laughs as the naughty twins from my carriage on the train are pushed out of the room, Mrs Bostock's hands firmly on each of their shoulders.

'I'll take this one,' announces another woman, pointing at a fourteen-year-old girl with pigtails and lurid, swollen spots. 'Mr. Birtwell's not likely to take an interest in a lump like 'er and she'll be useful in t'shop.'

'Jolly good,' sings Mrs Prendergast.

The selection goes on, but no one chooses me. I am now slumped on the floor with half-closed eyes. The room is emptying and I'm wondering where the nice lady is, the one who helped me off the train.

Suddenly, a giant shadow falls over me. I look up. She is the tallest and widest person I have ever seen. She looks like a man. Her eyes are very small, disappearing into great pockets of flesh around her nose. Her mouth seems petrified into a permanent frown and she has a dark fluffy moustache. She is definitely the most terrifying person in the world. I don't move.

'Right, young lady, I'm Mrs Wiggins. Let's get a move on, child. I don't want to be late back t'farm. We get up very early for the milkin'…not that you'll be 'owt use, except for the extra money and rations.' With that, Mrs Wiggins turns on her heel and strides out of the hall. I stay where I am.

'Go on with you, love,' cajoles Mrs Prendergast, 'Or you'll not catch her.'

We ride to the Wiggins farm in an open cart, pulled by a magnificent carthorse, who is called Derek. He has large fluffy legs and a gleaming white star in the middle of his forehead. The journey passes in silence, except for the occasional snort from Derek, whose white calves flash as we plod down the lane. I am comfortable around horses. My dad works with them and the horses seem to like me. I look forward to feeding Derek sugar lumps, although they are harder to come by at the moment, as Mummy often reminds me. When we finally reach the farmhouse, it is almost dark, but I can just about make out a brown timber house with a barn next door to it. It is low built, with a door painted long ago in bright blue paint, but which is now chipped, peeling and muddied. Mrs Wiggins asks Derek to 'whoa' and ties him to the post outside the barn. She doesn't give him any hay, or any water. Then she lifts me down from the cart, sighing deeply. 'Sooner you grow, the better,' she moans. She undoes the latch on the rickety wooden door and clomps into the kitchen. I follow as far as the threshold, where I stop. Looking through the door, I can see a small wooden table with four hard chairs, a stove and a coal fire, which is unlit. Dirt and ash from the fireplace covers the floor, mingled with bits of mud and straw. There is a faint smell of dung. My mother would have a fit if she saw this place. Mrs Wiggins lights a couple of oil lamps and then turns her huge frame around slowly. 'Christ, child, get in here and shut that ruddy door. It's freezing,' she bellows.

I jump and then dart into the kitchen, turning to close the door. I try to shut the latch, but I'm too short to reach it.

'Oh, give it 'ere. Why do I get left with the young'un who's nowt use to man nor beast?' she growls, shoving me out of the way to fire the latch. 'Don't know why I bothered even going down there. Bleedin' waste of my time. I've got enough to do without some scrap of nothin' hanging around me legs!' Mrs Wiggins walks around the filthy kitchen, complaining to herself. 'For Christ's sake, child, don't just stand there. Fetch a knife and plate for our tea.'

I look around. It's not like our kitchen at home, where my mother keeps the plates displayed neatly on the dresser and the cutlery arranged by knife, fork and spoon in a drawer. Here, there is just a large chipped sink, inside which are piled stacks of dirty plates, cutlery and what appears to be an enormous pair of greying bloomers. I'm unsure what to do, so I pick up two plates and two knives, wipe them on the bloomers and carry them over to the small wooden table.

'Sit down!' commands Mrs Wiggins.

I sit and wait, whilst Mrs Wiggins drags some coal out

of the cupboard at the end of the kitchen and attempts to light the fire. I watch, not daring to move a muscle in case I annoy her even more. Eventually, the flames begin to lick around logs in the fireplace and shadows start to dance around the kitchen walls. Mrs Wiggins brings over two small pieces of bread and some lard in her hand, which she throws onto my plate. She also gives me a mug of water. I realise that I'm starving, having not eaten all day, and I put the first slice to my saliva-filled mouth, but before I can take my first bite, Mrs Wiggins slaps the bread out my hand. 'You little heathen! We say our prayers before we eat in this house. Well, there's nowt for you now. Bed! Now! Let's go.'

I stare at the bread, which now lies covered in mud and coal dust on the kitchen floor. I'm so hungry that I want to eat it regardless, but Mrs Wiggins is already marching me up the stairs, her large paw on the back of my neck. She shoves me into a tiny room with a small camp bed and a ewer on the side table. Other than that, the walls are bare whitewash and there are no curtains on the small window. 'Right, you get up at 4.15, breakfast is at 4.30, you collect the eggs at 5 and then I'll give you the rest of your chores after. Lav is in the yard.' With that, Mrs Wiggins slams the door shut and leaves me in total darkness. Hot urine stings my legs and runs into my shoes. I wriggle out of my tights and lie down on the cold bed, clutching the photograph from Blackpool.

'Mrs Stein, Annie…' The lady with the blonde hair is shaking my shoulder. I cry out.

'Oh, I'm so sorry, Annie. I think you nodded off, so I'll leave you now and come back next week. Please don't get up.' She backs out of the room, looking embarrassed. I'm not sure what time it is, but I'm tired and it's dark outside, so I think I'll go to bed.

Mrs Wiggins pulls my threadbare coverlet off me at 4.15 the following morning. She splashes water on my face and hands, whilst I stand there shivering in my thin slip. Breakfast is a slice of bread with lard and a glass of milk, ladled directly from a churn in the kitchen. I mumble my prayers and stuff it in my mouth before she can stop me. Mrs Wiggins pulls back my chair, hands me a basket and shoves me outside, barking at me to collect the hens' eggs. I don't know my way in the dark. I fumble across the yard towards an outhouse. It's very cold. I open the door and the hens flap around me. They frighten me. I feel about for the eggs and put them in the basket. I want to get out of there as fast as I can and, as I come skidding back across the yard, I drop an egg in the doorway of the kitchen. It spreads out yellow, white and sticky onto the dirty stone floor. Mrs Wiggins slaps me across the back of my head and drags me over to the kitchen sink. She holds my head under the kitchen tap for a couple of minutes and then shoves me, wet and shivering, into the coal cupboard.

Joe

She had a difficult war and arrived home broken. Her parents tried to put the pieces back together again, but they could not align all the shards and she was left with jagged edges, shredded nerves. Evacuation left her more shell-shocked than if had she remained in the city for the duration of the war. Doctors, frazzled by fighting and famine, fazed by nothing, told her to pull herself together, but she couldn't catch onto the edges of herself. She jumped at her own shadow. Nighttime was worst – the darkness, black as coal, constantly dragging her backwards.

Sasha

I could have done without Sarah coming that afternoon. I was late on a deadline for my awkward client, who had already changed his mind a thousand times about what he wanted, the washing machine had broken down and needed a new part, so the dirty laundry was piling up, Zac had left his sports kit at home and had begged me to trek across town to deliver it to school, which took up half the morning – he didn't even thank me when I got there! – and Stanley had walked mud all over the house, so I'd had to mop the floors before Sarah arrived. At least I didn't have to worry about cooking for Jeremy that evening. He had gone to New York again and wouldn't be back until Sunday. Yet another working weekend, but apparently, clients must be wined and dined. It irked me that we spent less and less time together and that Jeremy saw Zac so little, yet oddly, I had become accustomed to it. Sometimes I couldn't decide if I wanted to see more of Jeremy, or if we were happy enough the way we were, waving to one another from a distance, sending the occasional metaphorical postcard.

The other major benefit of Jeremy absenting himself quite so regularly was that he was oblivious to the extent of the parcel issue. A combination of the ease of on-line shopping and working at home meant that we received quite a number. I justified this easily – why drag yourself to the shops, when you can order something from the comfort of your own home, while at the same time enjoying a cup of tea and a naughty piece of cake? Our food now came by van to the door, as did our cleaning products, Stanley's enormous bags of kibble, toiletries, you name it – everything arrived courtesy of a man in a van. All this meant was that I was freer to concentrate on other more important things in life, although Zac's prodigious appetite meant that I still could not avoid emergency top-ups. Yet I never admitted to the more insidious purchases, when I was tempted by special offers on my favourite designers on discount clothing sites, which meant that buying that extra, superfluous jumper, or irresistible pair of shoes, was just too easy. These were the parcels which I preferred to receive when Jeremy was elsewhere, if only to avoid the inevitable accusations about 'What are we buying now?' and 'Does the post office van drive itself to our address on autopilot?' When he was out or away, parcels could be unwrapped, items stored away to be revealed later as something I'd had for absolutely ages, and packaging torn up and well hidden at the bottom of the recycling bin.

The doorbell rang, breaking my concentration on a lovely white shirt, which appeared to be a steal at thirty percent off. Stanley raced downstairs to peer through the glass to assess the visitor. He was, as usual, upstairs when he should be down, but in reality, he was always where

I was, and I loved my faithful fluffy shadow. I followed behind and grabbing his collar, pulled him out of the way to let Sarah in. It was pouring with rain and despite her umbrella, Sarah was drenched, her jeans soaked in uneven patches and her shoes blotchy with water. 'Come in, do come in. What a disgusting day! Here, let me take your coat. I'll put it in the airing cupboard to dry while we chat.'

Sarah removed her shoes in the porch, while Stanley greeted her with sneezes. 'Hello, Stanley. How are you?' His maximal tail wags answered her question.

I returned to the hall. 'Do come through, Sarah. Please ignore the mess. I've had rather a mad morning.' The dirty dog towels, which I'd used to clean Stanley after our very wet walk, were still in a pile at the bottom of the stairs and there was an assortment of items in plastic bags, some of which were due to be unpacked, and others destined for the bin.

'No problem, I've had a ridiculous morning myself. I seem to have been stuck in traffic wherever I've gone today.'

I settled Sarah into the most comfortable armchair in the lounge by the window, as on her last visit, she'd decided that the light would be better in there for filming. At some point, the chair had been cream, but now it was more like beige, its arms and cushions pockmarked with brown stains incurred from too much chocolate and red wine. I really ought to get it cleaned, or better still, replaced. I'd discuss it with Jeremy the next time our signals crossed. By the time I'd assembled the tea and biscuits and placed them on the glass coffee table, Sarah had assembled her paraphernalia and was ready for action. I sank down in the armchair opposite her. I never sat in the lounge during the day. The chairs were too sleep-inducing and somehow, I felt guilty if I wasn't in my office, even if I was only internet shopping. 'How did you get on with my mother?'

'Oh, absolutely fine. She was charming. I think she found the process somewhat tiring, and we might have to film in small chunks at a time, you know, take baby steps, so as not to overwhelm her.' Sarah accepted her mug of tea with a polite thank you and coiled her hair back behind her ear.

'Yes, she does rather tire easily and sometimes goes a little off topic. Hopefully, I might be more lucid, but there's no guarantee these days!' I sighed and reached for a biscuit. Then I put it back again. Chewing on film was probably not that attractive.

'Right, I thought we'd start at the beginning with your childhood. Is that OK? I'll start filming now if you're ready. Just relax and answer my questions, as if we are having a friendly chat like last time. I'll edit it later'

'Sure, OK, well, where to begin? I was born in Manchester in the Sixties, only child to Joe and Annie Stein. Dad was forty five when I was born and Mum was only twenty eight, so there was quite an age gap. I wasn't really aware of it as a child. It was only once, when I was a teenager and a friend of mine asked me who the old man was. Of course, he meant my father, but I was shocked nevertheless. I never thought of him as old until much later, closer to the end of his life. And, of course, I was also a bit surprised that this particular guy didn't recognise my father.'

'Yes, that is a little odd, but maybe not all your friends watched current affairs at a young age.'

'I'm sure you're right. I was so immersed in it. I had no choice, really.'

'And you are an only child?'

'Yes and oddly enough, so is Jeremy.' And Zac, of course. 'But it never bothered me. The house was always so full of people and I was always treated as one of the adults. I guess I missed out on sibling games and sibling rivalry, but what you don't know, you don't miss, right? I think it's easier for today's generation, as there is so much more readily available entertainment, with all its associated pros and cons.' I laughed nervously. No, I had avoided sibling rivalry, but not the mother-daughter variety; less common, but far deadlier.

'And where did you go to school?'

'I went to the girls' grammar in the centre of Manchester. It took me about forty five minutes by bus. I liked school and I suppose I was reasonably academic. Mum and Dad had great hopes for me and desperately wanted me to go to Oxford or Cambridge. I applied to Oxford the year I took my A Levels, but I didn't get in. I had a dreadful interview with two men in a darkened room, who seemed to be taunting me from behind a tall pile of books. It was really quite intimidating and rather bizarre, to tell you the truth. Anyway, my mother was devastated when I failed to get a place. Dad wanted me to apply all over again the following year, but I was more than ready to fly the nest, so I went to Bristol instead.'

I came home from school one day in early December. The silver birches lined the road like arctic sentries, gleaming under the streetlights against the cold winter sky. I shivered as I hurried up the drive, my head tucked down into my scarf and my ears aching from the biting wind. It was quite clear that my mother was drunk again. I could see her framed in the front doorway, waiting for me, her face swollen and blotchy, rivulets of black mascara leaking from her eyes, the perennial wine glass in hand. 'You rang, didn't you? You couldn't wait. You just had to ring when I'd asked you not to.' I stormed past her into the hallway, which smelt of a strange mix of Dettol and Liebfraumilch.

My mother slammed the front door and trailed behind me, as I catapulted my school bag onto the marble floor and unwrapped my many layers, dumping my coat and scarf over the bannister rail. 'Sasha, Sasha, listen, darling. I rang because we hadn't had a letter yet. And so many people were asking me. I needed to know.' My mother began to cry again. Deep, angry sobs.

'Well, it looks like you've got your answer.'

'Sasha, you have to understand. I'm so upset, I'm so very disappointed. You've failed us. So many people were expecting you to get in.' She blew her nose loudly into her sodden handkerchief and took a slug of wine. 'I'd already told everyone that you were going to Oxford. It's just so embarrassing for your father and me.'

'So embarrassing for you? Well, I *am* sorry that I've turned out to be such a disaster, and to have placed you both in such a difficult predicament.' I snatched up my bag and pushed past her to flee to the sanctuary of my bedroom. As I moved, the edge of my bag knocked her elbow. Her wine glass fell from her hand, splintering as it hit the hard floor, shards and droplets scattering in every direction. For months afterwards, my father begged to retake Oxbridge, but I had to escape. I took up a place at Bristol and never looked back.

'So did you meet Jeremy at Bristol?' Sarah asked, glancing up from her notes.

'No, I met him after I graduated at a party in London. He knew a friend of mine, who was a great guy – very camp, and rather eccentric – and he used to throw fantastic parties, especially around Eurovision. The wearing of weird and wonderful costumes was de rigour.'

'And what about at university? Did you have many boyfriends there?'

'Well, I'm not sure I should discuss my ex-boyfriends on a film for my son, do you?' I suddenly felt rather warm and was aware that I was laughing a little too loudly. 'More tea?'

'Yes, that would be lovely, thank you.'

'Let me go and freshen the pot.'

I'd met Neil in The Cooler on Park Street in Bristol, a grotty club with a pungent aroma of stale beer and urine and a penchant for the latest pop and indie rock. I was with my friend, Clare, and we'd gone there to listen to a band, who are long gone now and whose name I can no longer remember. It was a typical student venue for gigs, where you had to shout over each other to be heard and when you finally went home, your ears would vibrate weirdly as they adjusted to silence. I wouldn't usually have frequented somewhere like The Cooler, but Clare was wild about music and dragged me anywhere and everywhere around Bristol to hear different bands. She also got noticed wherever she went. Clare was very much the rock chick, with her dyed jet black hair, deeply kohl rimmed eyes and ripped leather-look trousers. I would trot behind wearing my frayed jeans and checked shirt, hoping to remain inconspicuous.

We were drinking Baileys at a small table in the corner of the bar. I was entertaining myself by peeling the top off one of the sodden beer mats, when I became aware of a guy on the other side of the bar wearing a faded Elvis Costello T-shirt. He was tall, thin, not really my type, yet he had something about him. At first, I thought he was staring at Clare, which would have been normal, but eventually I realised that he was peeking at me. This threw me slightly off guard. Most of the evening was spent playing a game of sly looks and smiles, before he eventually summoned up the courage to saunter over, so that we could scream at each other over the din. He was a fresher like me, but studying Engineering, not History. He bought me a drink and then another – vodka and Coke was my tipple then – and after an hour or so, he asked me if I'd like to go for a walk with him up to the Clifton suspension bridge. The night was clear as we gazed up at the stars, which twinkled merrily above Brunel's construction. Neil put his arm around me and whispered engineering secrets. Apparently, the two towers which stood proudly at the each end the bridge were not identical and, despite the fact that the structure appeared solid, it was, in fact, made up of twelve vaulted chambers working together in silent harmony. I was hooked. I shivered slightly in the cool of the night and Neil wrapped his pea jacket around my shoulders. Then he kissed me. We stayed there suspended for hours, before walking home as the sun rose above the Avon. From then on, we were inseparable.

Our first phase of love was decadent, lazy, exciting. We lay in bed together until late most days, eating cheese on toast under the duvet and drinking steaming mugs of tea laced with whisky, and smoking a little weed. He confided in me that it was his dream to work for Rolls Royce and I revealed to him that I didn't have a dream, which was what worried me. I bought Neil silly little gifts: cookies, a cuddly toy, a mug with a funny slogan. I spent more and more time in his halls and less in my own, forgetting my other friends in my haze of passion. Clare kept trying to coax me out with her, but after a while, she gave up and we drifted apart. I've often wondered what happened to her. Neil and I were so completely happy as a unit that we felt no need of the outside world.

So the first time it happened, it came as a total shock. We returned to Neil's room one night after a few drinks in the local pub and Neil couldn't find a particular book, or a pen, or something he was looking for. He started to shout at me, accusing me of hiding whatever this thing was, or losing it. The next thing I knew, he'd shoved me and I ended up on the floor, hitting my head on the corner of a stool as I fell. Hot tears sprang up in my eyes and when I touched my head, my fingers came away coated in blood. Neil was immediately contrite, picking me up, holding me, stroking my hair, saying he was sorry. I was too stunned to talk, but somehow, I ended up staying the night. The next day, I went to A&E to have some stitches sewn into my gash, claiming to have fallen off the kerb on the way to lectures. After that, small rages and cruelly inflicted indignities became more frequent – a shove, a slap, a Chinese burn, a bite and one day, a knife – thrown whilst Neil was paring an apple – which narrowly missed my head. Yet I stayed with him. I don't know why I didn't just run away, why I didn't attempt to escape from him. I suppose I felt totally paralysed to act. Bristol was too small and Neil knew where to find me, so there was nowhere to hide. I had cut my friends loose in favour of Neil, and now, I had no support network, nor any strength or confidence to believe that I could walk out and live without him. I relied on the very man I feared. I hated myself for it, and I blamed myself for my inability to act. I wanted someone to ask me if I was alright, to intervene, to rescue me, but of course, no one ever did.

I broke away only when we left Bristol. Neil got his coveted job at Rolls and I went to London to work as a copywriter for an advertising agency. The physical distance emboldened me. I threw myself into my job and found a thousand excuses as to why I couldn't visit Neil, and even more as to why he couldn't come to see me. Neil bombarded me with letters, gifts, and phone calls. The more he pleaded, the stronger my resistance. One night, however, he arrived unannounced at the house I shared with three friends in Kings Cross. It was a tall, thin terraced house with a large lump in the wall, caused by the terrible damp on the stairs. During our residence, this tumour grew larger and larger, until we had to limbo past it to access the kitchen. Neil had spruced himself up, wearing a crisp white shirt and clean jeans. He lingered on the doorstep, his face partially obscured by a dozen red roses. Before I could utter a word, he went down on one knee, right there on the front step, produced a ring and proposed. I couldn't answer him, but I let him come in, more out of pity and sheer embarrassment than anything. He looked so forlorn, begging on the dirty, grey stone step in the drizzle.

I prepared a meal of cheese on toast for old times' sake and, after a bottle of wine, we made love under my Winnie the Pooh duvet in my cold attic bedroom, while the rain pounded heavily on the skylight. Neil fell into a deep post coital sleep, but I couldn't. I watched over him until it grew light, my stomach twisting itself into tight knots. In the morning, I told him as gently as I could that I was so sorry, but I couldn't marry him, that even though I loved him, I was scared of him, and that I couldn't commit to a life of uncertainty and fear. He punched a hole right through my bedroom door. Blood and flesh spattered the paintwork and carpet. My heart froze as I waited for him to turn on me, but he sank down onto the carpet deflated, as if exhausted by his anger. I took my chance to race past him out of the bedroom, banging on my flatmate's door, loudly enough to wake the whole house. Tony, a huge bear of a rugby player, ran out wearing nothing but a pair of boxer shorts and quite literally picked Neil up, throwing him out onto the street. 'Get out and stay out. Come near Sasha ever again and I'll call the police,' he commanded before slamming the front door.

Several hours later, the doorbell rang. Tony said he'd answer it and when he returned, he was accompanied by two police officers. As soon as Tony led them into the kitchen, I started to scream. Neil had walked up to Kings Cross station and thrown himself in front an oncoming tube train.

I took a fresh pot of tea into the lounge and placed it carefully onto the tray on the coffee table. 'In answer to your question, I didn't really have a boyfriend at Bristol, well no one serious anyway. I just had a great group of friends and we hung out together. I did a bit of writing for the University magazine and played a lot of pool. It was the usual dissolute lifestyle of a student. Otherwise, it was fairly uneventful. When I left Bristol, I got a job as a copywriter in a small ad agency in London. Jobs were very difficult to come by, as we were just emerging from recession, but to be honest, I think they knew who my father was and it helped get my foot through the door, much as I hate to admit it. More tea?'

'Yes, thank you. And you are still a copywriter?'

'Yes, although I've worked for myself for years now. Working in an ad agency was very different to what I do now, because I worked with an art director and we bandied ideas around between us, whereas I work by myself these days. When I started in advertising in the 80s, it was great fun. Business was booming and we wouldn't even look at a brief from one of the account handlers without insisting that they took us for a long lunch first. Then we begged another lunch from them when we presented the ideas, and another one if they sold it to the client. So it was hard work, but we played hard too. And the parties were amazing. At Christmas, the agency would hire a nightclub with a hot band. One year, they commandeered a huge warehouse and installed a giant funfair. The following day, I was badly bruised from the dodgems, as well as nursing a horrendous hangover at a nine o'clock meeting. Even at the end of every week – every single Friday night – a crate of champagne would arrive in our department to celebrate something spurious. It was a million miles away from agencies today. Today, I think it's all work and very little play.'

'It sounds amazing. Do you miss that life?'

'Actually, no, not really. While it sounds exciting, it became boring quite quickly and also, rather claustrophobic. You felt compelled to stay late, to drink until the small hours with colleagues – you know, you had to play the game – and if you didn't, somehow you were seen as not committed, no matter how hard you worked.

It was manageable for a while, when I was fresh out of university, but it wasn't a sustainable lifestyle for me.'

'So, what changed?' Sarah smiled at me encouragingly, pushing a stray hair back behind her ear.

'Well, I suppose real life overtook me. I met Jeremy, I married him, Zac arrived. Jeremy travels all the time and I didn't want to be the sort of mother who was never there for her children – child, I mean – yet I still wanted to work. Setting up as a freelancer seemed to be a good compromise. Of course, it's not easy working for myself, as I'm sure you are only too well aware. I fret constantly about where the next piece of work is coming from and I have no one to bounce ideas off, but overall, it's worked out well for me. I've been able to carve out a decent living and be there for Zac after school, so, well, you know, it's OK. And of course, I have Stanley to keep me company.' At the sound of his name, Stanley lifted his head up from the rug and wagged his tail softly. I threw him a piece of biscuit, which he caught deftly in mid-air, before lying back down with a contented flump, emitting a cloud of blonde fur, which floated skyward. I looked at my watch. 'Sarah, do you mind very much if we leave it there for today? I'm afraid I'm rather behind on a deadline for a client and I need to crack on with it before Zac gets back.'

'That's absolutely fine. Can we schedule some time for next week?'

'Yes, of course. I'll just have a look at my diary.'

Joe

I watch her re-run the horror show in her head. It's tortuous to watch your child suffering, but I couldn't step in then, or certainly can't now. Why is it that so often we are paralysed to help the ones we love the most? Certain barriers cannot be crossed. We discuss everything, yet we speak of nothing. And she never asked for help. A father is perhaps not the person a daughter should seek out for advice on *les affaires du coeur*…too much testosterone and protective spirit. Mothers should be the ones to counsel their daughters.

Annie

I can't sleep. I must get up soon to fetch the eggs, and I hate it, because it's so cold and so dark in the yard. Then it'll be time for school. It's such a long way to walk and my legs get so tired. And I get wet when it rains, and there's nowhere to shelter on the way. In the winter, it's pitch black on the road and sometimes, the noises in the bushes frighten me. And at school, no one likes me, because I don't come from round here, I'm only visiting. My desk is by the door and a cold breeze whips round my knees all day long. I haven't got a coat and my jumper is too thin and has a hole at both elbows. I've got sores on my skin and they hurt and itch me. Sometimes, yellow stuff comes out of them and if I scratch them, they bleed. The other children are mean to me and I have no one play with in the playground. One of the girls will wander over and pretend to be nice, and then another one will come up behind me and pull my plaits and call me names. This makes me wee my pants, and then they sing nasty songs about me.

I really hate it when the nit nurse visits. She makes me sit in the middle of the classroom and rakes through my hair with a metal comb. Then she finds a nit and announces to the whole class that I'm riddled with them. Everyone laughs, and they make up another nasty song for the playground about me being dirty. Little Miss Itchy Annie, they call me. I try not to cry, I really do, but sometimes, I can't help it. I take a nit note home to Mrs Wiggins. She yanks me down onto the milking stool in the yard, pours a bucket of cold water over my head and takes the rusty kitchen scissors to my hair, shearing me with gusto. She takes more care of her precious sheep than she does of me. The next day at school, the people in my class make fun of my bare scalp, which is scabbed in places from Mrs Wiggins' handiwork. I try to hide it by putting my hand over my head, but it doesn't work and I don't have a hat or a scarf.

I feel stupid at school. I don't know anything and I can't learn anything. When the teacher asks me a question, I shake. Sometimes, I cry and sometimes, I wet my pants. Then the teacher throws chalk at me, or tells me to go to see the headmaster, who hits me on the hand with a ruler. I try not to cry, because if I do, he hits me again, but I can't help it. It hurts so much. I like nursery rhymes and often sing them to myself when I walk to and from school. 'Baa Baa Blacksheep' and 'Pop Goes the Weasel' are my favourites. If I get home from school and Mrs Wiggins is out, I have to wait in the yard, because she won't allow me in the house if she's not there, and often it's very cold. It gives me a very bad cough and then Mrs Wiggins gets cross, saying she's sick of listening to me hacking my guts up. When it gets very bad, she shuts me in the coal cupboard, so she can't hear me as easily. It's funny, but the coal cupboard just makes me cough even more. If the barn is unlocked when I get home and Mrs Wiggins is out, I go to have a chat with Derek. He bends his head down to nuzzle me and I give him a big cuddle. I love his huge brown eyes and I wish he could talk. He nods though, and that's how I know that he agrees that we must run away together, far away from the farm. I whisper in his ear that we will set up our own business. I will drive a pretty cart painted with flowers, which Derek will pull, and we will offer rides to people in the town, who want to travel around in style. Derek will be paid two sugar lumps per journey and I'll get a piece of cake. When I tell Derek my plan, he licks his lips.

Sometimes, Mrs Wiggins receives parcels and letters that have my name on them. I can read my own name, so I know. Usually there's money in the envelopes, which Mrs Wiggins immediately stuffs into her apron pocket. If food parcels arrive, Mrs Wiggins never shares them with me. She crams them in the top cupboard where I can't reach them and I know she eats them when I'm in bed. There is always a letter to read, but Mrs Wiggins never even looks at it. She just throws it onto the fire. I'm not sure she can read. On my eighth birthday, a doll arrives from my mother. It is the most beautiful thing I've ever seen. The doll has wide smiling eyes, a tiny black painted nose and a pink smile. Her dress is patterned with blue cornflowers and she's wearing shiny patent shoes. Mrs Wiggins dangles the doll in front of me, but I can't reach it. Mrs Wiggins has very thick legs with big red veins crisscrossing up and down them and they make me feel a bit sick when I look at them.,

'So, what 'ave we got 'ere then, young Annie. A bloody doll! Doesn't your damned mother know there's a war on and that she'd be better sending us summat useful, like money, or clothes, or anything, 'cept a stupid puppet.' She swings the doll carelessly by her golden hair. 'This doll's of nowt use to me! And here's me, taking you in, feedin' and clothin' you. Where's the bloody gratitude, I ask you?'

I wait, silently, holding my breath and my wee. Mrs Wiggins starts shouting again.

'No bleedin' use at all. You know what? Happy bleedin' birthday, Annie. Here you go.' Mrs Wiggins tosses the doll towards me and it somersaults through the air. I hold out my arms to catch her, but as I reach forward, she falls through my fingers onto the hard stone floor. Her beautiful face smashes into a thousand splinters, which scatter amongst the dirt. 'You little wretch, you ungrateful little sod,' screeches Mrs Wiggins, grabbing hold of my hair and pulling me towards her. 'Your mother scrimped and saved for that doll and this is how you repay her!' I start to howl and a hot trickle runs down the inside of my legs. 'Oh, you disgusting little brat!' cries Mrs Wiggins, 'You filthy, filthy child! It's pathetic that you are still wetting yourself at your age!' She wrenches me over to the other side of the kitchen, where she flings open the door to the coal cupboard and forces me inside. 'So you can stay in there, yet again, until you learn to appreciate what you're given.'

It is so black and so cold in the cupboard. I hug my knees to my chest and try to stop shaking so much. The coal dust makes me cough. I wriggle in my wet pants. I shiver, I cry, I shout, but no one comes. I might be in here for an hour, or for a whole day, or for however long, I just never know. When she lets me out, I'll be smacked for blackening my dress and sent to bed without food, or worse, without water. I try to remember Mummy and Daddy, but I can't and the picture I had of us in Blackpool has long since dampened and curled, so I can't look at that anymore either.

I must have fallen asleep. There's light through the curtains and I can hear the birds chirping in the garden. I turn my head slightly and the large numbers by the side of my bed blink 05.30. I can feel dampness between my legs and realise that I need to change my pants. I struggle to lift myself from the mattress, tugging on the ugly grab rail by my bed. I hate the way it mocks my infirmities. As I swivel round, I knock the wine bottle off the side of my bed, but it's empty, so no harm done. There's a drop left in the glass, so I drink it down, as my throat feels dry, before I hoist myself off the bed.

Joe

In the evening sunshine, The Midland Hotel shimmered like a Jaipurian Palace on the edge of St Peter's Square, its art deco façade of interlaced pink and dark granite, edged in dark terracotta, foretelling of the exotic splendour within. The two towering seahorses, which flanked the giant doors to the lobby, stood stoically, guarding its majesty. The glitterati, of which I was one of the shiniest, flocked to this magic kingdom in their sharp suits, gorgeous gowns and perfect perfumery. It was a place to see and be seen, a voyage of discovery, beckoning to the citizens of this grey and gloomy city. With champagne coupes in one hand and cigarette holders in the other, men in black tie and slicked back hair laughed a little too loudly at their companions' jokes. The ladies tinkled and glowed in response.

The string quartet in the corner of the room played 'Stranger in Paradise' as she entered, a goddess in emerald green. Her skirt fanned out with layers of chiffon and net, like a peacock preening itself, and her stilettos of the same colour enhanced the curve of her calves and ankles. Her eyes were the same intense green and her mouth popped in Indian pink. It was the witching hour and I was beguiled.

Sasha

'So you're going ahead with this film nonsense, are you?' Jeremy peered at me over his reading glasses. We were sitting on the sofa after dinner, half-chatting and half-watching an episode of some long-running Danish drama. Jeremy had thrown all the cushions on the floor. I had long since given up explaining the point of cushions on a sofa to Jeremy and merely replaced them each night when he'd gone to bed. As I sat at one end, resting my feet on Jeremy's lap, while he sat at the other, I thought how handsome he was looking tonight. Something was different about him, but I couldn't quite tell put my finger on it. His hair was graying at the temples, which rather suited him, and he had recently grown some trendy designer stubble. I suspected that he wasn't thinking such attractive thoughts about me, as I slouched in old fraying sweatpants and a baggy T-shirt, with nappy rash cream covering a large spot on my chin, while eating the remains of a chocolate bar.

'Yes, I've spoken to her a couple of times. We just had a general chat, really, Childhood, university. She's a good listener. I like her.' I wiggled my toes, hoping Jeremy would take it as a cue to massage my feet, but instead, he removed his glasses and wiped his hand up and down his face, his usual signal of exasperation. He replaced his glasses, pushing them firmly up to the bridge of his nose.

'Right, so you've covered all the general stuff, eh? Are you stopping there? What the hell will you say next? Remember Zac is going to watch this.' He glared at me and I imagined him in court with me in the dock, ready to be slaughtered by his superior intellect.

'Do you think I'm a complete idiot?' Jeremy stared at me, not answering, letting the witness hang herself. The case for the prosecution rests, M'lud. 'I'll just skim over stuff. So far, we've talked about me growing up with a famous father, how the house was always busy with celebrity egos, studying at Bristol, how I met you. You know, the usual.'

'So, no mention of your wonderful mother's gradual descent into alcoholism, or your relationship with that psychotic nut job, for example?'

'Obviously not. Why on earth would I go there? You know I never choose to talk about Neil to anyone, and the reality of living with my mother is only suitable for a horror film, not a family one. I suspect next time we'll talk more about us, you know, how you and I met, our wonderful romantic life together – ha bloody ha – having the lovely Zac etcetera. I thought it might be nice if you joined me for one of the sessions. Sarah said she would come at a weekend, if it suited you better.' I stroked Jeremy's leg with my foot and he flinched. I consoled myself with another piece of chocolate.

'I've told you, I'm having nothing to do with this

vanity project. I don't want to talk about our private life with strangers.' Jeremy stared at the television and grabbed the remote control to turn up the volume, even though the programme was sub-titled.

'Jeremy, you're being ridiculous. Why can't you just do this for Zac? For whatever reason, it's important to him and it might just make him feel a bit happier, more included.'

Jeremy turned and glared at me, brandishing the remote control like a weapon. 'You should have knocked this whole thing on the head when Zac first mentioned it. This won't do you, or any of us, any good. You might see it as some form of cathartic exorcism of previous demons, but all that will happen is that you will dredge up every ghost you don't want to face; your father, your dear mother, Neil Fuckface and of course, well, you know. I – well we – just can't go there again and Zac – well, he doesn't know, and he can't, and we always agree that he never would.'

My chest constricted as I fought to stop the tears forming. The effort made my throat burn. 'I never intended to speak of it. We said we would never tell Zac, or anyone for that matter, so do you really think that I would suddenly reveal all to a complete stranger? And if I ever were to tell Zac, why the hell would I do it via film, for Christsake?' I was screaming now, up off the sofa and standing in front of Jeremy, who regarded me placidly. It made me even madder. 'Do you really think I'd be that cruel? Do you?' I bellowed. Tears lashed down my face, blinding my anger.

'Calm down, Sash. That's not what I meant. I just don't think any good can come of this, that's all I'm saying. It's just a stupid, vainglorious idea.'

'Oh, so that's what you think this is? It's not me doing something nice for our son. It's me doing it for myself, taking centre stage. Is that it?' I walked around and around the coffee table like an entrapped tiger. 'Because, of course, that's all I've ever wanted, isn't it… to be in the limelight.'

'Well, possibly, yes.' Jeremy sighed and tried to look past me at the TV screen. All hope of following the Scandi noir plot had been lost some time ago.

'You really are a bastard, you know that? I spend my whole time looking after Zac, while you gad about, Christ knows where, and now I'm a bad mother, am I?' I sobbed until it hurt. Each word escaped in staccato.

'Oh, here we go again with the bad mother crap. I never said you were a bad mother. I said you're turning this into something about you.' He glared at me, daring me to contradict him. I stood there, a red, swollen mess, with snot running out of my nose, tears smearing my cheeks, chocolate caked round my mouth, spot cream melting. I stared back, but I couldn't answer. I stalked out of the room and into the kitchen, where I began to unload the dishwasher noisily. Then I poured a glass of water and headed upstairs. Thank goodness Zac was out staying with a friend this evening. I would have hated it if he'd heard us arguing over his film, his present to himself and to us. Why did Jeremy have to be so bloody awkward? Why couldn't he just put up a front and say a few nice things for the sake of his son? Why couldn't he just tell a few white lies like the rest of us?

I lay in bed trying to read my book, but I couldn't concentrate. The words tormented me and settled back down in an alternative order on the page. I switched off the light and attempted to sleep, but I just kept rehearsing my argument with Jeremy in my head. He said X and I said Y, when what I should have said was Z, but I didn't think of it at the time. I heard Jeremy come upstairs and head for the spare room. He slept there quite often these days, especially if he had a very early plane to catch the following morning. I didn't mind that much, although I knew it was a bad habit to have started. We hadn't made love in months and now, I wasn't sure how to broach the subject anymore, and he never did. Even before this, our sex life had been sporadic, slowly eroded by having a child and work and well, just by life, I suppose. Maybe we should try to get away for a weekend, just the two of us and talk like we used to do when we first got together.

'So you met Jeremy at a party?' asked Sarah, nibbling on a piece of marble cake. Stanley lay at her feet, staring unblinkingly. 'Tell me more.' She smiled at me, the arc light behind her head highlighting all my flaws, inside and out. I smiled back and ploughed on.

'Well, as I mentioned, I had a very good friend from work, also a creative, an art director. Philip was very eccentric. He would turn up to work each day wearing a velour jumpsuit, usually shocking pink, but sometimes orange, or flaming red. He was gay, but I think you might have guessed that already, extremely camp, always happy. Above all, he was a great listener and he was the one I turned to after, well, what I mean is, whenever I was unhappy about anything, I could chat to Phil. Anyway, every year, he threw a Eurovision party. It was around the time that *Eurotrash* was on the television – do you remember that wacky, rather risqué programme presented by Jean Paul Gautier every Friday on Channel 4? We used to go to the pub and then back to Phil's flat to watch it. Well, everyone had to dress *a la Eurotrash* for this particular party, so it was pretty outrageous, as you can imagine – quite a bit of rubber and leather. Anyway, of all the places you would not imagine that I would bump into a future QC, I met Jeremy there. He was dressed like something out of the Village People. Do you know that band? They were very bizarre. Anyway, Jeremy was the builder one. I don't know how Phil knew Jeremy, but that's where we met anyhow. I seem to remember it was a very drunken party and Jeremy escorted me home at the end of the evening. And I must say that he was a real gentleman. No kissing or anything. He just made sure I was safe, planting a small peck on my cheek as he left. He was the archetypal tall, dark and handsome man. He made me feel safe. Yes, he made me feel as though no one could hurt me, that he would protect me and I guess he has.'

That's what I'd needed at the time – a safety net – and Jeremy had provided it for me. He took me to dinner, we went to the theatre and to the cinema. We went shopping together. Jeremy was a great shopper. He'd send me into the changing room and then bring me a selection of outfits to try. He had exquisite taste. He dressed me up like a doll and I loved it. Three months later, he proposed, I said yes, and we got married six months after that. We loved each other, but more importantly, we were good friends. We supported each other. We used to talk for hours and fall asleep hugging each other. I'd had enough passion for a lifetime, what with Neil and everything, and more than enough drama with my parents. I couldn't live with such intensity anymore, so I dialled it down. Sex wasn't really that important to Jeremy and me. We were best mates, and so far, that had been good enough for me. After all, no marriage maintains passion for very long, does it?

'And Jeremy is now a very well-respected QC working in human rights, as I understand it?' Sarah scrunched up her nose as she peered down at her notes.

'Yes, well, Jeremy is a very brilliant man. He went to Cambridge and came out with a double first, entered an excellent set of chambers and it's all been an upward trajectory from there. The downside is that he travels a great deal. He's often in New York, or Brussels. But I'm so proud of him and everything he has achieved. Really, I am.'

'Do you ever travel with him?'

'Oh no, never. He's always so busy with clients, or he's in court, or he has dinners. You know how it is. I'd just be in the way. And anyway, I have to be here for Zac.'

I used to suggest to Jeremy that I could accompany him on trips, but he always said no. I'd be bored in the hotel room, I'd have to eat alone, he'd be travelling between cities. In the end, I stopped asking and we settled into a routine, where he went away whenever he needed to and I stayed at home all the time. He rarely told me his plans in advance and often went away with only a few hours' notice. One time, he flew to New York for an emergency meeting and forgot to tell me. I had no idea where he was, this being in the pre-mobile era, and I spent much of the night contacting the police and local hospitals in London. Eventually, he called me from his hotel in America, totally unabashed. There simply hadn't been time to call before he flew, not a single moment. His assumption was, quite simply, that I would always be at home and be fine with that. After all, what else would I be doing?

'And you work from home?' Sarah shifted position and pulled one of the cushions out from behind her, placing it under her left arm.

'Yes, well it's much easier that way. I get to be here when Zac gets back from school and of course, I have Stanley, so I don't like to leave him for too long, do I, Stanley?' Stanley glanced at me momentarily, wagging his tail, but stayed steadfastly next to Sarah, who had not yet finished her cake.

'And what does Zac plan to do when he leaves school?'

'Well, go to university hopefully. We've visited a few places recently, some of which he liked and some less so. We'll see where he decides to apply. He works hard, so hopefully he'll do well and get where he wants to go, but you never know these days. Marking is so erratic and everyone can have an off day, but he's a good kid.'

'He is absolutely charming. He's a real credit to you, I mean it. I bet you'll miss him when he goes?'

'Well, of course, but I know it's important to let him go and I'll just have to adjust. Take Stanley out for more walks!' Stanley raised his head expectantly. 'Sorry, Stanley, not right now.' Stanley put his head on his paw and sighed heavily.

I was trying hard not to think about life without Zac in the house. Even the vague idea of him not being there made me feel tearful, but I knew I had to put a brave face on it. I would have to move on to a new phase of life, and Jeremy and I should be planning this together, but at the moment, we seemed to be drifting further and further apart. My rock was slipping away and I had been feeling unmoored now for some time. Jeremy and I were no longer best friends, rather, for the most part, amiable flat mates, but that wasn't going to be enough once Zac had moved on. It would be fine for Jeremy, because he had a life outside of the family home, but I was about to be marooned on an island.

Joe

They leave you. They brush you aside and move on. Even when you think that you can survive the breaking of the last thread in the weft, you don't. You educate them, feed and clothe them, encourage them to do well and bask in their success. The result is that you lose them. Never again will their tiny hand slip into yours. Never again will they run to you, throwing their arms about your neck and tell you, without a care in the world, that they love you and that you are the very best. We teach them to think independently and thus, they realise that we are imperfect mosaics of neuroses and flaws. They love us, yet they pity us and maybe even despise us, just a little. In the end, we need them more than they need us. We wait for them to call, or to visit, as they head into the world and we retreat from it. Our offspring replace us. Thus it has always been.

Annie

Joe talks to me all the time at the moment. He wakes me at night and sits on the end of my bed. We reminisce about the old times – the people we met and the places we visited. He tells me stories about his own childhood, things he has never talked to me about before.

'I've been listening to you relive your old war stories,' Joe says, chuckling to himself. 'We all had a bit of a rum time back then, didn't we? You evacuated to the back of beyond and me running around Manchester trying to keep people indoors. Somehow it was easier to forget about it after the war, wasn't it? We just got on with everything and concentrated on future fame and fortune. No point in looking back, eh? But now we're old, it's all we seem to do.'

I nod and reach out to hold his hand, but somehow I can't quite grasp it. My head sinks into my pillow. 'Tell me a story, Joe.' I want to suck my thumb. I look up, but Joe doesn't reply. He's disappeared again – off on one of his missions, as he likes to call them – but he'll be back soon. I do love our little chats, and I miss him when he goes away, but he's busy and I know that. He is always at work and tied up with his little dalliances, which he tries to keep from me, but never can, especially when they are plastered all over the tabloid press. He loves me, I know he does, but I can never, well you know, *love* him in some of ways he needs, so he finds it elsewhere. Sex always seems a bit dirty to me, difficult, and reminds me too much of the other thing, the thing I can't tell him about. It's just easier if he takes himself off somewhere else. He's probably gone to find one of his floozies now, but he'll be back later. He always comes back to talk to me in the end.

Joe

Men need sex. Fact. Not just sex, but interesting sex, with a partner who enjoys it too. Reciprocity. That's what many people don't understand, the difference between love and sex. You can love someone, but they can disappoint you sexually. You can have sex with many people, none of whom you could ever love. But if you find that perfect pairing, where you love someone deeply, and you can't keep your hands off each other, then you are indeed a match made in heaven. But how often does that really happen, beyond the initial passion? Annie was a good woman, but she was damaged by war, by life. Making love was clearly something she dreaded, because she associated it with unfortunate consequences. I never had the patience to try to mend her. Truthfully, I think it would have been impossible.

Sasha

A robin hopped onto the window sill, and tapped on the glass with its shiny beak. 'Hello, Dad,' I said, addressing the chirpy little bird as it puffed out its red chest. 'How are you doing today?' The robin twisted its head from side to side, its beady eyes alert, ready to fly away at any sign of danger.

The robin is my father. As we stood in the anteroom at the Jewish cemetery in Cheshunt with the hum of the M25 rhythmically sounding in the distance, a robin hopped onto the rafters, a red flash of colour and hope in a cold, bleak space. It was my father looking down on us, listening to the speeches by the rabbi, and of the great and the good, who had gathered to bury him. The robin listened and chirped when he liked a particular phrase or cadence of voice, but he was silent during the Kaddish. There was too much finality about that particular incantation for him. He was also absent at the grave, as we lowered my father down into the filthy ground, as we shoveled soil on top of him, our tears turning it to mud.

The day after my father died, I wandered into the living room, exhausted and numb from the day before and I spotted the robin again. He tapped on the French windows, and then, as he flew away, the photograph of my father and I walking up the steps of the registry office at my wedding fell to the ground and smashed. My father was making it known that he was still going to watch out for me. Since then, I see the robin most days, regardless of the season, flitting around my garden, or accompanying Stanley and I on our walks. I talk to him as he flits past and I ask him questions, but I am no longer sure of the answers. I guess it's what I miss most, our chats. I used to call my father every day, and we'd natter about nothing in particular most of the time, yet we'd always have plenty to say. But if I needed something, if I couldn't make a decision, he was my sounding board, and that's the void I feel.

And I wish he could see Zac and the wonderful boy/man he has grown into. He is so like my father. The way he suddenly starts to dance to music when it pipes up on the radio, his total lack of a sense of direction, his keen eye for a beautiful woman, his generosity of spirit. Zac had barely known my father and the memories he does have of him are of a different man entirely. He only met him in his demented dotage, unable to walk, incapable of feeding himself, or identifying who we were. Zac remembers only a man in a bed with a baby sippy cup who barely spoke. He experienced his grandfather's former glories by watching re-runs of his various talk shows, as the anchor man of *Stein at Seven*, or *Stein on Saturday*; confident, superbly erudite and ever so slightly arrogant, yet with a Northern charm, which somehow meant he could get away with the risqué, or even the deeply personal question. He would introduce a particular guest on one of his shows, then upend them and turn them back over, before they'd even had a chance to take a breath. He would not allow celebrities onto his show to promote their latest blockbuster film or book. He wanted them to talk about themselves as people. My father peeled them open, little by little, as if he was slowly revealing the nutritious contents of a sardine can. He created a televisual art form all of his own and even now, I read reviews of more current talk shows, where the final summary is that the presenter had not managed to 'do a Stein.'

Yet at home, my father was gentler, his inquisitorial demeanour diminished without the arc lights. He would remove his jacket and tie, take off his highly polished shoes, replace them with his slippers and announce, 'I am now going casualty.' That was his regular little joke. He would pour himself a large Scotch, add a little water and sink into his armchair, reading the paper cover to cover, or watching old war documentaries on the television. Oddly for an educated man, he never read novels, as he claimed they did not hold his attention, and he hated the theatre and the cinema, which I thought was distinctly strange for a man who ruled the airwaves. Yet when he had to prepare for a show, he was scrupulous, shutting himself in his office – a tiny room with unpleasant flock wallpaper, a noisy fan heater and a faint whiff of cooking smells from the extractor fan on the wall where it abutted the kitchen – and he would prepare meticulously. Sometimes, if I was very lucky, he'd ask me to stand in as the guest. I enjoyed this very much and it made me feel important. Sometimes, I would go to the dressing up box and don a wig or a tie to set the tone. My father would ask me questions and I would do my best to answer them, but truthfully, I'm not sure I was of much use. I just didn't know enough about the world to metamorphise into a politician, or a film star, but it was good fun trying.

My mother was never the guest. In the early days of their marriage, my father often asked her to help him practise, but she always replied, 'No, Joe. I don't think so. I don't know how to answer those questions. I'll just look silly. Anyway, I need to go to buy the food for dinner' and she'd run away. In the end, Dad stopped asking her and worked with his latest 'assistant' on his shows, of whom there were a great many over the years. It was only much later that he asked me to help him, but this seemed to upset my mother.

'Sasha, don't you have homework to do?'

'I've done it.'

'Well, you can't have done it very well, can you, if you're already in here disturbing your father. And anyway, how can *you* possibly help with his show? Go and empty the dishwasher for me and tidy your room. Do something useful, for Christsake. You're a lazy good for nothing, Sasha.' She stood in the doorway, nostrils flaring like a frustrated thoroughbred.

'Sasha, you'd better go and help your mother,' my father would sigh.

'But why can't I help you prepare the rest of the show and then do it?' I bristled.

He turned back to his desk and started marking his script with his red ink pen. He was never one to provoke an argument. My mother tugged at my jumper, dragging me back over the threshold of the office and into the kitchen. 'You really need to learn when you're not needed, Sasha. Now go and get on with your chores.' She turned and took a slug of wine from her ever present glass on the kitchen table and then reeled back to me again, as I stood hovering between the kitchen and my father's office. Out of his earshot, she hissed, 'I said, get out of here, you little bitch!'

Joe

I heard the story of a man. He was so in love with his beautiful young bride. Then she gave him a daughter, whom he loved more than he could articulate. His daughter grew into a pretty young woman with a good mind. She grew more beautiful every day, while his wife perceived her own beauty to be fading with every passing hour. The daughter moved towards her prime, whilst the mother left her best years behind. The daughter began to menstruate, the mother stopped. The bond between father and daughter was purely paternal. The mother knew this, but could not control her jealousy. Every time she saw the father with the daughter, anger misted her mind. Every time she spent time with the daughter alone, she could not control her cruelty. The man was torn between the two loves of his life. He did nothing. He watched them rip each other apart.

Annie

The blonde lady is back eating my biscuits. For a thin little thing, she does seem to get through them. She's nosey, too, asking me more questions about when I was young.

'So, how did you find it when you returned home to Manchester after the war?'

'Well, I wasn't too well for a while. I couldn't go to school. I didn't go for a year or so, in fact. Then when I did go back, I had missed so much that I never really caught up again, so in the end, I left when I was fifteen.'

'That must have been very difficult for you?' The lady smiles at me and fiddles with her hair.

'I think we all just had to get on with it,' I say, staring at my lap. I've got a loose thread in my cardigan. I pull it and it unravels.

My mother is waiting at Victoria Station. The smoky air in the concourse hangs thickly, stinging my eyes. I don't really recognise my mother. Well, I do, but she looks thinner, older, greyer, and if I'm honest, slightly shabbier than I remember. I stand there, hopping from foot to foot. My mother seems to recognise me immediately, however, running over and grabbing me in a lengthy embrace. I let my hands hang by my sides.

'Annie, love. Oh, Annie. My, how you've grown, but you're so thin. Didn't they feed you? Did you get the food I sent to you? I never heard from you, but no bother. It's been hard for all of us. But now, we're going home, love. Your dad can't wait to see you. He would have been here, 'cept he had a problem at the yard. He should be home by the time we get there. We're very lucky we've not been hit, you know, as the rest of the street wasn't so lucky. Your room is ready for you and...' She gabbles ten to the dozen, but I can't hear what she's saying. The station is so noisy. I'm not used to it. There are people running every which way, trains steaming, whistles screeching. I want to put my hands over my ears.

'So, did you then, Annie? Did you?' I look down at my shoes and feel the tears pinching the corners of my eyes. 'Hey, love, what's up?' asks my mother, putting out her hand to hold mine. I flinch. My mum's eyes widen, but she says nothing. 'C'mon, you. Let's get you back home, eh?'

We travel back on the bus in silence. I stare out of the window on the top deck, tugging at my hair and watching small scruffy children playing on the broken shards of houses, digging for buried treasure amongst the rats. There are no fields or animals. Mum sits next to me, holding onto my small threadbare bag as if it was a small kitten about to escape. She keeps glancing at me, like she's checking it's really me, or if I'm some alien child who has returned from the countryside. Mum suddenly presses the bell on handle of the bus and jumps up. I jump too, but remain sitting. 'Come on, Annie, love. We're getting off here.'

I get up and follow my mother down the twisting stairs of the bus, struggling to keep my balance. As the bus stops, I stumble down the last step, crashing into my mother's back. 'Sorry,' I mumble, expecting a slap, which doesn't come.

'Don't worry, love. Buses take some getting used to, and they drive like the clappers round 'ere. Are you OK?' She pats me on the shoulder and I flinch.

'I'm fine,' I mutter as I pull away from her.

The trees are in full blossom, and showers of pink and white confetti rain on us as we pace down the narrow street, coating the cobbles. The grey terraced houses close in on me from both sides. I concentrate on the cracks in the paving stones.

'Here we go,' says Mum, as we turn into the path leading to our door with its peeling red paint. The door number is missing and the net curtains look faded. I don't remember it.

Before Mum can find her key in her bag, the door bursts open. 'Ta da! Hello, Annie. How's my baby girl?' shouts my dad, skipping down the front steps and scooping me up in his arms. He twirls me round and round, until I feel quite sick. I just want him to put me down. 'Right then, well, don't just stand there. Let's get inside. It's nippy out 'ere,' says Dad, holding out his arm. I stand stock still. Mum and Dad exchange a glance, then my father ushers my mum into the house ahead of him. They leave the door open and after a few moments, I follow them in. The house smells vaguely familiar, of vinegar and bleach. 'Right, our Annie, let's get your coat off,' said Dad. 'Your Mum's gone to put the kettle on. We've saved our coupons and made you a special malted loaf and some almond biscuits. You'd best be quick, or I might eat 'em all!' Dad chuckles and I just keep looking down at the floor. 'Right then, come in. Come on then. I won't bite.' Dad shoos me into the small living room and sits down at the wooden table on one of the three chairs. It's scratched and there's a crocheted mat in the centre which tries to hide the worst of it. The carpet is threadbare and the remnants of the blackout blinds are still in the windows. I linger in the doorway. I need the toilet, but don't want to ask. 'C'mon then, love. Sit down and let's get reacquainted. You must have so much to tell us!' beams Dad. A hot trickle run down my legs and I start to cry.

I can hear my parents arguing in the back kitchen.

'I'm at my wits end, Jim. What are we going to do? She won't eat, she doesn't sleep, she shakes, she cries, complains of headaches. And her hair is falling out. I just don't know what's up. And she won't talk to me. Nothin' at all. She's like a bleedin' church mouse when I ask her anything about Carnforth and that Wiggins woman.'

'Look, Dee, this was never going to be easy. She's been away so long, and now she's back, we all have to get to know each other again. Give it time, eh, love? Now let's have a nice cup of tea.'

'One of your bloody cups of tea won't solve this, Jim Brewer. She's my child and I abandoned her to Christ knows what, and now she's returned a total nervous wreck. I don't know how to talk to her. We can't just go on ignoring how this and pretending she's OK. I've got to get her to a doctor.'

'And what's the doctor going to do, eh?' My father's voice is louder now. 'Tell you there's been a war and you all have to straighten up and crack on. They've got proper things to worry about, you know, like disabled soldiers and people what's been bombed. They don't need you troublin' them with such trivial nonsense.'

'Trivial nonsense?' screams my mother. 'She's not right, Jim. You can't just pretend it's not there. It's all fine and dandy for you, eh? You just bugger off with your mates at the brewery and drink beer out of your precious barrels and you just don't see it.' I hear sobbing.

The surgery is dank, with cracked plaster and torn posters warning of the dangers of tuberculosis and whopping cough. The receptionist barks at Mum and me to take a seat on one of the grey plastic chairs. She is a pudgy woman, whose eyes sank somewhere into her face long ago, but it's hard to tell exactly where. She pulls her files just a little closer to her drooping chest, just in case I might commit some random act of espionage. The waiting room is full, yet silent, the air punctuated only by the occasional hacking cough, spit of phlegm, or files being stamped with ferocious determination by the woman without eyes. Every so often, the doctor pokes his head around the surgery door and beckons to the next patient. The wait is so long that I wouldn't be that surprised if one of the patients expires before the doctor actually sees them. Finally, the weary-looking doctor emerges yet again and called 'Brewer' without looking up from his notes.

The doctor's surgery is small and smells of surgical spirit. Dr. Flanagan –his name is on the door – speaks without looking up at either of us. He wears a stained white coat with a stethoscope hanging around his neck. His teeth are yellow and crooked and his hands look yellow too. He smells of cigarettes. His small desk is covered in over-stuffed files and random bits of paper. We sit opposite him on two small wooden chairs, my leg shaking up and down vigorously.

'What appears to be the trouble'? asks Dr. Flanagan, still looking down at his notepad.

I say nothing, so my mother launches into the whole story: my evacuation, my health problems since I got back, my hair loss, my apathy. Dr. Flanagan, a willowy man with jaundiced skin to match his teeth and deep dark circles below his eyes, takes copious notes, but still makes no eye contact. Occasionally, he makes a sound. 'Hmm.' After what seems like hours, he finally looks up and stares at me. 'Hmm,' he mutters more decisively, rising from his chair, his head almost scraping the low mustard surgery ceiling. 'Hmm.' He walks over to me and I flinch. 'Hmm.' He leans over and put a hand on my head, gently examining my bald patches and the thin wispy tufts which still remain. 'Hmm.' Dr Flanagan folds himself back into his chair and starts to write in his yellow notepad. 'Hmm.' When he finally speaks in a soft Irish lilt, both Mum and I jump. 'Well, young lady, I think you've been through the wars, as have we all, hmm?'

We stare at him.

'Mrs Brewer, it is clear to me that Annie has been severely adversely affected by her sojourn in Carnforth. Her symptoms are not unlike many of the soldiers I see returning home. Stress and nervous exhaustion caused by an inability to process the situation in which she finds herself. This has been exacerbated by the young age at which she was evacuated, and the lack of care and possible neglect she has suffered whilst away. Did you suffer neglect, Annie? Did you? Hmm?'

I remain fascinated by the pockmarked wall behind him. Dr Flanagan turns to address my mother again. 'Hmm. So, my belief is that she is suffering from some sort of nervous breakdown, which will explain the crying, screaming, loss of appetite, inability to leave the house, etcetera, etcetera. Hmm. The hair loss is due to alopecia, also a symptom of a disturbed nervous system. Hmm. Now, with regard to treatment, I know that's what you're after, hmm? Well, there's no quick solution, I'm afraid. Ointment for the hair with regular application will help eventually. It may take a year or two. Hmm. And with regard to the nervous breakdown, just lots of love and attention, that's the ticket. Nothing else for it, I'm afraid. Hmm.'

'And school?' ventures my mother.

'Hmm, school. Well, no point in school for a good while yet. Not until she can cope a bit better. Come back and see me in three months and we will review her then. Hmm?'

I sleep with the light on. Whenever I close my eyes, walls move towards me, pavements fall away, ceilings spin and voices crescendo, orchestral cacophonies boom in my ears. I reach for my beautiful china doll. I stroke her hair and kiss her pale cheek. The doll smiles back impassively. She moves her face closer and closer to mine, smiling, until she rears up, before crashing to the floor. I start to scream.

I jump in my chair.

'Are you OK, Annie? Mrs Stein? Can I get you anything?' The blonde lady looks concerned. She has a deep wrinkle in the centre of her forehead. She should try not to frown. That wrinkle will only get worse.

'Oh yes, I'm perfectly fine, thank you. Would you like more tea?'

'No, I'm fine, thank you, Annie. Are you happy to continue?'

'Yes, of course.' I pull at another thread in my cardigan. I need to darn it later, or it will just get worse.

'What else can you remember when you got back home after the war?'

'Well, one thing I do remember is that, on my twelfth birthday, Mum and Dad gave me a surprise. They came into my bedroom with a big cardboard box and put it on my bed. The box wasn't shut properly, and suddenly, this little nose appeared out of the top of it. It was a puppy, a small black and white terrier, a tiny ball of black and white fluff with thin dappled legs and very pointy ears. I stared at that dog, and that dog stared back at me, her head cocked to one side, and I knew that she would be my best friend. I called her Tina.'

'Tina, what a lovely name,' says the blonde lady.

'Yes. We were inseparable. We ate together, slept together and went out together. She was my best friend.'

The blonde lady looks a bit sad. Maybe she's a little hungry.

'Would you like another biscuit?' I ask, proffering the plate. 'Glass of wine?'

Joe

People cannot co-exist without passion, anger, jealousy, deceit, love and grief. We hurt those whom we love the most because we can. We cheat and lie. We live in fear of revelation. I cheated, she knew, we stayed together. My sister ran away as a GI bride. The night she left, my mother cried. My family said that she had died.

Sasha

My father spent the last four weeks of his life in a nursing home. Up until that point, my mother was adamant that he would be cared for at the house, but eventually, even with twenty-four-hour carers, the fitting of winches to lift him, stair lifts to transport him and chairs to wheel him, he needed even more help.

On the day my father died, I shot up to the home in the early morning. I visited every day, usually in the afternoon, before I had to collect Zac from school, but this last week, my father had been fading fast. Somehow, on that particular day, I knew that I had to get there as soon as I could. I drove erratically, barely able to see the road through a torrential downpour. When I entered his room, my father was tangled in his sheets, breathing heavily with a gruesome rattle. It was a terrible sound – one I had never heard before – and it terrified me. It just went on and on and on, growing louder and ever louder. My father stared straight ahead, unseeing. I didn't know what to do, so I went out into the corridor to see if I could spot a nurse, or a care assistant, or anyone, who might be able to help him, but there was no one to be seen. I crept into the room, leaving the room ajar so that

I could catch someone if they passed by. I squatted by my father's bed and held his hand, talking to him about Zac and what he was doing at school, about Jeremy and his most recent cases, about just about anything that came into my head, as I willed the horrible noise to stop. My father kept his rheumy eyes on the ceiling. 'Dad, can you hear me? You're going to be fine. I think the nurse will be here in a moment. Don't worry.' A tear leaked from the side of his eye and I rummaged in my handbag for a clean tissue to wipe it. He still didn't blink. I paced around the room, folding a towel, putting a chair straight, fidgeting. I wondered what my father was thinking, if he was thinking, whether he could think.

After about an hour, my mother returned. She'd gone home to change and shower after sitting with my father through the night. She was wearing funereal clothing; a black coat, a dark polo neck and black jeans, which were damp at the hem from the continuing deluge outside. As she entered the room, she shivered dramatically, taking off her coat and hanging it precisely on the back of the door. When she came over to the bed, she smelt of wine. 'You know what this is it, don't you?' my mother whispered to me. 'It's the death rattle. I heard it when your Grandma died. He's going.' My mother took hold of father's hand and stroked his face. 'You're leaving me, aren't you, my darling Joe. How can you leave me alone?' She stared into my father's eyes with such overwhelming affection, that I marvelled at the strength of their love, which had endured for so many years, despite so many infidelities and myriad twists and turns. Yet, here they were, still united. My palms were damp and I was shivering, despite the heat of the room.

'I tried to find the nurse, but there is no one about. It's ridiculous. No one had been along the corridor in the whole time I've been here.' I heard my voice rising, going too fast.

'It won't make a difference now.' She seemed lost in my father's face, unable to take her eyes away from him. 'You should go to work now and come back later.' My mother was strangely calm – calmer than I'd seen her in a long time. She straightened up and moved over to the window, refusing to meet my eye. She did not hug me, or hold my hand, or console me in any way. She did not comprehend that I was losing my father. Her own grief was all consuming and there was no room for mine.

'I'll come back later this afternoon,' I murmured, 'after I've collected Zac. I'll drive straight back.' I leant over to kiss my father on his forehead. He was so shrunken now, wizened and wasted by old age and illness. There was so much I wanted to say to him, but I could not speak the words in front of my mother. A tear rolled down my cheek and I wiped it away quickly. 'Love you, Dad. I'll see you a bit later on, OK?' As I spoke, Dad nodded his head imperceptibly, but it was a definite movement and he looked straight at me. I knew that he was saying goodbye. 'Bye, Dad,' I whispered and I fled from the room, tearing down the stairs and out of the home. When I reached the car, I slammed the door shut behind me and then I drove too quickly towards town, struggling to focus on the road through my sheath of tears.

I had been driving for around twenty minutes when my phone rang. I hesitated, before pressing the button to answer. I already knew what my mother was going to say. 'He's gone. He's just gone now,' Mum announced in a flat voice.

'Mum, I'm so sorry, I'm so very sorry. I thought I'd get back to see him again. I really thought I would.' The line went dead. I pulled over to the side of the road and stopped the engine, clutching the steering wheel very tightly. The person I spoke to every day, the one I revered and admired, my rock, my eternal supporter, was no longer with me to help me through my days. My throat constricted, I struggled to breathe, thumping the steering wheel hard as my tears stung the back of my throat.

'I'm so sorry, Sarah. I tend to get rather emotional when I think about my father, even though he's been gone for fifteen years. It seems so long ago in some ways, but in others, it seems like yesterday. There's a whole part of my life which I've lived without him, yet I still chat to him occasionally. You probably think I'm barking mad.'

'No, not at all. It's very hard losing a parent. It's like losing a part of yourself, like finally being cut adrift, even when you think you've already been independent forever. Somewhat rudderless, if that makes sense? I don't think people truly understand what it feels like until they've lost a parent themselves.'

'I think you're absolutely right. So you've lost a parent too?'

'Both, in fact. They died within a very short space of time. I really don't think they could bear to be apart for too long.'

'How awful for you.'

Sarah was dry-eyed, but I passed her a tissue.

We sat in companionable silence, until I suddenly realised that Zac would be home soon and I hadn't even thought about dinner. I had about five minutes to rummage for something vaguely nutritious in the freezer and heat it up in the microwave before his text came summoning me to the bus stop. It used to be the one part of my daily routine which I relished – well, that and walking Stanley – the five precious minutes I had with Zac in the car on the way home from the bus, when he'd fill me in on his day, his homework, the work he'd had marked, silly things which had occurred during the day, irritating events, even more irritating teachers. I used to listen to him offload and I cherished it, in the full knowledge that once home, he would be enveloped again by life, food, Stanley, homework, PS4, Sky Sports, Twitter and whatever other murky entertainment lurked on his phone and laptop. At least at the moment, he was quite keen to make conversation about the progress of the film. He regularly wanted to know how we were getting on and what specifically my mother and I had revealed to Sarah.

I made my apologies to Sarah, found a spaghetti bolognaise, which I quickly removed from its carton and pierced with a sharp knife, before throwing it on the mercy of the microwave. I called Stanley, snapped his lead onto his collar and bundled him into the back of the car. I had an old Golf convertible and on dry days, I rolled the roof back and Stanley would sit on the back seat with his film star looks, smiling at adoring fans as we drove along. If he could have performed a royal wave, he would have done so. Zac was just stepping off the bus as we pulled up. He looked even more disheveled than usual. Stanley went berserk when he saw him, his tail wagging uncontrollably as he pirouetted on the back seat. Zac sauntered over and patted Stanley on the head, before slinging his school bag onto the back seat next the dog and jumping into the front.

'Good day?'

'Not bad.' He looked out at the street, away from me, as we drove along. I wittered on about everything and nothing. Zac was clearly tired, so I didn't press him on his day. It was the weekend, so we had plenty of time to catch up. He could rest a little, the weather was glorious and I was in the car with my two favourite boys. Later on, my third one would be back from his latest trip. A wave of warm contentment washed over me and I thought how lucky I was to have all this.

'Mum, do you ever wish you'd had another child?'

I turned the steering wheel slightly too fast and the car veered towards the curb. I straightened up, my heart beating wildly. 'Um, well, I suppose it might have been nice if you'd had a brother or sister, but we have always felt blessed to have you, and that's been enough for me.

Why, would you have liked to have a sibling?' I suddenly felt very hot. Sweat trickled down my back.

'Maybe. It might have been fun to have someone to play with. If you had had another child, what would you have called him, or even her?' he added quickly.

'I, well, I don't know. I've never really thought about it. I. Why do you ask?' I couldn't look at him, so I kept staring straight ahead.

'No reason. I just wondered, you know, out of curiosity? And what would you have liked to have had if you had the choice? A baby boy or a baby girl?' He was looking right at me.

I pulled into the drive, relieved that we were home and we could stop talking. I noticed Jeremy's car was already there, which was highly unusual. 'Oh look, Zac, your father's back early. That's good. Let's go in and say hello.' I grabbed my handbag and Stanley's lead, pulling the car seat forward to let him out. I unlocked the front door and Stanley ran inside. 'Hello?' I called. 'Jeremy?' I dropped my bag down on the table in the hall and hung my jacket on the overladen coat rack in the corner by the front door.

'In here.' Stanley pulled ahead of me, his head and tail wagging in opposing directions in his joy at seeing Jeremy. 'Hello, Stan,' Jeremy said. He was sitting on the sofa and leant over to tickle Stanley's tummy, which was now on show. Then he looked up. 'Hello, Sash. Where's Zac?'

'I assume he's gone up to his room. I'll call him down for tea in a minute. I just need to heat up his spag bol. I need to talk to you about him later. He's asking some very odd questions.' I slumped down onto the sofa, suddenly exhausted, and leant my head back into the cushion. 'Anyway, it's lovely to have you home early. What's the occasion?'

Jeremy stared at me, then ran his hand over his face. He was unsmiling. 'We need to talk.'

'Yes, I know, but can we do it later after dinner? I've got to sort the food out and finish off a piece of copy before we eat.'

'We need to talk now. It's important. Can you close the door?'

I stood up and closed the door. My hands were shaking slightly. 'What's the matter? Has something happened at work?'

Jeremy shook his head. He stood up and walked over to the mantelpiece, where he studied his reflection in the mirror. Without turning to face me, he said, 'Sasha, I'm leaving you.'

I don't know why, but I laughed.

Jeremy turned to face me. 'I'm so sorry, but I can't lie to you anymore. I'm leaving the house today and I'm not coming back.'

I felt the settee moving away from me. I opened my mouth, but nothing came out, so I just sat there gawping. My first thought was that, if he was having an affair, couldn't he just pretend and not tell me about it?

'I've wanted to speak to you for such a long time, but I just didn't know how to start. I've hoped that, over the years, my feelings would change, that I could be normal

– whatever that is – but I've realised that I can't. I've got to take control of who I am. I've got to admit it, finally, to myself, to everyone. So there's no easy way to tell you this, but the fact is, I'm gay. I suppose I've always known it. I've tried to pretend for so many years. The effort has almost killed me. But now I've met someone, someone I can be myself with, someone I can be happy with, and I have to admit finally that he – another life – is what I want and it's what will make me truly happy.'

I leapt up and stumbled on the rug as I lurched towards him. I grabbed the lapels of his jacket and I started to scream and sob simultaneously. 'You're leaving me for another man?'

'Sasha, I'm so very sorry. If I could be someone else, I would be, but now I have to be me.'

I let go of him and sank into a chair. 'Now you have to be *you*? How long have you known?'

'For a long time. Forever, I suppose. But it was only when I started going to New York so regularly that I realised that I could no longer live, well, here with you.'

'And how many have there been?'

'How many?'

'How many men? Exactly how many men have you cheated on me with?'

'Only one. The one I want to be with now. I swear, Sash, just him.'

I slapped him hard across the face. I'd never struck him before and Jeremy appeared stunned. 'You're a bloody liar, Jeremy. No one walks out and leaves their wife of over twenty five years for just one man. Not after so long. You must have been with others. I don't believe you, Jeremy. I just don't believe you.'

Jeremy said nothing. He was crying now and his face looked puffy and ugly.

'And you just said that the effort has nearly killed you. The effort?' I was shouting now. 'The effort of being with *me* for all these years? Or of being with your son? It's been an effort to be with the two of us? And now you want to be truly happy. Well, terrific, good for you, Jeremy, but what about me, and far more importantly, what about Zac? What the hell is this going to do to Zac?'

Joe

Is there any father who's ever lived who thinks there is a man in this world good enough to marry his daughter? Can there be anyone else who will love and cherish her, look out for her always and shield her from harm? Of course there isn't. All you can do is hope for the next best thing. So I did and I thought she had found it. She married an intelligent, stable man, who provided her with a good home and a beautiful son. He would look after her, whatever life threw at them. If I could kill him, I would.

Annie

Sasha has come over to see me and she's given me the news. I think Jeremy's disgusting. How can men do that to each other? Well, it doesn't bear thinking about. I wish Sasha would join me in a glass of wine. She'd feel better, loosen up a bit. 'I always thought there was something odd about Jeremy. I always said he was a bit shifty. He never really looked you in the eye.'

'Mummy, you love Jeremy. You always have. You think he's charming, debonair, a real gentleman. I was so lucky to find him. Remember?'

'I never said anything of the sort and if I did, it was only to be polite. I never knew he was as gay as a nine bob note then, did I?' My glass is empty. I have another bottle in the dresser, but Sasha doesn't know it's there.

'Mum, for Christ's sake!'

'Don't you swear at me, Sasha. What would your poor father say if he knew Jeremy was bent?'

'He worked with loads of gay people, Mum. He adored them. It was the nature of the business.'

'They weren't gay, Sasha. They were just theatrical. They never actually, well, you know, did anything.' She thinks I don't notice how she belittles me... Miss Hoity-

Toity. 'Anyway, much more importantly, how do you know if it's catching?'

'Catching?'

'You know, Zac. What if he…?'

'I'm not staying here listening to this crap from you.'

'How dare you talk to your mother like that!' Sasha turns on her heel and walks out. Just like that. I'm not surprised he left her.

I'm clearing up. Sasha can't even take her coffee cup into the kitchen and wash it up when she leaves. She's always been lazy. She'll be OK, though. She'll cope. I've had to cope with much worse. I've been without Joe for so long now, for so very long. We didn't have it easy, Joe and me. At least I help Sasha, support her. Not like Joe's mother. She hates me.

Joe drives me round to his mother's house in his brand new Rover. The leather seats are roomy and comforting, but this evening, I'm fidgeting. I can't seem to calm myself. We should have stopped off for a drink on the way. We pull up outside a large red brick gabled house. It's in Salford, miles away from the part of Manchester where I come from. The men ambling along the road look like they're in fancy dress, wearing long black coats and fur hats, ringlets of hair hanging down their faces. They mutter quietly to each other in a language I don't recognise, as we make our way up the gravel drive. Joe opens the front door – he has his own key, even though he doesn't live here officially anymore – and leads the way into the sitting room. The house is spacious, yet the family appears to convene in its smallest room with its old musty brown leather sofas and chairs and a four bar gas fire, which pumps out heat like a blast furnace.

Joe's mother is holding court, a doll-like, diminutive figure enveloped in a massive armchair in the corner of the room. 'Hi, Ma. How are you?'

'Joseph, darling, I'm fine,' she says, rising from her chair. 'I've got you a nice bit of hen for your dinner.' Then she spies me as I peep around the door, looking me up and down as if Joe has dragged a filthy carcass in from the street. 'And who's this?'

'Ma, this is Annie Brewer. Annie, please meet my mother, Peggy.'

I step forward to shake her hand, but Peggy stands up and moves straight past me. 'Joe, I didn't know we were having visitors. I've no more food.' She turns to face me. 'I'm sorry dear, but you'll have to go home.'

'Annie, ignore her. Ma, Annie's staying for dinner.' Joe reaches over and takes my hand in his.

Peggy raises her head to consider me again, ostentatiously assessing me from the top of my head right down to my shoes and back again, as if I am a prize cow being readied for market. 'She's far too tall,' she barks, storming out towards the kitchen. Joe squeezes my hand to steady me.

'Now what can I get you to drink?' Joe asks me and I suggest a whisky to steady my nerves.

Peggy suddenly returns. 'Time to eat,' she announces, looking straight through me.

We troop through to the dining room, which is set with gleaming gold-rimmed plates and sparking crystal. An ornate, if somewhat faded, chandelier hangs from the ceiling, emitting a disappointing amount of light. 'Sit', Peggy instructs and we sit. I am aware of how much I tower over her, even when we are seated. I am to her right and Joe is on her left. Peggy spends the majority of the meal with her back turned decisively against me and towards Joe. Despite the fact that Joe lives with his mother on and off during the week, and that she speaks to him several times a day, she appears to have a great deal to discuss with him, all of which is conducted in a fierce whisper. David, Peggy's nephew, is seated next to me and regales me with intimate details of his sciatica, neuralgia, hiatus hernia and a particularly difficult in-growing toenail. He fails to mention his rampant dandruff, which coats his shoulders and floats into his soup when he bends his head to slurp it loudly. I feel quite nauseous, partly due to David's proximity and partly, because the hen Peggy has served is so tough that I fear for my teeth.

Joe excuses himself for a moment and Peggy swivels around rather violently to face me. 'So, you're the shikse who wants to shack up with my Joe, are you? Couldn't find one of your own kind then,' she hisses.

Sweat begins to run down the back of my neck and the air around Peggy's head seems to fragment. 'I...'

'Ttt, not even got a tongue in your head. Listen, my girl, go out with him if you must, but remember, you're not a Jew and you never will be. Once a shikse, always a shikse. And if you do marry – I say if, as you never know, you never know – God forbid my Joseph makes such a foolhardy decision – but *if* you do…he will never be happy with you. Never.' She turns her head towards the door, searching for Joe, and then turns to assault me again, frowning. 'And you make sure that you feed him the food he likes. None of your goy rubbish.' My tongue refuses to navigate the contours of my mouth. My hands begin to shake and I sit on them quickly, after taking a hefty slug of wine. 'You really don't say much, do you? And why are you so tall. You're just far too tall.'

Joe

I told my mother that I'm marrying Annie.

'You're doing what?' she shrieks. 'I don't think so, Joseph! A shikse, in my house! Isn't it bad enough that your sister ran off with that bloody yank and now you want to shame me further by marrying a goy?' Her tiny frame trembled, a small volcano spurting red molten rage.

'Ma, I'm forty-three, for Christsake,'

'Don't you swear at me in my own house, Joseph Stein!' She pulled at the long string of pearls around her neck, as if they were a rosary.

'I've never met anyone else that I want to spend my life with until now. You should be happy for me.'

'So, there are no decent Jewish girls in the whole of England for Joe Stein? Are you meshuggah?' She crashed down into her armchair, beating the armrests into submission. The antimacassars struggled to stay put.

'Annie will convert. We will be married in synagogue under the chuppah. It'll be fine.'

'Oy vay, under the chuppah. Yes, under a *Reform* chuppah. Not the same, not the same at all. Men and women sitting together!' She clicked her tongue and rolled her eyes far back into her head. 'Your father, your poor father. If he wasn't dead already, you'd kill him. I'll probably go and join him from the shame. Watch me. I'm about to have another hemorrhage right here!' She held her head in her hands, moaning loudly.

'Ma, stop it. I'm marrying Annie and you're going to have to get used to the idea. I've proposed, she's accepted and she's seeing Rabbi Goldberg next week to discuss conversion.'

'Rabbi Goldberg. Who's he? Some Mickey Mouse rabbi? Did he even graduate from a Yeshiva? Never heard of him. What will Rabbi Solomon say?'

'I should think he'll say Mazeltov, as is customary at weddings.'

'Mazeltov? He's more likely to say Kaddish. You're killing me Joseph Stein, killing me.' She leant back in the armchair, closing her eyes.

'I'm going to leave now, but I will bring Annie back to see you again later in the week and you will be nice to her. Do we understand each other?'

'If I'm still alive, please God. My head, it's terrible. I might not make it through the night.'

Sasha

I've been an utter fool. All these days and nights and weekends Jeremy had spent away from me and yet I never realised – never even suspected – that Jeremy could be unfaithful to me – and with a man, with anyone. I keep re-running the evening he left on a constant loop in my head. Our row had been so terrible. We said things we never should have said. And now I have to recognise that my whole marriage has been a complete sham. For the past twenty five years, I've lived a lie – unknowingly – or was it knowingly? I can't bring myself to admit it. I don't know. I just can't work it out. I need to get a grip, for Zac's sake, if nothing else, but I can't seem to ground myself. I'm spending my waking hours in a half-daze. I can't concentrate on work, or on the housework, or on anything very much. I can't sleep. I wander the house like a spectre unable to cross over into the next world.

And then there's Zac. He heard us screaming, tearing into each other. I was crying uncontrollably and so was Jeremy. Zac walked in to see us both raging, falling apart. No child should have to watch his parents' marriage disintegrate. We were supposed to be there for him, to love and support him, to set an example to him. How can we command any future respect after he saw us scrapping like animals without a shred of dignity? There would be no reason why he should look to either of us for advice or comfort ever again.

After Jeremy finally left, I sat exhausted on the sofa. Stanley lay with one paw over my foot, his eyes never leaving my face. During the row, he'd hidden under the coffee table shaking. I don't know how much later it was, but eventually Zac came in and sat beside me.

'I told you,' he said quietly.

'You told me what?' I sniffed.

'I told you, or at least, I tried to warn you. I kept asking you where Dad was at night, at the weekends. It was bloody obvious he was having an affair. It was staring you in the face.' Zac was trembling, his skin drained of all colour. I reached out and held his hand. He did not pull away.

'I just thought he was busy working. I never thought he'd leave me, us. Not after so long. We've been together for so many years,' I blew my nose in my sodden tissue.

'But he was never here, was he? And you just put up with it.'

I stared at him.

'Well you did, didn't you? You let him walk all over you. And now he's walked out.' Zac stood up and strode over to the mantelpiece to pick up a pen which was lying there. He started to press the top open and shut, click, click, click, facing away from me. I went over to him and reached out to hug him, but he ducked out of the way.

'I just never thought he's have an affair, Zac. Your

father has never been the type. He's too reliable, loyal and well, faithful. He never so much as glanced at another woman while we were together.' I guess now I know why. I laughed despite myself.

'It's so humiliating!' Zac suddenly shouted. 'What the hell am I supposed to tell people? That my dad has a boyfriend? That I might have two dads? Christ. It's just unbelievable. Surely you must have known. You must have. You've just been lying to yourself and to me. It's just another one of your horrendous lies.' Zac paced the room. He came up to me and grabbed me, shaking me violently by the shoulders, before shoving me down onto the sofa. Stanley leapt up and barked at Zac. 'You're just a bloody liar. You're a real idiot.' screamed Zac.

Zac ran from the room into the hall, grabbed his anorak from the rickety hat stand by the front door and stormed out of the house into a lashing rainstorm. I called after him, screaming up the street like a banshee. All the neighbours must have heard me. Zac just kept going, his long legs striding away from me under the street lamps. I stood there and watched him go. 'At least take an umbrella!'

Zac returned much later on. I was lying on my bed, having called him repeatedly, only to get his answer message on repeat and sent him a million texts. He replied to none of them. I felt sick and exhausted. He could be under a bus, or he might have jumped from a bridge, or been mugged. My head pounded with dread. Hours later, I heard him return, slamming the front door and then I heard nothing. He didn't appear to have come upstairs, so I wrapped my dressing gown around me and tiptoed downstairs to find him. Zac lay on the floor with Stanley by his side. Zac was crying. Stanley lay with his head resting on Zac's leg, comforting him. I went over to them both and knelt down, reaching out for Zac's hand. He touched my fingertips and we sat there together, I don't know for how long. 'I'm so sorry, Zac. I'm so very sorry, but we'll get through this. We'll sort it out, I promise Somehow, we will manage.'

Joe

We lie to protect the feelings of others. We lie because we are ashamed of what we have done, or of what we have not done. We lie to ourselves. Sometimes, we convince ourselves that those lies are truths. But lies are heavy and in the end, most of us will buckle under the weight of them. The pack of cards comes tumbling down.

Annie

'I was very sorry to hear about Sasha and Jeremy. I haven't seen her since he left. Is she OK?' The blonde woman is fishing for the nitty gritty.

'Oh, she'll be fine. I never thought it would last, if I'm honest with you. They were both wrapped up in their own little worlds. Perhaps if Sasha hadn't insisted on working and had spent more time paying attention to Jeremy, he never would have run off with a…well, no matter. Do have another biscuit, a glass of wine, maybe?' I thought that would shut her up.

'No, I'm fine. Thank you so much. So, Annie, do you mind if we carry on with the interview? I know Zac's keen to progress it, regardless of what's happened. I think it might be a good distraction for him, actually.'

I say nothing, but if you ask me, that boy's got a lot to deal with as it is, what with having a poof as a father and nervous wreck of a mother. I can't see how a poxy film is going to help, but I say nothing.

'I thought we might pick up where we left off. You told me last time about meeting Joe. How long did you go out with him for before you married?' She smiles and picks up a biscuit from the plate on the coffee table.

'Oh, it was for a very long time. Joe was Jewish, you see, and I was, well, I wasn't. And he'd lived at home for his whole life and had a cushy number there. His mother cooked and cleaned and did his washing for him. He had another home, but he barely used it. Why did he need to get married? But eventually, I gave him an ultimatum.'

'Gosh, that's very brave of you. How did that go?'

I am cocooned in a darkened velvet booth at the back of the Cabin Club off Deansgate, waiting for Joe to arrive. I chose this spot deliberately, as it is discreet and can't be overlooked by other drinkers. I have dressed carefully in a fitted satin dress in dark red damask, which allows me to blend chameleon-like into the maroon chaise longue. I fiddle with the slice of lemon floating aimlessly at the top of my gin and tonic, my second. It's impossible to know what to do with my hands without a cigarette. I had an X-ray last month, which revealed a shadow on my lungs. I haven't had a drag since. I find I've made up for it by having a bit more than usual to drink, even though it's bound to make me gain weight. Joe is late, and I want to get this conversation over and done with. Having geared myself up, I need to spit it out before I lose my nerve.

Eventually, Joe saunters in, dapper as ever in his light grey suit, red silk tie and jaunty trilby. He looks up and his eyes search across the tables as he moves towards the back of the club. He starts to peer into each of the recessed booths. 'Oh, here you are! I couldn't see you tucked away in there. Wouldn't you rather sit nearer to the bar and listen to the band? They're rather good tonight,' he asks me, leaning over to give me a peck on the cheek.

'Actually, no, Joe, I don't, not tonight. There's something I want to talk to you about and it's too loud out there... and you're late,' I bark, furrowing my brow.

'Yes, sorry about that. I had a problem at the studio with one of my assistants. She couldn't get her brief straight and I had to help her.'

'Well, never mind that, I've got you your whisky and water. That should cheer you up.' I smile wanly.

'Thanks, my darling, thoughtful as ever.' Joe pours the water into the whisky until the glass is half full and takes a large gulp. I drain my gin and tonic and wave at a passing waiter for a refill.

'Ah, that's much better. Now what did you want to chat about? Is everything all right? You look a little pale, my darling.'

I smooth my dress and uncross and cross my legs. My drink arrives and I take an unladylike swig. 'The thing is...the thing is...the thing is, Joe, things can't go on like this.' I look down into my glass, feeling real empathy with my drowning slice of lemon.

'What things can't go on?' asks Joe. He pulls his silver monogrammed cigarette case out of his top pocket and taps one out on the lid as he closes it. He lights it and I lean towards him to inhale the forbidden smoke.

'*We* can't go on, Joe. Like this. It's not working. I'm twenty seven years old, and we've been going out for six years, and I want to know where we are going with this relationship. I know there are difficulties with my not being Jewish, but you've had plenty of time to think about that, and if you can't tell me what's what, then I think we should call it a day. I want children and if I have to start again with someone else, I need to know now, or I'll run out of time.' The words, pent up inside me for so long and corked by anxiety, gush out in a breathless rush of air. Joe suddenly appears very interested in the bottom of his own glass. 'Well, say something!'

'What do you want me to say?' asks Joe, looking me straight in the eye.

'I want you to answer me, to tell me what you're thinking. You might be able to continue to have your cake and eat it, going out with me, living at home to all intents and purposes, and making no decisions, but I just can't do it anymore. Are you just using me, or do you actually love me?' I raise my voice more than I had intended.

'What do you mean, am I using you? Using you? Is that what you think of me, after all this time? Is it really?' Joe's face contorts strangely as he spits my words back at me. I can feel tears stinging the back of my throat.

'Well, it feels like that. It really does. How much longer do you expect me to wait? I'm not superhuman. I just really need to know. I need to know now, or I warn you, I will go. I need you to tell me if we've got a future.' Tears trickle unbidden down my reddened cheeks and I bow my head to hide my weakness from Joe.

'Well, you're not going to get an answer by screaming at me like a fish wife in a public place,' retorts Joe, rising from his chair and throwing some money on the table.

'There. That should cover the drinks,' he growls. He plants his trilby firmly on his head and strides out into the night, while the eyes of the Cabin Club stare into the ruby cave where I weep silently.

I'm at home and Joe hasn't called for two weeks. I've cried every day. Suddenly, I hear my dad calling up the stairs. 'Annie, love. Phone call. Get a move on. It's your bleedin' beau.'

I shoot down the stairs, my hair standing on end with static from my pillow. Out of breath, I grab the phone off my father. 'Hello?'

'Hello, Annie. It's me, Joe. I think we should talk.'

So we get married. The wedding is very low key with just three guests; Joe's mother and my mum and dad. We get hitched in a registry office, as we've not had time to sort out my conversion properly as yet. Joe's mother is extremely vocal in her condemnation of the event. 'So, I have to schlepp all the way into the middle of Manchester to watch you marry this shikse in a registry office, do I? And I suppose I'll have to make small talk with her goy parents? What do I know about barrels? Are they both too tall as well?'

Mum and Dad are not much keener. They like Joe, but they don't like the age gap and the Jewishness. They're not so much anti-Semitic as nervous. Mum asks, 'An' what about his mother, Lady Muck? We've not met her, but she sounds really awful, from what you've said. Is she still calling you a trickster?'

'A shikse, not a trickster, Mum! It means non-Jew. And yes, but I just try to ignore her…and I try to stoop as much as possible, so that I'm not too tall!' We giggle.

In the end, the wedding goes off smoothly enough and we repair to The Midland Bar to celebrate. Joe orders a bottle of champagne, a whisky and water for himself and a Guinness for my dad.

'Well, it's a relief to see that you're short,' Peggy says to my mum. 'I mean, it's alright in a man, like your husband, and goys tend to be taller anyway, but in a woman…well, it's just not ladylike, is it?' Peggy shifts on her chair, her legs dangling down in the absence of any available poof.

'Well, I don't suppose we can control our 'eight much, can we, Mrs. Stein. I mean, we're just born with it, aren't we?' counters my mum carefully.

'Nonsense. You've just fed her the wrong stuff. Now, I like to feed my children a good piece of hen. Can't go too far wrong with hen'

The next day, we flew to Nassau for our honeymoon.

Joe

And then there were three. Marriage is often followed by children, but not usually as soon as the honeymoon ends. A man feels many emotions when he is told his wife is expecting. Pride in his potency, fear of the future, and pressure to provide. He waits for his wife to swell and pop.

Sasha

I was at the supermarket and I couldn't remember what I needed to buy. People tore past me in a mad dash to grab and go. I stood inert by the reds, greens and yellows of the vegetables, unable to make a decision. Tears stung the corners of my eyes. And then I saw him. He was at the end of the aisle with his own trolley, picking produce off the shelves with cold calculation and ticking items off his list systematically as he went. He looked well. He'd lost a little weight, but it suited him. Jeremy slicked back his grey mane and frowned at his list. My heart flipped over and I gripped the rail of my trolley so tightly that my fingers hurt. Should I turn and hide in another aisle, or should I drift towards him? We hadn't seen each other in a while now. We only spoke occasionally on the phone to sort out housekeeping matters. It was all very business-like. Jeremy addressed me as he would a work colleague, brusque and factual.

This was ludicrous. I gave myself a stern talking to. This was my ex-husband of twenty five years. I should be able to say hello, for goodness sake. But what would we say after hello? Make small talk over the washing up liquid? I told my wobbly brain to steel itself and forced my trolley forwards into battle, steering it towards the soothing smell of baking bread. He didn't see me coming. 'Hi, Jeremy, how are you?'

He looked up and the Shredded Wheat he was holding slipped out of his hand onto the floor. 'Hi, Sasha.' He bent down to retrieve his cereal and dropped the box into his trolley with practiced nonchalance. 'I'm fine, thank you. How are you?'

'Fine, yes, I'm fine, thank you. You?' I wanted to hide my face, my body. I'd come out without a scrap of makeup, in old sweats and grotty trainers. I resembled a bag lady who had come into Tesco to look for handouts.

'You look a little tired,' Jeremy remarked, a faint look of concern on his face.

'Well, thanks for that, Jeremy. You, on the other hand, look bloody fantastic. Your new life must be agreeing with you.' Stop it. Stop it.

Jeremy looked down at his list, clearly hoping that the next item on it might give him a clue as to what he might say next, anything which might not be inflammatory. Sweetcorn, tuna, lettuce, innocuous things to say to your ex-wife should your trolleys happen to bump into each other. 'How's Zac?'

How's Zac? Well, he's a basket case actually, Jeremy, I wanted to shout. But can you blame him? He gets trolled on social media because his dad has a boyfriend. He won't talk to me about it, because I can't give him anything close to a satisfactory explanation as to why it happened and when I do, I just start crying. He goes out drinking until all hours, I'm fairly sure he's taking drugs and he skips school. 'He's struggling. I've found a counsellor and I hope she'll help him, but he's not keen to go.'

'No, well, I can understand that. It's hard to talk about your feelings at his age.'

'It's hard to talk about feelings at any age for some people.' We stood in silence, two gunfighters facing off against each other, yet without ammunition. Hostilities had ceased temporarily only to spare the feelings of other shoppers.

'Well, I'd better get on,' said Jeremy. 'I need to get back.'

I said nothing and was about to turn and walk away, when a man emerged around the corner of the aisle. He walked up behind Jeremy and put his hand on his shoulder. 'Jez darling, do you think this might go well with the fish for dinner tomorrow evening?' he asked, flashing him the label on what looked like an expensive bottle of Chablis. He was much younger than I'd expected, slight, dressed in jeans and a T shirt, achingly good-looking, mid-twenties at most…just a few years older than Zac, I guessed.

'Well, what do you think?' he crooned. Then he looked up and saw me. He noticed Jeremy bowing his head, his colour rising. With more self-possession than either Jeremy or I could muster, he stepped forward and held out his hand. 'Hello, I'm Guy. You must be Sasha. It's *so* lovely to meet you. I've heard so much about you from Jez.'

Jez? Guy's almond eyes smiled at me from under a long dark set of lashes, which a woman could only dream of possessing. I was clearly no competition. I stared from Jeremy to Guy and back again. Then I turned and ran, discarding my trolley, which came to rest in a tall display of toilet rolls. I pushed strolling shoppers out of the way as I made my escape. When I reached the car, I started the ignition and drove through sheets of tears to the neighbouring car park of the toy superstore, where I stopped in a remote corner and cried for a very long time, while happy families packed their cars with playthings all around me. I cried for me, I cried for Zac, I cried for the failure of my marriage. I heaved and sobbed and racked my body until I had nothing left.

That evening, I curled up on the sofa with Stanley, who had been the only real beneficiary of Jeremy leaving. He was now allowed on all the chairs and sofas, and into my bedroom, where he snored and snuffled on the deep pile carpet in canine bliss, while I tossed and turned all night long. 'Oh, Stanley, I've got to get a grip,' I said, stroking his soft head and passing him a piece of my chocolate biscuit. Most evenings we shared a packet. Stanley licked my hand and stared at me with his dark amber eyes. 'What would I do without you, Stanley?' I sniffed. Stanley put his head on my lap, as if to say that I shouldn't worry on that score, as I would never be without him. I heard the front door opening. 'Zac? Zac, is that you?' I called.

'No, it's a burglar with a key! Who do you think it is?'

Stanley abandoned me, leaping off the sofa to pay homage to his returning brother and I listened as he and

Zac played tug of war with Penguin. I walked slowly into the hall, hugging my ratty cardigan around myself. 'How was your day?

'Fine.'

'Fancy a take-out tonight?'

'Again?'

'Yes, well, I didn't get a chance to get to the supermarket. Well, I did, but…oh well, it was complicated.' Zac tickled Stanley's stomach without looking up.

'I think I'll just go round to Ben's house and eat with them.'

'Haven't you got homework to do?'

'Not much, no. I'll do it there.'

'Zac, I don't think you can keep imposing on Ben's family. They've got enough mouths to feed. And anyway, it would be nice to spend an evening together. Watch a film or something?'

'Ben's mum says I can go there whenever I want. She's so cool. And they've got a huge TV where we can play PS4 for as long as we like. Really, it's no big deal.'

'Well, let me call her and check.'

'Don't you dare call her. I mean it.' Zac glowered at me, and I didn't have an ounce of fight left in me. He slung his bag back over his shoulder and re-opened the front door.

'By the way, I'm going to see Dad tomorrow. He's picking me up after school,' Zac remarked, glancing back at me.

'Well, that's a first. Where's he taking you?'

'He's invited me to see his new flat. He's just moved

in and says he's decorated a room for me, if I want it. I said I'd have a look, decide, you know.'

'He's decorated a room for you?' I pulled my cardigan tighter round my ever-thickening middle.

'Yes, for me to stay whenever I want to…if I want to. So I'll see you later, Mum, or tomorrow or whatever.'

'Zac, please stay. I'd like to chat.'

'You always want to chat, Mum, but you're never honest with me and we go round and round in circles.'

'Honest about what?'

'About Dad and all the other stuff that's happened. You just can't face up to it. You won't answer me about other things.'

'What other things, Zac? What are you getting at?'

'I know you're hiding something from me. I'm not an idiot. I've seen a photo at Grandma's of a baby who's not me.'

'I don't know what you're talking about Zac. Seriously, what do you mean?'

'I saw a photo of a baby, but it was dated two years before I was born, so I know it's not me. So who is it?'

'Of course it's you, Zac. Who else would it be?'

'I don't know, but I intend to find out. I've been trying to find out for ages now.' He slammed the door and I stood there staring at it for a very long time.

Joe

The object of the game Happy Families is to collect as many complete families as possible. Every player starts with an equal number of cards. Players ask each other to swap cards to create a family. The winning person has a whole family, or more than one complete family. The loser is left only with pieces.

Annie

Joe has asked me to go away with him for the weekend, even though we're not even engaged yet. I know he's slept with many other women. They throw themselves at him in his job, so it's not really his fault. But if I want to hang onto him, I know I can't put it off forever, which is why I've said yes. I'm really nervous about it. My parents are apoplectic.

'This man is twice your age, old enough to be your father and a Jew to boot! You know he's only after one thing and when he's got it, he'll bugger off and you'll be left deflowered, or even worse, up the bloody duff! You can't go!' Dad is puce in the face. He paces the length of our small living room, wearing the threadbare carpet to a wafer and waving his pipe in the air like a lethal weapon.

'Annie, love, your father's right,' ventures Mum.' Once you've been away with him, that'll be it!'

'I'm 23 and I can make my own decisions. I love Joe and I am going away with him, whether you like it or not.'

'Well, don't come blathering to me and your mother if it all goes belly up, my girl.' Dad stomps out of the living room, his pipe forming angry smoke signals.

Mum slumps into her armchair, defeated. 'Well, if nothing else, please at least take precautions.'

I desperately want to ask Mum what I should expect, what men actually do, what they look like, whether it hurts, but I can't. We never discuss intimate matters. I remember my first period years ago. It was a complete shock, waking to find my sheets covered in blood. I checked myself all over for cuts, never dreaming it could come from between my legs. I screamed and Mum changed the sheets, giving me a huge wad of cotton, which I was somehow supposed to put in my knickers. I couldn't walk properly. Mum said this meant I was a woman now and not to let men touch me. If they did, I'd get a reputation. I guess that's her worry now.

Joe is throttling his brand new MGA with the roof down. Traffic is light and we make good time, stopping for lunch at a picturesque pub just outside Rugby, where I have a couple of gin and tonics and Joe sticks to whisky. Then we drive straight down the A1 to The Dorchester, where we are greeted by the magnificent spreading plane tree in full blossom in the courtyard. A liveried doorman opens my door and I step out of the car, but having been blown about by the convertible for hours, I feel more bedraggled than elegant.

'I'll bring your luggage, Mr. Stein,' says the doorman.

'Thank you, Arthur,' Joe replies, slipping him a pound note with a magician's sleight of hand.

The splendour of The Dorchester makes The Midland in Manchester look like a country hotel.

Towering flower arrangements stand proudly on marble tables and porters glide effortlessly across the lobby with trolleys piled high with expensive luggage and designer shopping bags. Joe marches to the front desk, where the manager walks around to the customer side of the desk to shake his hand. 'Welcome back, Mr. Stein. Good to see you again. I have your suite ready for you, as always. If you'll both follow me, please.'

'Thank you, Michael,' says Joe, shaking the manager's hand warmly.

Michael turns to me. 'Welcome to The Dorchester, Madam,' he says, bowing slightly and taking my glove in a slippery handshake. We follow Michael to the left of the lobby and the lift operator whisks us to the top floor. When the doors slide open again, we step into a long corridor with plush carpeting, large highly patterned Ds woven into it. Michael leads the way to the far end and opens the door to our suite with a large heavy key, which he then presents ceremoniously to Joe, as if he were giving him the keys to London itself. He turns to me. 'Madam, this is one of our most luxurious suites, designed by the famous theatre designer, Oliver Messel.' Michael steps back and bowed ostentatiously.

I giggle, then mask it with a cough. 'Excuse me,' I mutter into my handkerchief.

'Thank you again,' says Joe, slipping some money into Michael's seemingly closed hand.

'My pleasure, as always, Mr. Stein,' simpers Michael, walking backwards out of the door.

As soon as Michael leaves, Joe grabs me by the waist and swings me round. He takes my hand and drags me from room to room. I follow him open-mouthed. The front door leads straight into a monumental living room, with two chaise longues with intricately carved wooden arms covered in royal blue damask. In the centre of the room stands an exquisite flower arrangement, which reaches all the way to the ceiling. There is a large cocktail cabinet with exquisite marquetry and on it sits a bottle of champagne on ice, and two crystal champagne coupes. The windows flow from floor to ceiling, offering a spectacular view of Hyde Park. I watch a glorious chestnut horse putting his rider through his paces in the distance. Through a large set of double doors is the master bedroom, which houses the largest bed I have ever seen. What's more, it's circular and covered in a heavy cream silk bedspread. There are enough pillows to make a family of ten comfortable. Off the bedroom is a walk-in dressing room, with a spectacular Louis XIV dressing table. On the other side, the bathroom hosts a marble bathtub, raised off the floor on four golden claws and there are his and hers sinks with gilt cherub taps. 'This place is larger than our whole house,' I marvel, smiling at Joe.

He comes towards me and takes me in his arms, kissing my neck and sliding his hands down my back and over my bottom. I pull away and move towards the window. 'Joe, I've never been to London. Can you take me to see the sights?'

'Well, I thought we might do that a little later,' says Joe, grasping my waist. I twirl away.

'Let's go now,' I laugh, smoothing down my skirt. 'while it's still so light. Then we'll be back in time for dinner.'

After our grand tour, we repair to the bar, apparently one of London's most glamorous drinking holes. Joe tells me that this is where Harry Craddock, London's most famous barman, invented three of the world's most well-known cocktails: the Martini, the Manhattan and the White Lady. We try one of each. The alcohol starts to take the edge off my nerves and when we stagger back to our suite, I let Joe un-peel me layer by layer. I feel as though I'm watching a film, in which I'm slightly out of focus, almost fuzzy. It's all over rather quickly and when Joe falls asleep, I lie there with an unpleasant stickiness between my legs.

Joe

For me, it had always been about the thrill of the chase. Can I? Can't I? Will she? Won't she? I never dreamt I'd settle down. But then, no one can foresee the future. Sometimes events just happen and when they do, they force you to alter your course. Even those of us who have remained steadfastly single-minded – selfishly so perhaps – ultimately need to do the right thing.

Sasha

During my time of crisis, internet shopping had proved a great solace. I had filed for divorce, but while I still had access to the joint bank account, I made full use of it. Whether sitting at my desk in my office surrounded by ever rising piles of paper and files, old coffee cups and half-eaten packets of biscuits, or lounging in my fraying pink onesie in front of the television, or even lying awake in my lonely king-sized bed, hot water bottle on my stomach for comfort, I replenished my wardrobe from top to bottom. I found smart shirts and comfortable cashmere sweaters and bought them in every colour. I purchased straight leg, boot cut and cropped jeans. I splashed out on high heeled boots, low heeled boots, ankle length and knee length boots, trainers, and naturally, high fashion wellingtons for walking Stanley. I felt like Jay Gatsby preparing to impress Daisy. Zac was not forgotten and he received not only new clothes, but also a spanking new cricket bat, bright red football boots sponsored by Ronaldo, several football kits with his initials monogrammed on the chest and I invested in every paid-for sports channel available. Zac had not yet started driving lessons, so I pre-paid for a course of forty, as well as organising and paying for his theory test. No doubt, at some point, this would prove to be an enormous bone of contention between our respective lawyers, but I was guessing that Jeremy would be feeling a reasonable burden on guilt and therefore might just let it go.

Yet no amount of comfort shopping could stop me obsessing about Jeremy and the lies he had told. I wanted to know the truth about when he had first realised he was gay. Was it before we got married? Was it before we even met? Was it after we met and if so, when? How had he realised? When had he realised? Who had he realised it with? How many men had he slept with? How could he make love with them and still – albeit occasionally – sleep with me? Did he feel guilty now, or merely relieved? Had he felt guilty then? Did he ever miss me? Had he ever loved me? If I had been a better, or more attractive, or more interesting woman, would it have made a difference? These thoughts tortured me, invading my every waking hour.

I discovered Jeremy's address from Zac –an apartment near Marylebone – and I started sending farewell gifts to him. I began low-key, buying slightly risqué magazine subscriptions to both girlie and gay magazines. These elicited no response from Jeremy, despite the fact that I knew he would have instantly checked on the origins of these sudden arrivals. So I upped my game. I sent small kitchen appliances at first – hand whisks, juice makers, soup makers, popcorn and ice cream makers. My former better half maintained radio silence. So I procured him a complete state of the art kitchen, or at least, the main white goods elements of it. Jeremy's doorbell would ring and a man would stand there with a stainless steel American refrigerator with built in freezer, two ovens which could be switched on remotely via an app, a microwave and dishwasher. All had the highest level of extended warranties and guarantees and I had even paid for installation.

My mobile rang and Jeremy's younger face flashed up. I let it trill until just before it tipped over to answerphone. 'Sasha, what the hell is going on?'

'Hello to you too, Jeremy. How are you?'

I heard a deep sigh – Jeremy's equivalent of counting to ten. 'I'm fine, thank you, or at least I would be if you stopped sending me all this crap!'

'That's extremely ungrateful of you, Jeremy. I've sent you some beautiful housewarming gifts –exquisite and top of the range, I might add – and all you can do is be rude and ungracious about them. Really, it's too much.' My mouth twisted, as I tried to stop my voice from rising.

'Sasha, I know you're angry, but this ridiculous nonsense has got to stop. Let's try to deal with this like adults, shall we?' I heard someone speaking in the background. Jeremy mumbled, 'In a minute, Guy. I'm on the phone.'

'Like adults? I can't believe you're saying that to me, Jeremy, of all people. Did you treat me like an adult during our marriage? Did you tell me about your feelings at any point? No, you didn't. You brought my whole house down in one fell swoop. You gave me absolutely no warning. On the contrary, you unleashed a devastating avalanche and now you expect me to behave like an adult. Well, I've got news for you, Jeremy. I'm not going to make it easy for you to walk away and ruin my life after all these years.' My voice was cracking. I needed to stay strong. I really didn't want to cry until the call was over.

'Well, I'll make it easier for you then, Sasha, shall I? As of an hour ago, I've closed the joint bank account and cancelled all the credit cards. I will pay you a monthly allowance to cover the household bills and subsistence for Zac until we agree a final settlement. That should settle the matter.'

'You can't just do that, Jeremy. Not without my agreement. I'm sure you can't just…'

He interrupted me. 'I think you'll find that I can and I have. The money in that account comes solely from me and I alone can stop the flow. So, let's stop the silly games, shall we? My lawyer will be in touch.'

The phone went silent and it reverted to my home picture of Zac and Stanley smiling out at me from the beach at Littlehampton. Jeremy had cut me off, quite literally.

Joe

They say that love conquers all, but even love cannot conquer an empty bank account.

Annie

I am very sad today. My friend Gill is dead. We have been friends since school, and now she's gone. She is my last friend, maybe my only friend. I don't know why, but I seem to lose a lot of friends as I go through life. I like them, sometimes a great deal and then, one day, I see them for who they really are, and I don't like them anymore. People take offence so easily. You can say something totally innocuous, they look at you oddly and then, you don't see them again. When I'm with Joe, we have people around us all the time. Of course, most of them are groupies or hangers-on, who think that some of Joe's stardust, or money, will rub off on them. It rarely does, and if he does rub against them, it's only ever temporary and he always returns to me like a homing pigeon.

Someone told me Gill is dead, but I don't think that's right. Only yesterday, we went to the pictures to see *An American In Paris* with Gene Kelly for the second time this week. We link arms and hoof down the street.

'I don't think we will ever get to dance with Gene Kelly, do you?' I laugh.

'You'd need a few more dance lessons before you do, my girl!' mocks Gill. 'C'mon Cyd Charisse, let's go to the Kardomah and get a coffee before we go home.'

'I said I'd be back by eight.' My parents are terrible worriers if I'm not home straight after work.

'Are you seventeen or seven? Did you or did you not live without them for five years when you were evacuated?' Gill squeezes my arm and I nod.

'Right, so my guess is you can stay out for an extra half hour' She steers me down towards Albert Square, negotiating our path across the road to avoid the drivers who tear around its perimeter.

We push open the door to the Kardomah Café, the bell tinkling over our heads to announce our arrival. The heat slams into our faces as we enter and the smell of stale coffee fills our nostrils. A rather stern middle aged waitress in a black dress and lacey apron, who is standing close to the door, cocks one eyebrow at us. Her makeup is pale, thick, almost white, and has set in the crevasses around her eyes and mouth. Her lips, by contrast, are scarlet. She looks like an aged clown. 'Can I help you?'

'Table for two, please,' replies Gill.

'Follow me,' sniffs the waitress. She wobbles down the room, her notepad flapping out of her apron pocket, her pen clicking open and shut. We follow, Gill sticking out her backside to mimic the waitress. I have to stuff my hand into my mouth to stop myself from cackling.

'What can I get you?' asks the waitress, tapping her foot and barely bothering to feign an interest in us – two young girls unlikely to leave a tip.

'Two black coffees, please,' I ask, smiling sweetly.

'Is that all?'

'Yes, that will be all,' replies Gill grandly. The waitress turns on her heel and waddles away, our laughter no doubt ringing in her ears.

'So, do you want to go to the pictures again next week?' asks Gill, stacking sugar lumps one on top of the other, until they all fall down and she starts the whole exercise again.

'S'pose it depends on what's on, though I don't mind seeing that Gene Kelly in Paris again. He's so dreamy.' I pretend to swoon and almost elbow the sugar bowl off the table. We burst out laughing again. The waitress returns with the hot drinks, slamming them down onto the table with more force than is strictly necessary. Coffee slops into the saucers and splashes onto the table.

'We'll just slurp it out of the saucer than, shall we?' calls Gill after the waitress, who appears to have become suddenly deaf.

I lift my cup and blow gently on the remains of my coffee.

'Are you back in the shop tomorrow then, Annie?'

'Yes, of course I'm back in the bloody shop. It's so boring, but what else am I qualified to do? I can barely add up the right change for people's fags.'

'Well, it's better than working in the textile factory. I come home every night coughing up bits of cloth.' Gill, pulls out a rather dirty handkerchief from her sleeve and blows her nose like a trumpet.

'Very lady-like!' I scoff.

I meet Gill at school when I go back aged thirteen. I missed the rudiments of Mathematics and English and no-one at school appears particularly bothered about helping me to catch up, so I sit at the back of the class with the other boys and girls, who struggle to learn, or who choose not to. Gill is one of the latter. She is far too interested in acting the fool, playing practical jokes on the teachers and on her classmates, and messing about with the boys in dark recesses of the playground. We make an unlikely pairing. I feel so shy, so nervous around boys, despite the attention they give to me. Gill is the exact opposite; confident, brash and a little too keen on sexual experimentation. Yet she's such a softie at heart – even if she appears armoured in a cast iron exterior – and she defends me against bullies and admirers alike. I know I would never have survived my return to school without Gill.

'Excuse me for interrupting, ladies.'

We break off our chattering and look up from our spilt coffees to see a man of about thirty-five in a shiny grey suit and a pink cravat with a matching handkerchief folded into the top pocket of his double-breasted jacket. He wears a large gold ring on each of his fingers and has chunky gold bracelets and a massive gold watch.

'I know this is going to sound a little forward, but do you mind if I join you for a moment?' Before either of us can answer, the man sidles onto Gill's banquette, forcing Gill into the corner and placing himself facing me. I look down, running my finger over a large dent in the off-white Formica table.

'Excuse me mate,' says Gill, shoving his arm. 'This is a private party.'

'Please, do not be alarmed. I'm not going to bother *you*, my dear. I just want to talk to your friend here for a moment.' The man stares straight at me, ignoring Gill. I feel my face glow red.

'That's what they all say,' Gill retorts. 'You lot are all the same. You see a beautiful girl and you can't keep your trousers under control.'

I still think of myself as a rather undernourished, stubby-haired ugly duckling. A year ago, I was five foot two and my chest was as flat as my mother's ironing board. Now I'm five foot eight with a decent pair of sizeable, if not slightly unmanageable, breasts, which tend to elicit a significant amount of male attention. It surprises me every time it happens. Gill, on the other hand, is five foot three, broad and essentially nondescript, but what she lacks in looks, she more than makes up for in personality, as my father so often comments when she's been over to our house.

'Look, sweetheart,' says the man, swivelling to address Gill directly, 'what's in my trousers is not generally available to the fairer sex – if you know what I mean – lovey.' He pouts and Gill is somewhat unusually lost for words. Turning back to me, the man introduces himself. I am transfixed by his many rings, which glint under the strip lighting. 'My name is Syd Levine. My wife and I – yes my *wife*, sweetie – run a designer clothing agency selling very expensive gowns to very expensive shops, who sell them on to very expensive women. We are looking for an in-house model to show our clothes off to best effect and you, darling, are exactly what we are after.'

I raise my head to look at Mr Levene, aware that my mouth is hanging open slightly and that I can do nothing about it. Gill is winking at me and giving me the thumbs up. Syd beckons to the waitress, who straightens up as she comes towards us, wearing a rictus smile. 'Edna, love, please could we have three coffees for myself and my two new friends, if you wouldn't mind, my dear. Thank you,' he simpered.

'Yes, Mr Levine. Right away, Mr Levine.' Edna half curtsies to Syd, whilst simultaneously managing to glower at Gill. Gill stares gormlessly from Syd to the waitress and back to Syd.

'Now, where were we?' Syd asks me, turning his back on Gill.

So now I work for Syd and Freda Levine as an in-house model in their atelier in Lever Street, off Piccadilly Gardens. They represent a number of quasi-famous designers and show their samples to department stores and select boutiques around the country. Buyers book appointments by telephone, or sometimes by letter, and then Freda or Syd call the buyer in advance to find out about the type of dresses and suits they are looking to buy this season, and to advise them of what they have in stock. Prior to their visit, I help Syd and Freda to prepare the rails for that particular client. I try on the dresses beforehand to ensure they fit me, so that the clothes look as attractive as possible I love modelling all these beautiful gowns, swishing around in them in front of the clients, although sometimes I have to swerve away from the odd bottom-pinching or bosom-brushing customer. I imagine myself as one of the film stars which Gill and I watch at the Gaumont and I wonder how they cope with wandering hands. I often keep one of the dresses on after the clients have left, until Freda politely asks me to hang it back up. I get quite a number of offers to go out on a date, but I always refuse. I tell them that I can't mix business with pleasure, but if I'm honest, I'm rather afraid of going out with an intelligent man, in case they find out how stupid I really am.

Joe

We met via Syd. He tipped me off that he would be drinking at The Midland Hotel with a darling young girl and that I might find her rather attractive. I did, and the rest, as they say, is history.

Sasha

I called Sarah today and told her officially to put the film on hold. I had discussed it with Zac the week before and he had agreed that life was just too traumatic at the moment to attempt to play happy families on film. I suggested to Sarah that I very much hoped we would be able to resume at some point in the future, as she had been doing a fantastic job.

'Sasha, please don't give it a moment's thought,' Sarah reassured me. 'I know you're going through a difficult time.'

'Thank you for being so understanding and please do send me your bill for the hours you've incurred so far. I don't want you to be out of pocket in any way.' As someone who was self-employed, I knew how galling it was when a client let you down in the middle of a job, refusing to pay you for your time. I knew all too well that it was easy for people to walk away in life.

'Please don't worry, Sasha. Why don't we just postpone it and you can settle up with me later, or when you decide to finish the film? I'm very relaxed about it.'

I could imagine her at the end of the phone, smiling and pushing a stray blonde hair behind her ear.

'No, Sarah. I insist. I know what Zac agreed to pay you initially, but I intended to pay the bill one way or another, as he has no money, obviously. You know teenagers never think about practicalities like money. Please, I'll feel much better if you let me pay you what I owe for now. And thank you again. You've been brilliant.'

Stanley and I were sitting at my desk trying to compile an Excel spreadsheet of our finances. Well, I was sitting at my desk trying to input various figures, both set and discretionary and Stanley was lying on the carpet dreaming of set and discretionary food. I was trying to be realistic about our spending, but this honest reckoning was sending me into a paroxysm of panic. Even the basic food bills were enormous, never mind the energy bills, mobile phones, satellite television and so on. I shut my eyes after I'd totted up haircuts, hair colour, gel nails, clothes for Zac…the list was endless. I saved the sheet and shut my computer down, taking a few deep breaths to calm my nerves. That didn't work, so I finished off the last chocolate digestive aided by my furry assistant. I'd only started the pack an hour ago. I was now not only a nervous wreck, but increasingly an overweight monstrosity. Sugar coursed through my bloodstream and converted instantly to fat at the top of my limbs and around my stomach. Everything wobbled, including my nerves, which shrieked loudly at me, jangling whenever I drove the car, or went shopping, where I regularly forgot my pin number. I tried the Mindfulness app on advice from a friend and, whilst the man trying to mind my mind had a wonderfully soothing voice, I just couldn't concentrate on what he was saying. My brain was too full of stuff. I started to panic that I was going the same way as my mother, unable to remember what day of the week it was, or the name of any of my friends, although to be fair, my mother no longer had any friends. The combination of Jeremy leaving me, Zac's impossible behaviour, my mother's erraticism and the onset of menopause made me a prime candidate for therapy, but my Excel spreadsheet told me quite categorically that this was an unaffordable luxury. I briefly considered resorting to alcohol, but after so many years of watching it transform my mother from Doctor Jekyll into Mrs Hyde, I had sworn never to drink alone. I stood up from my office chair and lay down under the desk with Stanley. He wagged his tail as I placed my arm over the top of him and we lay there in companionable silence, apart from the occasional grunt of pure contentment from Stanley. Stanley would save me.

I don't know how long we lay there, but the setting sun had thrown long shadows across the room. The clocks had gone back the previous weekend. I never understood how we apparently gained time, yet lost so many hours of precious light as a result. Mind you, at the moment, the darkness suited me. I rather envied bears their period of hibernation. I wondered if I might try it and when I re-awoke in the spring, everything would have righted itself. It seemed unlikely. Stanley lifted his head and nudged me softly with his nose. I looked at my watch. It was four o'clock, Stanley's dinner time. People say that dogs have no sense of time, but believe me,

Stanley does. He knows when it's time for his dinner, when it's time to wake up and when it gets past eleven at night, he rises from his place on the rug in the lounge in front of the television and pads off to bed, tucking himself in surrounded by his cuddly toys. If I am in the kitchen after Stanley's bedtime, he looks up at me with sleepy, bloodshot eyes, imploring me to hurry up and turn off the light, but not before he's had his rusk. He is an enormously spoilt creature of habit. 'C'mon then, Stanley, let's get you fed before you waste away.'

I eased myself off the floor, stretching my arms out in front of me. Stanley leapt up, knocking his head on the underside of my desk in his eagerness to reach his bowl – he appeared not to notice the bang – and followed me downstairs to the kitchen. I poured out a cup of kibble and some seaweed powder to keep Stanley's teeth clean and healthy, added some water and placed it on Stanley's food mat. He gobbled it greedily. He was a messy eater. Pieces of kibble shot out of his bowl in all directions in his eagerness to beat the world speed record for eating dog food, but he always cleaned up every fallen morsel at the end. If only Zac was as tidy.

Zac had stayed overnight at Jeremy's flat. He seemed to like his occasional evenings there and enjoyed long hours playing PlayStation with Guy, who was closer in both age and temperament to Zac than he was to Jeremy. The irony appeared to be lost on all three men. Zac would be back home soon – I hoped that he still thought of my house as home – so I busied myself sorting out his dinner. I prepared two salmon steaks in teriyaki sauce, placing three huge rosti potatoes next to them and putting the whole concoction into the oven. Next I put some carrots, broccoli and sugar snap peas into a bowl and covered them in Clingfilm ready for the microwave. Finally, I cut Zac a large slice of cake, stealing a sliver for myself to nibble as I worked and hulled some strawberries, which I washed and placed on the plate by his cake. Long before culinary programmes became the smash hit on television, I loved to bake cakes and muffins. I would often start late at night. I found the beating and the folding so relaxing. It used to drive Jeremy insane, yet he was always happy enough to polish off the results.

I heard the key turn in the front door while I was making myself a cup of tea. I no longer collected Zac from the bus stop. He said he preferred to walk. This small rejection cut me to the quick, but I said nothing.

'Hello, Zac,' I called. 'How was your day?'

Zac walked into the kitchen. His hair was wet from the rain –what is it about boys and refusing to wear a hood or carry an umbrella, as if doing so strangles their masculinity? – and his face was as pale as the oyster-coloured paint on the kitchen walls. He shot me a murderous stare. 'I know everything.'

I stopped stirring my tea and turned off the oven down. I had a feeling that we wouldn't be eating immediately. 'You know everything about what, Zac?' I asked, licking the back of the teaspoon.

'I know about Sebastian.'

I dropped the spoon and it clattered to the kitchen floor. Stanley rushed over to investigate. I slumped down onto one of the kitchen chairs and put my head into my hands. Zac came over and sat opposite me. 'What do you know about Sebastian?' I whispered. My throat had constricted and I was struggling to breathe.

A tear fell from Zac's eye. He threw an envelope onto the kitchen table. 'I did a search online in the end. I should have thought of it ages ago, instead of suggesting that stupid film, which was taking forever. I was watching a programme online about tracing your ancestry and that's when I had the idea. I found Sebastian's birth certificate, and I also found his death certificate. I asked them to send copies to Dad's address. Have a look.'

Zac pulled out a chair to sit down and nudged the envelope towards me, but I couldn't pick it up.

'I had a brother and you never told me. Why the hell not? Why did you lie to me for all this time?'

Tears coursed down my face. I couldn't speak, so I just held out my hand to Zac and to my surprise, he took it. 'Oh my God, Zac, I'm so sorry. I don't know what to say to you. Your brother, he died when he was so tiny, just eight months old. I can't begin to describe how horrific it was to lose him.' I paused and reached over for the kitchen roll, pulling off a wad and blowing my nose hard. 'I thought I would never recover. No, I thought that neither your father nor I would ever recover. It hit both of us so hard. It's impossible to explain.' I squeezed Zac's hand and he started to cry harder. 'Losing anyone you love is unbearable, Zac, but losing a child is like losing a part of yourself. It's like a part of me died with him.'

'But I still don't understand why you didn't tell me about him.' Zac released my hand and got up, sniffing and wiping his eyes with his shirt sleeve. 'I can understand why you might not have told me when I was little, but I'm grown up now and I actually asked you to your face. But you still kept on lying. Why did you do that?'

I stared at Zac through my puffy eyes. 'I should have told you. I know that now, Zac, and I am really, truly sorry. But there just never seemed to be a right time. Fifteen months after Sebastian died, I fell pregnant with you. I managed to move on slowly, paranoid inch by paranoid inch. The first year after you were born was a nightmare. I slept in the nursery with you every night, and checked up on you every second, all night long. I never left you alone for a moment. And you survived. That's why you're so precious to me and to your father.' I got up and stood behind Zac, putting my arms around him and burying my head into his hair. It smelt of stale sweat. 'I've thought about it more times than I can tell you, especially after you started to ask me questions, but it just seemed too difficult to tell you after such a long time. And your father never wanted to talk about it. In fact, he point blank refused. Then he left and there was so much else to cope with. I didn't want to add this on top of you having to cope with Dad leaving -the way that he left. '

Zac broke away from my embrace and wheeled around to face me. Snot was leaking from his nose. 'But it's not as though anyone could have stopped it from happening, is it? The baby – my brother – Sebastian – he just died in his cot, didn't he? It's not like anyone's to blame. No one actually murdered him, did they?'

I started to cough and Zac slapped me on the back, a little too hard. I struggled to form my words. 'No, Zac, no one actually murdered him,' I gulped, 'but I had buried the pain away deep inside, locked it in a box and I just couldn't bear to re-open it, to relive it. I couldn't bring myself to discuss Sebastian with you, or to try to explain how and why he died. And what good would it have done to tell you anyway, Zac? How would it have helped you to know?'

Zac opened his mouth to answer me, but said nothing. He sat down at the table again and pulled his hoodie up over his head. We sat in silence together for what seemed like an age and eventually we ate the salmon.

I bury Sebastian every waking day and every waking night. I watch over him, motionless, an alabaster god, asleep in his cot. He is just perfect. His long black lashes frame his plump cheeks and his lips pucker as he dreams. His tuft of wispy fawn hair floats gently above his scalp. His tiny body is stretched out in his pale blue babygro, the one dotted with the sun and moon across its length. His skin is as smooth and unsullied as newly fallen snow, ice cold. I strain to touch him, but he moves further and further down, away from me, until I watch him sink slowly into the cold, damp ground. Hundreds of worms and maggots squirm through holes, crawling all over my beautiful boy, and I wake up screaming his name. Sebastian.

Part Two

Joe

The greatest moment of my life was holding Zac on the day he was born. His skin smelling sweetly of vanilla, he stared up at me with unblinking purple eyes, inquisitive and trusting. I was almost eighty years old, too ancient to be of any use to him, and sadly, I passed on when Zac was only five. But I visit him every day, obsessively. I recognise that, right now, he is suffering not only the painful passage from child to man, but also the trauma of family breakdown and the shocking discovery of long buried secrets. It's impossible for him to understand why the people around him have made the decisions they have. He will be able to put them into perspective over the years which follow, but at the moment, his world revolves around himself and everything that happens to him does so from a very personal perspective. This is not a criticism, but merely an observation about the way the young mind works. A broader view of the world comes only with time and experience, through love and disappointment. Every parent does all they can to shield their offspring from harm for as long as they can. Lying can be kinder than the naked truth, but eventually the truth will emerge from its hiding place and relationships can be damaged forever.

My own childhood was fairly brutal, not because my parents were unkind or mistreated me in any way, but because we had so little. Until I was twelve, I lived in a factory where my father worked as a tailor – myself, my three brothers, two sisters, mother and father – in a basement room, where we spent our nights coughing from the cotton fibres which got caught in our lungs. During the day, the benches we slept on were used to cut cloth using carefully drawn paper patterns, which was then sewn together by noisy sewing machines, their operators' fingers aching from overuse and chilblains. At night, their work would be folded away and we would roll up our coats underneath our heads as pillows and huddle together under thin blankets.

My siblings and I were the first of our family to be born in England. My mother, Peggy, was the daughter of Russian refugees, who fled the violence of the pogroms in 1892, arriving by ship as a toddler into the stinking docks in Liverpool. Her father, Ezekiel, had managed to arrange passage for himself, his wife Miriam and their six children, although they did not all land in Liverpool. At the port in Odessa, the family was separated and four of the children were placed in error onto a different ship, bound for the newly opened Ellis Island, the gateway to New York. The youngest two, Karl and Peggy, managed to stay attached to their parents, but it was the last time that Miriam and Ezekiel saw or heard of any their other four children, whose ages at the time ranged from fourteen to nine years old. We never managed to trace each other once they had landed on opposite sides of the Atlantic –

if, indeed, they survived the passage, which was perilous in those days. Passengers died from disease, starvation or sometimes, at the hands of other travellers. The problem with tracing family separated by the Atlantic Ocean was exacerbated by the fact that, on landing, families were given different surnames from the ones they had possessed in their native countries, by officials who could neither spell nor pronounce the bizarre names of the arriving immigrants. Officials truncated surnames to suit themselves and hence Avraam-Simkha-Mstislavsky became Abrams, Stenichkin became Stein and so on. Who knew what the small Katesenelenbaums were renamed, when and if they arrived in Ellis Island?

The same thing happened to my grandparents on landing in Liverpool, from where Ezekiel and Miriam, walking on shaking sea legs, boarded a train to Manchester as the newly abbreviated Katz family, with the aim of joining other members from their Russian village who had already settled in the busy industrial town. They travelled light, wearing their only set of clothes, having been forced to leave almost all their possessions behind. They moved to an area near Cheetham in Manchester known as the Red Bank, a slum area, so ill-lit that it appeared to be perpetual night. It was hidden away from the more prosperous areas of Cheetham by the railway tracks and warehouses, which polluted the River Irk on a daily basis, but even Cheetham could not escape the Red Bank's rotten stench of too many human beings herded together like cattle. The Katzs occupied one damp and airless room, but not alone. They shared it with another family of seven, clambering over limbs and stinking chamber pots whenever they needed to move. Russian life had been poor, yet they had at least had land and animals to tend and more importantly, fresh air. However, they had lived every day in fear of their lives. The Red Bank was harsh, smoke-filled and black, but they had arrived, they were alive and they were determined to begin again.

Ezekiel, my grandfather, like many of his fellow immigrants, was a tailor. He was particularly talented, however, with a keen eye for cut and style, which soon marked him out from the competition. A combination of hard work, excellent customer service and good tailoring meant that Ezekiel's business grew very quickly. Miriam, in addition to bringing up the children, took in washing and cleaned houses for the wealthier, more established households in Cheetham Hill and Broughton. The Katzs spent their first few years drowning in a well of exhaustion, rising daily at six from the cutting benches where they all slept together, and falling back onto its dusty surface very late in the evening. Friday evenings were the only time for pause, when the family would gather together for Shabbat, bowing their heads over prayers in thankfulness for everything they did not have. As soon as my mother Peggy could walk and talk, she began to assist her mother with cleaning and washing jobs, until her tiny hands were blistered and raw, whilst Ezekiel taught Karl the art of tailoring. After several years, the family was able to move into a small two roomed apartment, using one room as Ezekiel's workshop and the other for living and sleeping. They were creeping up in the world.

At the age of sixteen, my mother Peggy married Bernard Stein – coincidentally, or perhaps not, in the Red Bank – the son of another tailor also from Odessa. Despite having travelled so far, Jewish families still preferred to make a 'shidduch' between members of the same original settlements where possible, and 'shadchanits' or matchmakers, were as active in Manchester as they had been back East, shuffling between the crowded family groups, shrouded in their heavy shawls, making their lucrative deals as soon as the babies slipped from their mothers' wombs. Children quickly followed for Peggy and Bernard: Teddy and Peter, then yours truly, then Abigail, Moishe and finally, Esther, all efficiently spaced eighteen months apart. By the time all six of us had been born, my grandfather Ezekiel and my father Bernard – now partners in cloth – had managed to establish a small factory in Broughton, which meant there was plenty more space for us children to place our mattresses and blankets to sleep, plus we had access to running water and most exciting of all, our own toilet.

My grandfather and father continued to prosper, crafting expensive suits for leading businessmen in Manchester and beyond. The factory was now employed full time, filled with thrumming sewing machines and their swift-fingered operatives, as well as skilled pattern cutters and one over-burdened secretary. By 1928, my father was wealthy enough to be able to buy a large family house in Broughton, with four bedrooms; two of us children in each and a bedroom for my mother and father, as well as a kitchen, living room and dining room. It was a palace indeed. When we first moved in, I felt exhausted just walking around the house and wondered if I might get lost. My brothers and I went to the local school, where none of them particularly excelled academically, apart from me. I may sound boastful, but I won a scholarship to the grammar school in Salford, almost unheard of for a Jewish boy at that time. In contrast, my siblings all left school at fourteen, the girls helping my mother at home and Teddy and Peter working with my father in the factory.

No doubt the plan would have been for me and Moishe to have also graduated to the tailoring business after school, but sadly, my father died two days before my thirteenth birthday. On the evening before, I was rehearsing my Torah piece for my Barmitzvah with him in the living room. I had to stand by the hearth, which I enjoyed, as I could warm by legs in the fire, and my father sat in his wooden rocker, ebbing and flowing to the rhythm of the incantation. I was in mid–recitation when my father suddenly interrupted me. 'Joseph, we need to stop. My head is bad tonight. You carry on practicing and I will listen again tomorrow.'

I noticed that his father's face had drained of all colour, the circles under his eyes darkening. 'Shall I get you some water, Pa?' I asked.

'No thank you, my boy.' My father ruffled my hair. 'I think I'm just tired and need to get some sleep. It's been a long day and I have to finish up four suits tomorrow, so

200

it's probably a good idea to sleep now anyway. You keep practicing. Goodnight, Joseph. You're a good boy. I'll see you in the morning.' He never did.

I was woken very early the following day by my mother wailing like a wounded animal. She had woken up next to my father, who was stone cold, felled by a cerebral hemorrhage at the age of thirty one. We sat Shiva for a week, the mirrors in the house covered and our shirts ripped by the rabbi to signify our grief. I never did perform my Barmitzvah piece in synagogue and I always felt its loss, inextricably intertwined with the terrible absence of my father. I had so wanted to make him proud in synagogue, as Teddy and Peter had before me, singing my piece on the bimah, whilst my father stood beside me, encouraging, reassuring, a gentle hand on my back. I would have to prove myself in other ways.

I threw myself into my schoolwork, matriculating in English, Mathematics, Science, and History with the highest marks. Not bad for a boy who grew up sleeping on remnants of material in a textile factory. I won a place at Manchester University to study Pharmacy. On one occasion, after a long day in the lab, I was walking home to Broughton, which normally took me just under an hour, if I walked at a steady pace. I couldn't afford the penny for the bus fare in those days. It was early March and a bitter wind screeched around the streets corners. I didn't have a coat, but I turned up the collar on my thin jacket and settled my cap a bit lower, in a vain attempt to shelter myself from the icy onslaught. I was starving hungry and looking forward to whatever dinner Ma had made, as all I had eaten during the day was a slab of bread and cheese between lectures and lab work. I was hoping that tea was going to be a nice bit of boiled hen. That day at the university had been a bit of a treat. The canteen doled out a new drink, free of charge, to all the students. Of course, we all tried it. It was an odd liquid, black as coal, tasting slightly of treacle, and with bubbles which ran riot up your nose. If I'm honest, I wasn't convinced by this new American drink. It was bizarrely named Coca Cola and I couldn't see how it would catch on

Anyway, on this particular day, I rounded the corner into Peter Street and saw a large crowd gathered outside the Free Trade Hall. They were wearing black shirts with silver buckles on their trousers, which glinted in the street lamps, and they were all saluting with one arm raised skywards. They looked like trouble to me, so I stopped still in the shadows and waited. A man stood on a platform in front of the frenzied crowd. I couldn't make out everything he was saying, but I caught a few words, 'Fascism… Economy… Jews.' The black-coated crowd saluted and waved their truncheons. Behind them, another mob was forming, angry and determined. They clearly didn't want this sort of hatred being preached on their streets, but they had all come to fight.

I knew I couldn't get away, so I started to search desperately for a place to hide. Behind me was a shop entrance – I think it was the old Lewis's back entrance actually – piled high with rotting food and damp wooden boxes. It was pitch black, well away from the street lamps. I slowly inched into the doorway and from there,

I could hear the fighting as it began, the screams of baton on bone, of fist on flesh. My own heart seemed to be banging in time with the blows, and even though it was bitterly cold, sweat trickled down my back under my shirt. Then I heard whistles as the police arrived to join in the fray. Someone fell into the doorway, his head hitting my foot. I waited, crouching, concentrating on breathing soundlessly, desperate to move my cramped limbs. I can remember wondering whether my grandparents could have imagined that this might happen here in England, when they fled here to safety from the pogroms in Russia.

The man on my foot remained motionless, and I had no idea how long I remained in the doorway, but it was long after the square had quietened down. Slowly, I tried to move myself, but my arms and legs had lost all feeling. I wiggled my leg up and down and then nudged the guy with my toe, but I failed to rouse him. So I leant over him and then I vomited, because there was a large dent in the side of his head and his face was covered in congealed blood. The detritus of the scuffle lay all around me and straight ahead, the Free Trade Hall was daubed with a bright red swastika, welcoming the new dawn. A clock further off struck five a.m. and it was then that I realised I was going to be late for lectures if I went home, so I straightened my clothes, brushed down my jacket and put my cap straight. Then I just walked back the way I'd come hours before.

I took my finals in Edinburgh in 1934 – in those days, you could only sit the exams in either Edinburgh or London, which meant coping not only with the stress of study, but also with saving up enough money for the train fare – and on the journey home, I lobbed all my textbooks out of the train window, where they were shredded by the train wheels as it thundered south, thus signalling the end of my academic life, but not my thirst for research and knowledge.

Then the war erupted and I was exempted from military service, due the need for pharmacists on the home front. In those days, I made all my medicines by hand, measuring out the relevant ingredients with scrupulous care on the scales. In the small room at the back of the pharmacy, I ground the restorative ingredients in my mortar with my pestle before adding any liquid, always raising my receptacle to eye level in order to gauge the precise level of the meniscus for complete accuracy. This skill proved very useful in later life, long after my pharmacist career had ended, for ensuring I always poured the correct amount of water into my whisky. But my work was so dull – I often spent twelve hours a day, or sometimes longer, behind the counter – grinding, binding and serving. I knew I needed to do more to challenge myself intellectually and more importantly, to earn some decent money, but this was war time, so it was either pill manufacturing or soldiering, and I knew where my preference lay.

At night, I switched my pharmacy coat for blue ARP overalls and a black tin hat with a large 'W' on the front, often returning straight back to the pharmacy from my shift without a wink of sleep. I moved from house to house, knocking on doors and advising people on the correct precautions to take before, during and after raids, admonishing anyone who did not conform to the rules of the blackout. I helped people in and out of the shelters during raids and with the horrific clear ups in their aftermath, separating limbs and belongings from endless piles of smoking rubble. Of course, being an ARP warden did have its compensations. If I say so myself, I was an attractive man – many remarking that I bore a striking resemblance to the Hollywood actor, Robert Taylor – dark, dapper and rather debonair. So, if I met a good-looking woman either in the pharmacy or on my nighty tours of duty, I might invite her to one of the shelters later, luring them with the enticing offer of the chance to play with my gas rattle. It worked more often than you might imagine. The war was, after all, a time of sexual promiscuity. Husbands and boyfriends were away fighting, people left behind were losing their homes, and often their lives, to bombing raids and children had been spirited away to the country in Operation Pied Piper, including my Annie, but more of her later. There was little time to worry about inhibition – life was quite simply too short. I cut my sexual teeth during the war years, working hard and playing even harder whenever I could. Taking girls home was never a possibility, as they were impossible to smuggle past Ma, who had both eagle ears and eyes at all times of day and night, so instead, I made good use of the bomb shelters and if needs must, the rather uncomfortable pharmacy counter.

I was not Ma's favourite child. I have often puzzled

about why this might have been the case. Was it because I was brighter and more ambitious than my siblings, with a sharp, ready answer for everything? Or was it because I was somehow inextricably entwined with my father's passing? Or was it because I never trained as a tailor, nor supported my brothers in the business? It could have been any of those reasons, or one of a dozen others. Conversely, my eldest brother, Teddy, could do no wrong, yet he was lazy and work shy, living off others' coat-tails for his whole life. Peter was quieter and did much as he was told. Abigail was headstrong and less easy to manage, but she was a girl, so different rules applied and Moishe and Esther were always my mother's babies, getting away with almost anything.

My father had died in 1929, the year of the Wall Street Crash, which in turn plunged the world into the Great Depression of the 1930s. Peter, with grudging help from Teddy, kept the family business going – just about – and I continued at grammar school and then university, all paid for by scholarship awards. Ma, however, was forced to return to work, cleaning other people's houses and taking in sewing and ironing, which she very much resented. She felt that she had moved up in the world, but was once again looked down upon by the other residents of Broughton. When the Second World War began in 1939, the government commissioned the Stein factory to make uniforms for soldiers, which meant that it was constantly busy, ticking over with a meagre, yet regular income. Teddy and Peter were exempted from service, due to essential war work in the factory and, as I have already mentioned, I was similarly relieved in order to deliver key medical support to the local community. At home, we kept our own hens, which lay efficiently and we also grew potatoes and other root vegetables in our small garden, which meant that we could supplement our rations and of course, I was able to ensure that we had medicine if needed.

On one particular evening in 1943, I was walking home from the pharmacy, dragging my feet and smoking the butt of my Craven A when I heard someone running up the road. I turned to see my sister Abigail panting her way towards me, holding onto her hat, her flat heels clacking along the pavement. She was wearing her ambulance driver khaki uniform, with its belted jacket and Red Cross on the sleeve. 'Joe, Joe. Wait, will you?' called Abigail.

'What is it, Abby? I'm dog-tired and want to get home to eat before I go out on shift.' I had another ARP stint ahead of me and had planned a hot date at one of my shelters with a rather gorgeous nurse I had met recently.

Abigail caught up with me, breathing heavily and looking rather flushed. 'Joe, I need to tell you something important. And I'm going to need your help,' she said, trying to catch her breath and smile beguilingly at me at the same time.

'What it is now, Abby?' Abigail quite often got herself into scrapes, which had ranged over the years from giving a fellow school friend a black eye, to losing almost everything anyone have ever given to her, to - by accident - running over a patient's foot in her ambulance.

'I'm going to tell you something now, but you have to promise not to yell.' She glowered at me. 'Do you swear?'

'If it means I can get home quickly, I'll promise anything,' I laughed.

'Look, Joe, this is serious. So you need to listen, OK?'

'OK, OK, spit it out then. Or let me guess? You've run over another patient. You've strangled one of the hens by mistake. You've....'

'I've met a GI and I've agreed to marry him.'

Abigail stared me straight in the eye, daring me to object. I took a step backwards and gawped at my sister. 'You've done what? Have you gone insane? Who is this guy? I'm going to knock his bloody lights out.' I stopped. 'Hang on a sec. Are you up the duff?'

'No, I'm not in the sodding club!' shrieked Abigail, rather too loudly, so that an elderly frum couple on the other side of the street turned around to stare. Abigail looked down and opened her bag to pull out a pack of cigarettes. I noticed that her hands were shaking.

'Give me one of those, would you?' I asked, stubbing out the dreg end of my previous cigarette with my foot on the flagstone. 'I think I might need it.' I lit both cigarettes, handing one back to Abby, and we lent against the street lamp, silent for a moment.

'His name is Walter Klein. He's Jewish,'

'Oh, well, that's alright then! As long as he's Jewish, it doesn't matter that he's American and that you are buggering off with a complete stranger to God know where!'

'Shut up and listen. As I said, his name is Walter Klein, he's Jewish, he lives outside Milwaukee, where his family who own a lot of land. He's six foot tall, handsome and I love him.' Abigail looked down at the pavement and took another drag of her cigarette.

'And what else?'

'What do you mean, what else?' demanded Abigail.

'I mean, what else do you know about him? How long have you known him? Does he already have a wife and kids waiting for him in Milwaukee? Does owning a lot of land mean a small garden in the middle of Hicksville? These GIs with their smart uniforms and endless supplies of silk stockings and chocolate are all very attractive, Abby, but you're not seriously going to move halfway across the world to marry some guy you hardly know. C'mon, Abigail, pull yourself together.'

'That's exactly what I'm going to do and what's more, the ship leaves from Liverpool in two days' time.' She looked straight at me. 'And I need you to tell Ma.'

My mother took the news much as one might expect, with much screaming, wailing, shouting and tearing of her hair. Teddy and Peter were consulted and told Abigail flatly that she was not going. Abigail, however, had never heeded her older brothers' advice in the past and was certainly not going to start now. Amidst all of this, I had not only taken on the role of messenger, which automatically meant I was somehow implicated, but I had also decided to take Abigail's side, despite my own misgivings. 'Ma, listen. If she really loves this Walter chap and he's going to make her happy, then she's old enough to make her own decisions.'

'Joe Stein, how dare you speak to your mother like that. Ha! It's always you, isn't it, always you who's causing the trouble. For all I know, you put her up to this. Yes, that would make sense. How did she meet this Klein anyway? Was it through you and one of your shelter tramps?' My mother's face rippled with rage.

'It was nothing to do with me and I've never met the guy. If you'd just calm down, Abby can bring him to the house and you can at least decide for yourself if you like him.'

'Meet him? Meet some country bumpkin from Milwaukee? You've got to be joking. It'll be over my dead body.'

'Well, if you don't, Abby'll be gone and you'll regret it one day,' I counselled.

'Get out of my sight!' screamed my mother. 'Both of you!' My mother locked herself into her bedroom, from where her howls ricocheted off her walls for the rest of the night.

In the end, I was the only one of the family to meet Walter before they left for America. He turned out to be a pleasant man, who very much in love with Abby. I accompanied them both to Liverpool by train and saw them safely onto the throbbing ship, which would whisk my sister off to a strange world across the deep ocean. It was a perilous time to attempt to cross the Atlantic and I prayed that they would make it safely to the other side. Standing on the dockside, I shook hands with Walter.

'Take good care of her, please. She's a real handful, but one I'm quite fond of.'

'Roger that, Joe. I'm pretty fond of her too. No need to worry.' Walter launched his large American smile and thumped me heartily on the back, causing me to have a short, violent coughing attack. I turned to hug Abigail, who was struggling to restrain her tears.

'I think you're a complete idiot, you know that?' I hissed in her ear. 'If you get there and it's a complete disaster, don't come running to me for help…but you that know you can.' I kissed her on the head. Abigail just nodded, unable to reply. All she could muster was a wave.

As it happened, Abigail and Walter were very happily married for forty years, until Walter died of lung cancer. His family was indeed wealthy and held great swathes of fertile land in Wisconsin, so they lived very comfortably, raising three children. Abigail was lucky. So many *GI Brides* married men who looked supremely handsome in uniform, yet were, in reality, dirt poor and lived in highly remote places in the United States. Some were bigamists and some were wife-beaters. Many brides stayed in America and led miserable lives and some returned to England, if they could afford a return passage, often with small children in tow. In the late 1950s, Abigail and Walter also returned to Manchester to visit the family and reconciliation took place, although my mother always referred to Walter as 'that yank,' behind his back, as well as to his face, and she never forgave me for allowing Abigail to leave her.

The war finally ended and Broughton, like every

other place in Britain, struggled to pick itself up. For me, the end of the war heralded a momentous decision, which I revealed to my friend Bruno over a pint at The Empress on Cheetham Hill Road. Beer was still in short supply and often, the pubs ran dry before its clientele had drunk their fill, but on this particular evening, we were in luck. 'I've been thinking about what to do next,' I announced, as we sat in the corner of the dark, dank pub nursing our pints of bitter, sitting on two rickety stools, which were set against the peeling flock wallpaper.

'Really? And what did you decide?' asked Bruno, leaning forward to listen through a fog of cigarette smoke, which hung just above the table.

I had met Bruno in 1938, when he had arrived in Manchester from Vienna, one of the fortunate who managed to escape the city before the Anschluss by Germany. Like my own family, Bruno had come to Red Bank with nothing, where he joined his uncle, who, funnily enough, was another tailor. Bruno was red-haired, short, chubby and with a completely trusting and trustworthy disposition. When he smiled, his teeth bucked out to greet you like an over-energetic pony, and when he spoke, it was with a thick Austrian accent, which he never lost. He soon became a well-known and well-liked member of the Red Bank community, energetically running errands for various tailors. We met when he began to deliver cotton reels and needles to my brothers at the factory. We began to hang around together, smoking Craven As, playing football with old cans in the street and picking up girls. We rarely spoke about what Bruno had left behind. The rest of his family had perished in the darkness of Treblinka. We both felt guilt; Bruno for surviving and me for being British and having been powerless to do anything to stop the horrors inflicted on my fellow Jews just across the Channel.

'I'm thinking that there's no future for me as a pharmacist. It's deathly dull being in the shop all day long, listening to people drone on about bad stomachs, wicklows and styes. And what's more, there's no money in it. I want to earn real money and make something of my life.'

'I agree that you won't be happy in the shop for your whole life. But what else will you do? Maybe you could work with me and we try to get a van together? *Joe and Bruno. No job too small*,' suggested Bruno.

'Not the worst idea you've ever had, but no. I think I'm going to go into the entertainment business. What do you think?'

Bruno took a gulp of his beer, surveying my five o'clock shadow, which always appeared by one o'clock, no matter how much I shaved. 'The entertainment business?' Bruno appeared to be choking. 'Are you meshuggah?'

'Quite possibly, but hear me out. I saw an advertisement for BBC Radio. They are advertising for a production assistant on a new show called *The Third Programme*. It's going to be a mixture of classical music, drama, literature and discussion.' I was reading from the crumpled fragment of newspaper, which I had fished out of my jacket pocket.

'And what do you know about music, drama and literature, if you don't mind my asking?' Bruno snorted into his beer, shooting froth all over his moustache.

'Absolutely nothing, I grant you, but what I *am* is organised, ambitious and hard-working and I reckon that's more important. All I need to do is show a bit of chutzpah and I bet you I can wangle the job.'

And that, ladies and gentlemen, is how I got started in showbiz. *The Third Programme* was billed as a show 'for the serious-minded, for the educated and those who wish to be so.' I counted myself educated, even if I was not always serious-minded, so I emphasised the former rather than the latter when I went down to London for my BBC interview. I found London immediately exhilarating, with its glut of traffic and its crammed, filthy tube stations. Friends of mine who had visited London before me warned that I would be swallowed up in its terrifying jaws, but to me, it instantly signalled freedom and opportunity. The night before my interview, I stayed at a rundown bed and breakfast with grey dusty net curtains by Kings Cross station – it was clearly usually frequented by men and women for nefarious purposes other than sleeping – but it was all I could afford after the train fare down. Instead of staying in and listening to the illicit activities through the paper-thin walls, I wandered out for the night, walking miles from Kings Cross, down to the edifyingly seedy streets of Soho, through to Piccadilly Circus, which beckoned to me with its posters and bright lights. From there, I took in Leicester Square and walked through the market at Covent Garden, before reaching Waterloo Bridge at three in the morning, the magnificent meandering Thames laid out in front of me. I stood for a long time staring out towards Pugin's magnificent Houses of Parliament, mirrored in the black water. I threw a coin off the bridge and watched its long descent into the water. It carried with it my wish to get the job at the BBC and to make a successful life in London. I arrived back at Kings Cross around seven that morning, just in time to grab a quick cup of tea and to change my shirt. I'd asked one of the seamstresses in the factory to run me up a smart white cotton shirt and I'd chosen a striking red tie to set it off. My grey suit with its electric shine was a perfect fit. I settled my trilby at a jaunty angle on my head as I headed out into the foggy air to meet my destiny.

At the BBC, everyone ran everywhere in a suffocating fug of cigarette smoke. From the moment I arrived as the junior on the production team of *The Third Programme*, the pace was frenetic. We had content to source and deadlines to meet, and I ran harder and smoked faster than anyone else to make it all happen. I was very much a back stage player and was set to remain that way, largely due to my Northern accent. Everything at the BBC at that time had to be delivered in 'received pronunciation' or 'RP', and if you lacked it, you were 'not quite right, old boy'. The BBC certainly didn't want anyone with shortened vowels to address the public, but I knew that I didn't want to be a backroom boy forever, so I waited for my big break. And funnily enough, it was the Queen who gave it to me – well, sort of – long before she awarded me my CBE for services to broadcasting.

The coronation in 1953 led to a massive surge in the purchase of television sets, as people were desperate to watch their young Queen going through the motions with her sceptre and orb in Westminster Abbey. However, having bought their sets, they then had the temerity to demand other programmes to watch on them, ones which were not constant re-runs of Muffin the Mule, or the news headlines. After eight long years serving my time in dark basements, researching topics and writing copy, I was finally allowed into the light, but only by happy accident. Having worked on *The Third Programme* for what seemed like forever, I was well-versed in politics and culture. It was me who wrote the briefs for the interviewers, and me who told them what questions to ask, but it was never me who got to ask them, or even to meet the interviewees, except perhaps to take their coats, or provide them with a glass of water. In 1954, I was moved from radio to BBC Television to work on a new programme – *The Culture Club* – which would attempt to do for viewers what *The Third Programme* had done for listeners, namely interview politicians, writers, artists and the general great and good about their work and world views. My job was the same – to set it all up and watch someone else deliver it – except that on one particularly cold January evening, the presenter slipped on some black ice on the way into the studio and fractured his leg in three places. It was wonderfully fortuitous. And who stepped into the abyss, but yours truly. I didn't get to keep the job, as they brought in another presenter for the next show – one who spoke in RP and had two good legs – but someone else had spotted me and they liked what they saw.

The rest, as they say, is history. In 1955, ITV was launched and one night, sitting at home in my flat – I'd moved into a one bedroom flat in Kentish Town, which had a chipped sink in the room and a shared bathroom and privy, as well as a very friendly landlady called Kitty, who needed 'comforting' a couple of times a week – Kitty came to my door. 'Joe, darling, there's a telephone call for you downstairs. He sounds very important, so I'd come quick, if I was you.'

I ran down the stairs and into Kitty's front room, which is where the only phone was located. Kitty hovered in the doorway in her nightie and curlers, affectedly not really listening.

'Hello, Joe Stein speaking.'

'Joe, good evening. I'm sorry to disturb you at this late hour. My name is Phil Pratt. I'm a senior producer at ITV. I wonder if you'd like to come in to the office and have a chat with us. We've got an interesting proposition for you.'

'Well, thank you for calling, Mr Pratt, but I already have a production job at the BBC and I've just moved over to BBC TV, so I'm not sure I want to move again so quickly.' I'd heard through the grapevine that ITV were hiring, and I didn't want to sound over eager, but my heart had picked up speed under my shirt.

'Dear boy, you misunderstand me. We want to talk to you about *hosting* a new entertainment show, not producing.'

I didn't hesitate. 'I'm free tomorrow. What time suits?'

Kitty stood in the doorway, cigarette smoke curling around her lips. I picked her up and twirled her round. 'Let's celebrate, Kitty! I'm going to be a star!'

I was soon a regular fixture on ITV, graduating within a year or so to having my own shows, which were on the main schedule every week. I hosted current affairs on Sundays and various quiz shows during the week. I like to think that I paved the way to the small screen for thousands of Northerners and other hitherto ignored accented minorities everywhere with my Manchester warmth and charm, but the truth was far more clinical. My success was down to detailed and painstaking research, a skill I'd honed over the years at the BBC. I never went on set without knowing everything there was to know about the person I was interviewing. Even if I only ever used a tiny percentage of what I knew during the interview, I felt that nothing could surprise me, but more importantly, I was confident that I could surprise my guests. This allowed me to delve deeper into the personal lives of the famous and well-connected in a way which had never been done before. The public loved it, celebrities warmed to me and politicians were always respectful, if slightly wary.

With my new renown came money, and with money came the highlife. I bought a large house in St Johns Wood, by Regents Park, with its sweeping paths and fabulous foliage, although I was never one for walking. I preferred to drive my Jaguar with its walnut dash and constant supply of toffees inside the glove compartment to offer to my passengers, and I had the bar in the back for 'entertaining'. I spent many weekends on the French Riviera, each time with a different woman on my arm. I would sit on the beach at the Carlton Hotel drinking whisky, while my skin darkened in the soothing rays of the sun and in the evenings, I would head for the casino to try my hand at the Baccarat table. I was rarely lucky, but I loved the potent mix of risk-taking and refined elegance. People recognised me wherever I roamed, and I would always make time to talk to them, or to give them my autograph. Without my fans, I would be nothing again and I always cast an eye behind me as I went, conscious that all of this success could be snatched away from me at any moment. I was careful and I was rewarded, eventually being lured back to the BBC and given my own prime time slot on Saturday evenings at nine pm. Weekends became incomplete without watching 'Stein on Saturday.'

But I didn't forget my roots. I went home every fortnight and stayed with Ma. It kept me grounded. Back at home, I was just plain Joe. 'You're a fickle, lazy philanderer, Joseph. You're never going to settle down and give me grandchildren,' Ma shouted at me, as she put on the chinchilla fur I'd bought her in preparation for an evening out with me in a swanky restaurant, where she would be treated like royalty. 'You know, Joe, it's all OK now, while you're young and fit, to go stupping every girl in town, but one day soon, you'll wake up lonely and I won't be here to pick up the pieces.'

'You'll always be here, Ma,' I reassured her. I was serious. She was indestructible, a tiny dynamo, who would never run out of energy. She did break down eventually, but only at the age of ninety three and even then, she was still issuing instructions with her final breath. Yet I began to wonder if my mother was right about settling down. Of course, I loved seducing women and it wasn't very difficult. In the clubs and bars, girls would come on to me, just so that they could say that they had spent the night with a famous man – and I wasn't complaining. A flash of cleavage and a show of suspender was all it took to convince me to buy someone a free drink and something for the road. But a nagging voice inside –aside from my mother – was gnawing at me, telling me that it was time to settle down, or to think about it for a few minutes at least.

One evening in the Carlton Club in Manchester, after I had taken Ma home following a slap-up meal in one of the best Italian trattorias Manchester had to offer, I was sharing a bottle of whisky with a couple of Catholic priests I knew, when I bumped into my old friend, Syd Levine. Syd owned a dress agency selling to stores and private individuals with his wife Freda. He did well for himself, in business and in his marriage. Syd and I had been at Salford Grammar together – he was the other Jew in my year – so we formed a strong bond, although we were very different people. Syd was gay, but this was a time when such persuasions must be hidden. Enter Freda, who was a hearty girl, not much interested in either sex – 'I tried it once with one of each and I didn't like it' – so she was the perfect wife for Syd. Not only that, but she was the brains behind the business. Syd had an eye for fashion, but Freda converted it into cash. It was a blessed partnership. 'Syd, old man, how are you?'

'Grand, my gorgeous boy. I must say, you're looking fabulous on the small screen these days. Who's doing your makeup?'

'I don't need makeup, Syd. I'm just handsome as I am, you know that.'

'And modest to boot.'

'Obviously. Can I interest you in a whisky?'

'Just a large tumbler full, old man.'

I poured and we talked about the old days, and the current days, and mutual friends who had passed our way in between.

'I tell you what, old man, we've got the most beautiful young girl working in our office right now. She's very green around the gills, but there's something about her. She's twenty-one tomorrow and we've invited her to The Midland for drinks to celebrate. Freda's kitting her out in one of our fabulous samples. Why don't you lurk around there around seven? I'll introduce you.'

I needed no excuse to lurk in The Midland Bar, so I turned up around six thirty and Alphonse showed me to my usual table, bringing me a large Johnnie Walker, no ice, with a jug of cold water on the side. I raised my glass to eye level and poured the water precisely to half way up the glass. Perfect. I also asked him to bring me a chilled bottle of Dom Perignon and four glasses for my unexpected guests. I saw Syd enter first and watched him sashay across the bar, Freda and the young girl in tow. Freda had dressed her with ultimate care to ensure that she would not look out of place. The young woman was striking, her statuesque frame embellished by a couture cocktail dress of emerald green, with a tightly moulded bodice cinched at the waist. The skirt fanned out with layers of chiffon and net like a peacock displaying itself. Cream silk elbow length gloves and stilettos of the same colour enhanced the curve of her calves and ankles. Her face was a perfect oval, framed by her blonde hair and enhanced by a hint of green eye shadow to mirror the intense green of her own eyes. Her mouth was Indian pink. When Syd brought her over, I could smell Lanvin's Arpege on her exposed collar bones and on her wrists and maybe, I hoped, behind her knees. The band was playing 'Stranger in Paradise'.

'Joe, old chap. What on earth are you doing here?' Syd turned to the young lady. 'I hope you don't mind, Annie, but I'd like you to meet a friend of mine, Joseph Stein.'

I had already risen from my chair. I took her hand and kissed her glove. She blushed violently.

'Did you know, Joe old boy, that it's Annie's twenty first birthday today,' announced Syd, winking at me in a rather obvious manner.

'Happy birthday, my dear. Do have a seat. I'd be honoured if you'd join me for a glass of champagne.' I couldn't abide champagne myself.

'It would be a pleasure, Mr Stein,' Annie stammered.

'Well, children, I feel that we should drink this rather inviting bottle of Dom Perignon champagne, which just so happens to be chilling right here, right now,' announced Syd, beckoning a waiter over to open the bottle, which lay on ice next to me. 'One isn't 21 everyday!'

The next couple of hours passed in a haze, as I quizzed Annie about the atelier and what is what like working for such a pair of loveable rogues as Syd and Freda, where she lived, whether she had siblings and what her parents did for a living. Annie was reserved at first, but after a glass or two of champagne, she relaxed a little. I was beguiled by her. Unusually, I didn't want to seduce her immediately. I wanted to get to know her. It was an odd feeling for me. When I asked if I could take her to dinner, I was willing her to say yes.

I could not quite believe that I was drawn back so consistently to this young woman, but there was something about Annie which magnetised me. It began slowly, with a weekly dinner date, or a drink at The Midland, whenever I could get away from London. She knew nothing of my world, which was perhaps part of the attraction, but the age gap of eighteen years worried me and she was not well educated. On the other hand, she had perfect manners and a good work ethic, to which I could relate. More than anything, though, I found Annie easy to talk to. I had never really opened up to anyone before, not even to Bruno, who was supposedly my closest confidante, but with Annie, I could talk about my past; the harshness of my childhood, the coldness of my mother and losing my father so young, 'I guess I felt guilty somehow. You know, like I should have known that was the last time I'd see him alive, that I should have said something important, rather than just offering him a glass of water – that maybe if I'd called a doctor, he'd still be alive.' I lit another Craven A from the dying embers of my current one.

'You can't beat yourself up, Joe. You can't blame yourself. There was nothing you could have done.' Annie sat on my knee and kissed me on the head.

Annie seemed to feel equally at ease with me. She told me that I made her feel safe. She confided in me about her own childhood trauma – her evacuation and subsequent breakdown – something she said she had never told anyone previously. 'After I'd been to see the doctor, I felt that my situation was hopeless. He had no cure for my condition and he just suggested rest and recuperation. I was cooped up at home, looking like a half-plucked chicken, and bored out of my mind. Yet, because my nerves were in tatters, I didn't want to go leave the house. My mother was out at work all day and when she was home, she was a horrific combination of over-solicitous and overwrought. She became exasperated with me, and we grew further apart. It strained my parents' marriage as well. My mother thought my father didn't take my situation seriously enough, and my father thought my mother should lighten up. It was, in fact, my father who started to help me in the end.'

'How did he do that?' I asked, stroking Annie's hair. We were sitting at a secluded table at the back of the Midland Bar. Annie stirred her gin and tonic with a cocktail stick, supposedly lost in the movement of the liquid in her glass.

'He started to help me to sleep at night by slipping me an aspirin with a tot of whisky. My mother would have gone apoplectic if she'd found out, but fortunately she never did. He used to bring it up to my room, when he came to say goodnight, hidden inside his newspaper. It sounds like a totally irresponsible thing to do, I know, but it helped me to make it through what was a very difficult time. As I swallowed the pill down with the whisky, warmth spread through my veins and somehow, it slowed my brain down and stopped it jumping from nightmare to nightmare. As I got a bit older, I used to sneak into the cupboard where he kept the booze and take the odd sip during the day sometimes. It just took the edge of everything, if that makes sense. Do you think that's terrible?'

'No, not at all. We all need a drink to put a dent into reality from time to time, and there's nothing wrong with alcohol, as long as you know your limits. I think it's perfectly healthy, darling. It should be national health policy for all children should be given sherry in their milk from birth. It might solve an awful lot of problems, from teething to tantrums to adolescence.'

'Maybe you could suggest it to one of the politicians when you interview them,' giggled Annie.

'Good idea. I must jot that down.' We were silent for a moment, happy just to be together, an ordinary couple. 'So when did you start leaving the house again?'

'I guess it was a year or so later. Mum and Dad casually invited the occasional visitor to pop in, especially if they had kids of a similar age. At first I hid away, but my father slowly persuaded me to join in, just for five minutes at a time. He'd give me a taste of Dutch courage, as he called it, and tell me I didn't have to say anything. I could just be. So I tried, and eventually five minutes became ten, ten became twenty and so on. Sometimes I said something. The next time, I spoke more than once. I started to feel a little more confident and my hair started to grow back again. Then Dad suggested that I come down to sit with him at the yard. He told me I could come in disguise, as an adventure, so no one need know who I was. So I'd dress up like a boy – I still didn't have any chest in those days – and put a cap on my head and go down to the yard. There I fed the horses and carried bits and pieces around for my father. He called me Bob and let me sip the beer whenever I needed to. He swears to this day that the other coopers never knew it was me, but I'm pretty sure they did.'

'And when did you start school again?'

'Oh, not long after that. But it was awful – I was awful. I'd learnt nothing at school in Carnforth, because I was terrified all the time. I was scared stiff of that bully Mrs Wiggins and of all the other kids at school, who were so mean to me. I'm not surprised that I came home a nervous wreck. When I was ill, I didn't keep up with any schooling. My parents didn't have much themselves, and they were too busy to help me at home. I don't think it occurred to them, to be honest. So when I did go back to school, it was a disaster. I could read and write, but I was hopeless with numbers. The teacher used to throw the board rubber at us if we got something wrong, which for me was all the time. So I moved to the back of the class with the other dunces and reprobates. I was a total failure.'

It broke my heart to listen to her putting herself down. She wasn't a failure. She just hadn't caught any decent breaks in life, well, not until Syd ambushed her in the Kardomah.

'I thought I was going to spend the rest of my life selling fags and chocolate in the corner shop until I met Syd. He turned my life upside down. I'll always be grateful to him.'

And she had turned my life upside down. We were just so easy together and it was frankly a relief not to be locked in intellectual competition. I had spent my whole life striving for success, and would continue to do so, but I didn't seek a companion to challenge me as well. I wanted someone I could love and protect, someone with whom I could relax and who would care for me. I could see that Annie needed my love and protection desperately, and I wanted to be her strength and guide. I would look out for her and make sure she never needed alcohol, or pills, or props of any kind to be happy. I would be the one to ensure her happiness. All I wanted in return was affection, well that and also sex, to be brutally honest, and this appeared to be rather a stumbling block between us. Annie was happy enough to kiss and cuddle with me, but if I tried anything more, she froze. Initially, I was patient, reasoning that she was a good girl from a decent family and this was only to be expected. But a man can only wait so long, and I had waited far longer than I thought was physically possible. 'C'mon, Annie,' I coaxed one night. We were sitting in my Rover outside her parents' house, my arm draped around her shoulders. I could see the curtains twitching, as her mother peeped out to watch any possible shenanigans. We were both concerned that if she saw physical contact of any kind, she'd be outside with a shovel in seconds. 'Let's go to London for the weekend … or I could take you to Cannes? Show you off along the Croisette.' I whispered, kissing her cheek and sliding closer to her across the leather banquette.

'I don't think so, Joe. I don't think it's right, you know, before marriage. And I don't think my Mum and Dad would be best pleased.' She seemed terrified. The more I pressed her, the more she resisted.

'Annie, you're 23 years old and more than capable of making your own decisions. We've been seeing each other for two years now. For Christsakes, think about it, please. I'm only human, after all.'

In the end, Annie agreed to an illicit weekend and I treated her to a sumptuous stay at The Dorchester Hotel in London. Even then, despite the best suite in the joint and several drinks in the bar, it took me all day to break her down and when I did, it was all over far too quickly. Throughout our marriage, Annie was never a willing participant in the bedroom, tending to stare at the ceiling in the hope that it would all be over swiftly, whilst I pumped away hoping that it wouldn't. In the end, I had to seek satisfaction elsewhere over the years which followed. I loved Annie, but the physical disconnect between us always bothered me. I never understood why she could not give herself to me entirely and, if I'm honest, it hurt me just a little and definitely wounded my pride.

A month or so after our weekend away, I came off set one Saturday evening after a punishing interview with an American actor, who had clearly felt that I was probing too closely into his personal life. The show was tense, exhausting – great television. I walked back to my dressing room, my shirt sticking to my back. I always sweated profusely during a show. The makeup girl would rush on with regularity during the breaks to dust my head, attempting to reduce the shine into people's living rooms. Some thought I sweated due to the intense lights on set, but it was down to pure adrenaline. I loosened my tie as I opened my dressing room door and switched on the light. I jumped, dropping my tie to the floor. Annie was sitting at my dressing table, her face tear-stained, mascara blackening her cheeks. 'Darling, what is it?' I wondered where my dresser was and who had let her in. The BBC was normally very strict on security. Whilst I was pleased to see Annie, I would have preferred my usual half an hour cool down, to enjoy a shower, a smoke and a whisky.

I went over to her and Annie stood up. She was wearing old grey slacks and a cream polo neck. It was the sort of outfit she's usually only wear at home. I took her in my arms and she began to sob. 'Hey, c'mon now. It can't be that bad,' I soothed, walking her over to the couch. I moved a pile of shirts, which were lying there waiting for my dresser to hang them up – a gift from one of my

Saville Row tailors, which had arrived earlier that day – and I sat Annie down. She was shaking. I walked over to the decanter on the dressing table, where I poured us both a couple of stiff whiskies. I always had one pre and post show, the first for luck and the second for congratulations or commiserations, depending on how well or badly it had gone. 'Here, drink this, Annie. God's best medicine.'

Annie gulped it gratefully.

'That's better, darling. Now what's the matter? What are you doing in London? Has something happened? Is there trouble at work with Syd and Freda? Are your mum and dad OK?'

Annie shook her head.

'What then? C'mon, Annie. You can tell me.' I sat down on the couch and held the hand nursing the whisky. Annie raised her reddened panda eyes to me.

'Joe, I'm pregnant.'

Annie wasn't the first girl to come to me to say she was pregnant, nor was she the last. But she was the only person I wanted to bear my child, so there would be no secret appointments to be arranged. This time there would be a wedding, and a hasty one at that. I dried Annie's tears and took her back to St John's Wood, where we sat up and talked all night and in the morning, I brought her breakfast in bed, complete with a daffodil I plucked myself from the garden. While she sipped her coffee, I got down on one knee and proposed. 'Get dressed, Annie. We're going out.'

I drove Annie to Bond Street in the brand new Jaguar. Annie chewed toffees from the glove compartment all the way there and we discussed wedding plans. As soon as possible would be best. It would need to be low key. We had the religious problem to consider, or rather the problem of my mother, who would have to be managed. The rabbi could be persuaded to perform a quickie conversion, sweetened by a suitable donation to the synagogue. I also had to ask Annie's father for permission, and I knew he wasn't my biggest fan. It was a difficult show to produce, but we'd manage it. I parked the car right outside Tiffany's and we were greeted by the liveried doorman, who held open the massive doors leading to the greatest sweetshop for grown women on earth. The sales assistant on the front desk recognised me immediately – I had bought various trinkets for lady friends here in the past – and bolted around the counter to greet me.

'Mr Stein, what a pleasure to welcome you to Tiffany today. What can we do to be of service?'

'You can keep this just between us, for starters. Do you have a private room where we could view some rings? We don't want any prying eyes from the press all over us, now do we?'

'Of course not, Mr Stein. Right away, Mr Stein. Do follow me, please.' The sales assistant led Annie and I up the staircase to the first floor and into a small room with a small polished table, where we were met by the store manager. The large window overlooked Bond Street and occasionally, a red bus slowed outside the window. Its passengers stared casually towards us.

'Can we close the blinds please?'

'Certainly, Mr Stein, straight away, Mr Stein,' grovelled the manager, as he walked briskly to the window and pulled the louvers shut himself. 'Now what can I show you today?'

'Diamond rings, please. Nothing under four carats. Please show us some square and some round, will you? Princess cuts. Best you have. Oh, and bring me a whisky with cold water on the side, no ice for me, and we'll have a glass of champagne for the lady, please.'

We left an hour later, Annie's finger weighed down by a monumental rectangular diamond and my wallet considerably lightened. 'Breathe a word of this to anyone,' I whispered to the store manager as we left, 'and I'll return the ring and never shop here again.'

Jim was no bother at all. He was relieved that I was not leading Annie a dance and happily gave her away. Neither he nor Dee knew anything of the pregnancy. Neither did Ma, but she was more challenging. 'A shikse, Joseph. Of all the girls in all the world, you couldn't find a Yiddish one to marry?'

'No, Ma, I'm sorry, but I love Annie and she is going to convert before we get married. We've already seen Rabbi Goldberg.'

'Who's that? Some mickey mouse rabbi who does this sort of illegal shidduch? Really, you disappoint me, Joseph. And all your children, will they be as tall as her?' Ma wrinkled her nose, as if bothered by an obnoxious fume, and stalked out.

The wedding was a small affair; Annie and I, obviously, Ma, Jim and Dee. We all got through it without any embarrassing comments – if you ignored anything Ma uttered – and had a drink after the service at The Midland to celebrate. Annie and I flew off on our honeymoon to Nassau for a week that evening. After we returned, Annie looked slightly plumper and extremely radiant, which was clearly due solely to the sunshine in the Bahamas. A month later, we told all the grandparents that we were expecting and six months after that, Annie gave birth to a beautiful baby girl. If anyone could count, they certainly failed to mentioned it. Having never thought too much about marriage or fatherhood, I suddenly became enamoured with the whole idea of it. I was forty five and about to become a father for the first time. Annie, however, was subdued throughout her pregnancy. At first, I thought it was only because she was as sick as a dog all day, but when the morning sickness had subsided and the birth grew nearer, she grew more and more detached. She took no interest in the preparations for the nursery, nor did she wish to discuss the potential sex of the child, or alternative baby names. I had to ask the decorator to kit out the nursery in neutral shades of cream, installing a highly impractical fairytale cot, shrouded in lace. Dee helped me to pick out white babygros and to buy nappies, pins and cream in readiness. I asked Annie to tell me what, if anything, was troubling her, but she refused to discuss it. I reasoned that she was just anxious, maybe as a result of her own childhood traumas, so I didn't push it. I was sure she would love the child once he or she arrived.

On the night Natasha did appear, I was at an awards dinner. Annie was suffering contractions earlier that day, but fathers were not encouraged to attend the birth in those days – thank goodness – and her mother was with her, so I figured I may as well go as to my event as planned, as I was both presenting and receiving an award that evening. It was an entertaining night, with many old friends and colleagues in attendance, with whom I could share whisky and a few amusing anecdotes, as well as exchanging industry gossip. It was also a successful night. I picked up the award for Best Personality on Television, handed to me by a ravishing actress, whose dress appeared to have a mind all of its own. As I was at the podium making what I thought was a rather droll speech about one of the celebrities I'd interviewed recently – on whom I had accidently spilled whisky just before she came on stage – I was handed a telegram. 'Ladies and Gentleman, this is highly irregular, but I have just been handed an urgent telegram, so I hope you don't mind if I read it aloud, just in case it's more important than talking to you lot.' Laughs from the audience. I ripped open the envelope and stood there silent for a moment, my heart beating slightly faster than normal. 'Ladies and Gentleman, I am delighted to announce that I have just received another award. My beautiful wife Annie has delivered me of a baby girl, six pounds, six ounces.' I paused, momentarily unable to speak, which was unusual for me. I pulled my handkerchief from my breast pocket and dabbed at my eyes. 'Mother and daughter are doing well. Mine's a very large whisky. Thank you.'

But mother and daughter never did do well. Annie, it turned out, just wasn't the maternal type. Dee stayed with us for the first few weeks and mothered the baby. She fed her with powdered milk – Annie refused to have Sasha anywhere near her breasts, saying it made her nauseous and sore and anyway, she'd given the baby her stomach, what more did she want? – bathed her, changed her nappies and got up to her in the night. It became clear that we would have to hire nannies to help out – Dee was not going to stay forever – and I couldn't be too hands on. I was extremely busy and anyway, babies aren't really that exciting, if I'm perfectly honest. I think they need to get to the age of at least two before they can be of any real interest. So, we engaged a day nanny, and a night nanny, who brought up little Sasha between them. Annie was exhausted, or so she said, from cooking for the day nanny and the night nanny, although we also had a housekeeper and a chef. I thought that cooking was part of his job description. Annie paid lip service to the child, but no more. It was as though she couldn't bear to look at her. It was shocking, really, as Sasha was an angelic child, with deep brown eyes and curly auburn hair, but it was her laughter which endeared me to her most. She found the smallest things amusing and would throw her head back and cackle when I made a coin disappear behind her ear, or if we played hide and seek. Our antics merely served to irritate Annie further, who was harsh on the child, constantly telling her to be quiet, or to tidy up. It was me who read to Sasha when I was home, or played games with her. Annie could not abide any of that nonsense.

'I'm busy, Joe. You're out all day and night managing your shows, but I have to arrange dinners for when we entertain and manage all the staff. Frankly, I'm dog-tired.'

I noticed that she kept a small flask in her handbag. When I asked her about it, she grew defensive. 'It's a draft from the doctor for my nerves,' she'd tell me, before ferreting the bottle away in her bag and stalking out of the room.

As Sasha grew, it became clear that she was a quick-witted little thing. She excelled at school, winning the form prizes most years. Her head teacher advised that she should try for a place at the most competitive grammar school for girls in North London, so we found her a tutor, who worked her hard, yet she seemed to thrive on it. Yet the more Sasha achieved, the more resentful Annie became. 'I can't help you with that,' Annie barked at Sasha when she asked if she could read her a story she'd written for her homework. 'You know I'm stupid. Ask your father.' Annie had never been one to talk shop with me either. Politics and all that guff was, she told me often, quite over her head. I should discuss it with my researchers. Yet Annie was an integral part of my business life, as a crucial part of my job was to host dinners at home for the great and good. Annie was a truly welcoming hostess, wowing our guests with her good looks, fabulous frocks and copious supply of booze. She knew how to dress a room and how to dress herself for maximum impact, as well as making polite conversation with the men and women we entertained. As Sasha grew older, she also began to join us at dinner

– when she could no longer be herded off to bed by whichever nanny we had in our employ at that time. We did tend to go through them at a quite frightening rate.

Sasha turned out to be a remarkable dinner party conversationalist. 'She'll be taking over your job soon, Joe,' remarked the head of Light Entertainment at the BBC on one occasion. 'You'd better watch out!' Annie glowered more and more, while Sasha's confidence bloomed as she met so many interesting people from all walks of life at our table.

At fourteen, Sasha began to blossom in other ways, transforming from a cheeky child into a beautiful and accomplished young woman. She did not resemble either Annie or me in particular. Whereas Annie was tall, blonde, willowy and statuesque, Sasha was a few inches shorter than her mother, with an hour glass figure and molten brown eyes. I think she got her eyes from me, but sometimes, she looked like a total stranger. I used to joke that the milkman had left her on the front doorstep one morning. Annie was never amused. As Sasha matured and became more able to participate in our soirees, and in my life, Annie became more and more difficult. I noticed that she began to drink more heavily. She had always enjoyed a glass or two, and was often quite tipsy by the end of an evening, but now she was drunk more often than not, and Annie was not an attractive drunk. On the contrary, she became sharp tongued and sometimes, quite offensive to our guests and almost always unpleasant to Sasha. If someone complimented Sasha, or laughed at something she said, Annie would roll her eyes in plain disgust, or worse, say something embarrassing, or just plain offensive.

'Annie, you've brought up a delightful young lady. I really must compliment you,' drawled a Cabinet minister, who was due to appear on the following week's show.

'Thank you, Mr Carmichael, but if you knew her as well as I do, you'd soon realise that she's a tricky little bitch,' retorted Annie, as Sasha shot up to help clear the dishes to escape from her mother's venomous words.

Eventually, I stopped entertaining at home, both to prevent reputational damage and to be perfectly honest, to escape the tortuous atmosphere which now prevailed. I went to my club in town, or to restaurants. I knew we had a problem, but it was easier for me to ignore it than to confront it. I was extremely busy, I was out of the house a great deal, and Annie was usually in bed by the time I returned, which grew later and later, as I became reluctant to sleep in my own bed. My avoidance tactics were easy for me to arrange, but there was little respite for Sasha, who was remained at home alone to suffer her mother's tirades.

One Sunday, when I was relaxing in the conservatory watching salutatory repeats of *The World at War,* Sasha crept in, closing the door behind her. 'Daddy, I need to speak to you,' she whispered.

'Why are we whispering?' I laughed. Annie had gone out shopping and we had the house to ourselves.

'I need you to be serious for a minute, Daddy, OK?' She looked worried, a line appearing between her eyes in an otherwise perfectly smooth complexion.

'Sure, Sash. What is it?' I turned the television off and shifted around on the sofa to face her. Sasha paced the room, pulling at her hair.

'Daddy, do you know how much Mummy is drinking?'

'Well, I know she likes the odd glass of wine, Sasha, but I don't think it's anything out of the ordinary.' I looked down, pulling up my sock, which had wrinkled under my foot.

'Daddy, she's drinking all the time. There are bottles hidden everywhere – in her wardrobe, in the spare rooms, at the back of the sink behind the cleaning stuff, in the garage. I opened the boot of the car the other day and there were three cases of wine in there, four bottles of gin and a crate of empties. I've asked her not to collect me from school, because she is a menace on the road. She almost hit some children on the pedestrian crossing last week, and the week before that, she collided with a dog as we came off the flyover. The poor thing limped away. I think it survived, but I'm sure you're supposed to report hitting a dog to the police. Anyway, you must have smelt it on her?' Sasha spoke in a rush of anxiety.

'I'm sure it's not as that bad as all that, Sasha. She probably just has a couple of drinks occasionally and…'

'No, Dad, it's not just a couple.' Sasha raised her voice slightly, beginning to cry. 'She drinks all day and she's horrible to live with. She calls me names, and she embarrasses me in front of my friends. The other day, Geraldine came over and Mummy called me a cow right in front of her. She spends hours on the phone to her friends, telling them how I'm so vain, above myself, Daddy's little girl. And you're not here, Daddy, so you don't know. You're not here and you really don't know…' Sasha collapsed onto the sofa next to me sobbing. I reached over and patted her shoulder. I really wasn't good with female emotion and never understood why it was always accompanied by switching on the waterworks. Personally, I couldn't remember the last time I'd cried. I wished this conversation wasn't happening and I needed to find a rational way out of it. What I needed to do was to commission some hard research.

'Look, Sasha, I'll tell you what I'll do. I'll find the bottles and I'll mark them at the meniscus. Then when I see the level go down, I'll ask your mother who's been drinking them and have a chat with her? How's that?'

Sasha looked up, and blew her nose fiercely on a paper tissue, which she had pulled from the sleeve of her sweater. 'OK, Daddy, yes please. Speak to her. I can't get through to her, no matter what I do, and when she's been drinking, she seems to hate me. She looks at me as if I'm an alien or something. It's horrible.'

'I'll do what I can, darling. Now how about you go and make us a nice cup of tea and see if there is any of that lovely chocolate cake left. That'll cheer us up.'

I did look for the bottles and I found plenty of them, as Sasha had said I would. I marked the labels very discreetly and kept a note of the dropping levels, which were indeed dramatic. Yet I failed to tackle Annie on the subject. It was a phase, I reasoned to myself, and she'd get through it. It was what Annie did when she felt out of whack and unable to cope. It was difficult for Annie to watch her daughter growing up into a beautiful young woman while her own looks faded. There were too many female hormones raging around the house, and I was not equipped to sort it out. I was sure that, eventually, Annie would settle down and that she and Sasha would pull through to become the best of friends. Mothers and daughters always have a special bond which you can't really break, don't they? Just sometimes, it gets a little stretched, pulled out of shape, that's all. Anyway, Sasha never asked me about it again, so I assumed things had improved of their own accord, just as I had suspected they would.

Sasha finished school and left home to go to university in Bristol. We had hoped that she'd go to Oxford, but she didn't get in, which was a great shame. I tried to encourage her to attempt it again, after she got her excellent A-Level results, but she was adamant that she wanted to go to Bristol. She seemed keen to move on with her life, and I reminded myself that I had once been the same, a lifetime ago. Once Sasha left, she never really came back to live at home again. She tended to stay in Bristol during the holidays to work, or rather doss with that strange boyfriend of hers – Neil, I think he was called – odd bloke, very intense. When she graduated, she got a job in advertising and rented a flat with some other university friends near Pentonville Prison in North London. I used to joke about the inmates coming to stay, and Sasha would laugh politely, having heard the same joke many times before. It was a horrible house, but she said she was settled there. Then eventually, she met Jeremy – I'm not sure what happened to Neil, but hopefully she kicked him into touch – and settled down. They seemed to be very happy, and what more can a father ask, than that his daughter is happily married to a decent chap. Jeremy was solid – dull, serious, edging on boring – but a good guy, and someone who would provide for my little girl. I could relax a little.

And bizarrely Annie seemed much happier without Sasha in the house. I thought she'd be quite morose without her only child to keep her company, but she appeared to be far more content. She had a new lease of life and she even began to take more interest in my work again. We reinstated regular entertaining at home and went out to parties together. Annie shone. I'd forgotten so much of why I was initially attracted to her, and why I had chosen her over so many of the other options. I was proud to have her on my arm. We even stayed in together more frequently, watching films and drinking whisky together, something we hadn't done together in years. I wasn't getting any younger, and I became happier to take it easy in the evenings. Annie would make a TV dinner for us and we'd watch whatever was on, even if it was me – especially if it was me. And as I started to work less and when I eventually retired, we travelled more, taking a round the world trip for a few months, visiting places we had never had time to see before. Sasha was settled and we had not need to worry about her. I eased into older age comfortably and happily now that Annie and I had rediscovered each other.

Sasha and Jeremy appeared similarly content, but it took them a long time to have a child. They both had their careers – Sasha working in advertising and Jeremy as a barrister – and I did wonder for a while whether they would be one of those couples who sacrificed a family in order to press on with their career ambitions. The thought disappointed me from a selfish perspective. I was in my late seventies by now, and I had hoped to meet my grandchildren before I moved on to the next world. So you can imagine how delighted I was when Sasha did finally announce that she was pregnant. It was Christmas Day and she presented Annie with a gift-wrapped set of wool and knitting needles. Of course, the symbolism went right over Annie's head, and all she did was tell Sasha that she didn't really knit, so she may as well give the wool to someone who did, but I got it straight away. 'You're going to have a baby?'

'That's right, Dad. It's due in August, so I'm telling you very early – as it's Christmas. But please don't tell anyone yet. Not until I'm safely past twelve weeks. Get ready to be a Grandad.'

So inevitably Annie told everyone she knew immediately – and even those she didn't – that very same evening and a huge row with Sasha ensued. 'Why can't you respect my wishes just this once? What if something goes wrong before I get into the second trimester, and then I have to tell everyone I'm not having a baby? It's very selfish, Mummy.'

'Sasha, you are being ridiculous as usual. Nothing will go wrong. Believe me, once you're pregnant, you're pretty much stuck with that foetus, whether you like it or not!'

Annie was right and the pregnancy went to plan. In mid-August of the following year, Sasha was delivered of a beautiful baby boy, whom they named Sebastian. We lived quite close by, and popped in regularly to see Sasha and the baby. Annie used him as an enormous shopping opportunity and he was the best dressed baby in town. Yet it was hard for Sasha. She went back to work quite quickly, as the agency were very demanding and she was worried about losing her job, and Jeremy travelled quite a bit. I suggested to Annie that she might like to help her out, but Annie appeared to have little sympathy. 'We've all had children, Joe, and being a mother is tough. Sasha was a real handful, need I remind you.' She had forgotten that she had had nannies, and night nurses, and that she gave up her job as soon as we got married, but no matter. I had no desire to turn motherhood into another battleground between Annie and Sasha. We rarely babysat, as Sasha always seemed to have someone else at hand, and I was never too fussed about looking after the baby. He was very sweet, but after a few minutes, there was nothing much to say to him. He just smiled and drooled.

One day, however, when Sebastian was about eight months old, Sasha called me to ask for our help. 'Jeremy's client has invited us down to his house in Sussex for the night – apparently it's a very important client and we have to go, even though I need it like a hole in the head – and I can't get a babysitter. I wondered if you and

Mummy could stay over and look after Sebastian. It'll just be from late afternoon until the following morning, because I'll get back by elevenish at the absolute latest. Do you think that would be OK?'

'You're asking the wrong person, Sasha. You know I'm hopeless with babies, but I'm sure your mother will be more than happy to oblige. She's done it before, remember. I'll ask her when she gets back from the shops.'

'Thanks, Daddy, but you will come and stay too, won't you? Don't send Mummy alone.'

'Well, if you'd like me to, of course, but I won't be much use.' And I wasn't much use anymore. My legs didn't work very well and often refused to help me out of my chair. It took me some time to get upstairs to bed, and Annie and I had discussed getting a stair lift fitted. And Annie told me that was increasingly forgetful, but I could never remember if I was or not.

I forgot to ask Annie about the babysitting, but Sasha obviously called again and spoke to her and it was all arranged. We headed over to their house in the late afternoon and Sasha and Jeremy scurried off for a well-deserved night away. Annie fussed around Sebastian, feeding him breadsticks, bananas and rusks and cleaning him up afterwards. Then she bathed him and put him to bed around 7.30. She seemed so much happier with her grandson than she had ever been with her own daughter, although she was displeased that he was a boy. 'I just don't know what to do with his thing, Joe. And when I change him, he wees all over the curtain. It's gross.'

'He should go straight off and sleep through,' Sasha had told us before she left, 'but I've switched the baby monitor on in the kitchen, and in the spare room where you're sleeping, so you can hear him if he wakes up. And I usually check on him during the night anyway. Just in case.'

'Just in case of what, Sasha? For goodness sake, stop fussing and go away. He'll be fine with us. After all, I brought you up in one piece, didn't I?' Sasha shot a look at me, before Jeremy bustled her out of the house and they drove off.

With the baby in bed, Annie and I settled down in the lounge to watch television. We had a few whiskies and retired. There wasn't a peep out of Sebastian all night. The following morning, however, we were woken by screaming. I nudged Annie, who was still asleep beside me, snoring gently. 'Annie, what the hell is that noise? What time is it?'

Annie groaned and reached out her hand for the clock. 'Christ, it's quarter to eleven. Is that the baby?' Annie put on her dressing gown and went into the bathroom to use the toilet, while I fumbled on the side table for my glasses. At that moment, the bedroom door burst open and Sasha entered, carrying Sebastian, with Jeremy following straight behind her.

'Help me, Daddy, help. He's not breathing.' She placed Sebastian onto the bed beside me. I put out my hand to touch his face. The child was cold.

'Sasha, I've called 999. They're on their way,' intoned Jeremy, ashen-faced.

Annie came out of the bathroom, pulling a hairbrush through her hair. 'Sasha, what's going on? I can't believe it's so late and the baby slept right through. What on earth was all the shouting about?'

Sasha was sitting on the bed, holding Sebastian, rocking him back and forth gently whispering in his ear. 'C'mon, little man, wake up, wake up, please wake up.'

I began to recite the Kaddish prayer.

Part Three

Sasha

I'd started going to the gym.

It didn't seem to be doing my body much good – I walked as though I had been riding a horse bareback for a week and everything was wobbling just as badly as it had before – but it was helpful for me to get out and socialise with other people. Otherwise I sat at home every evening, becalmed, watching re-runs of old box sets on the television while scoffing chocolates, or spooning through an entire carton of ice cream. I didn't stay out for more than a couple of hours – it wasn't fair on Stanley, who always looked at me forlornly, as if I was leaving him for a fortnight, whenever I shut him in the kitchen – and I didn't like to be away from Zac for too long, just in case he wanted to chat. Things had mercifully settled down a little between us now.

Concealing the truth about Sebastian had been a long-held emotional burden for me, and now that his existence – however brief – was out in the open, I felt strangely released. I think Zac had forgiven me for withholding the secret for so long, or was at least trying to, and with help from Jeremy, I think he understood why we had originally decided to keep him in the dark.

Of course, he only knew that he had had an older brother, who sadly died in infancy. He did not know anything about the real circumstances of his death, and I saw no reason why he ever should. Zac had a good relationship with my mother, far better than I had ever had, and I felt that that was important to maintain that bond, as both of Jeremy's parents had passed away years ago and she was his only grandparent. If Zac knew that his grandmother had been in charge on that awful night, and even worse, that she had been inebriated…well, perhaps Sebastian would have died anyway, even if I had been there. I had no idea what time he had actually passed away, but that was not the point. My parents had been responsible for Sebastian that evening and yet, had been so unforgivably irresponsible. They never considered that they needed to stay sober, watchful. They would never have heard him cry out, even if he had. I blame myself for being stupid enough to ask them to babysit. I blame them for not taking it seriously, especially my mother. My father was an infirm old man, who needed looking after himself. But what was my mother's excuse? She couldn't lay off the bottle just for that one night? Who was I kidding? It was my fault and mine alone. I trusted her with my child – the woman who hated her own child– so maybe I deserved it.

At least when I was at the gym, I could stop tormenting myself with thoughts of Sebastian and Zac, and the ongoing divorce from Jeremy. I had to concentrate so hard on the basics, like continuing to breathe, that more complex anxieties became infeasible. I started off in the gym itself, trying out various machines. This was not a success. I couldn't last for more than a minute on the cross-trainer before the heart monitor bleeped, indicating that an attack was imminent. I tried the rower, but I couldn't keep my feet in the pedals and, when I did manage a couple of strokes, I put my back out for a week. When I attempted the treadmill, I pressed the wrong buttons, causing the belt to move at a frightening speed, one at which only Usain Bolt could compete. I fell off the end in my panic and landed in an embarrassed heap at the foot of a man on the bike behind me. After that, I tried the weights machines, but as all I could lift was a couple of kilos, I thought that I may as well stick to carrying the shopping back from the supermarket.

So I decided to try a class instead. Initially, I had avoided classes, assuming that I would be one of the oldest, fattest and most out of shape people in the class and therefore, by default, a laughing stock. However, there were a few beginners classes and I noticed in the changing rooms that not everyone had a beach ready body – mine hadn't been ready for anything for quite a while – so I figured that I may as well give it a go. I began slowly with yoga, but it was a little too slow. When I shut my eyes and breathed in deeply, I felt like I might nod off on the mat. Anyway, my body was going to take some persuading to bend itself into the shapes the instructor was demonstrating. I decided to leave downward dog to Stanley. Next, I tried a spinning class. Someone should have warned me about the potentially life-altering implications of the saddle. Then I spotted a poster for a new Zumba class. I thought this might be more up my alley and it turned out to a blast. Firstly, the instructor was a gorgeous Brazilian guy, barely older than Zac, but with huge energy and an infectious smile. I burned off calories just by swooning over him, while occasionally admonishing myself for being old enough to be his mother. The music pumped loudly and for forty-five minutes, my fellow classmates and I fell over our own and each other's feet and laughed a great deal. I had absolutely no rhythm or athletic ability whatsoever, but I enjoyed it, and that's what counted. The class was at seven in the evening at the leisure centre, not far from where I lived, so I could walk to and fro, which made me feel even more righteous. It was attended mostly by women, although there were a few brave and foolhardy men strutting their stuff as well. We all got to know each other well enough to exchange pleasantries. For the most part, I kept my head down, as I wasn't yet ready to answer the inevitable questions: are you married (yes, but not for much longer), do you have any kids (yes, one, but I used to have two) and so on.

At the end of the class, I usually bid everyone a hasty goodbye, grabbed my bag and headed for the door, but last week, one of the guys in the class came up to me as I was leaving.

'Hi, I'm Harry. I've not had a chance to say hello to you yet, even though I've seen you in the class a few times.' He was handsome in a quirky way, around six foot tall, thick set with a wide mono-brow and brown curly hair, probably in his early thirties. He had barely broken a sweat during the class and looked as though he was about to begin a workout than finish one. By contrast, I was melting. Sweat was running down my face and I could barely catch enough breath to answer him.

'Hi, hello, yea, I'm Sasha, hi, lovely to meet you,' I puffed. I sounded like Zac. I pulled my coat on, struggling to get my arm into the sleeve. Harry reached over and helped me find it. It was a while since anyone had touched me, and the intimacy of his gesture both surprised and embarrassed me. 'Thank you. That's very kind,' I mumbled. I picked up my bag and started heading for the door.

Harry put his hand on my shoulder, for a nanosecond, but long enough to make me pause. 'Would you like to grab a quick drink?'

I was so surprised by his question that my bag slipped from my hand. It fell to the floor and everything tipped out as per usual – the same old tissues, bits of paper, poo bags, my purse, an emergency tampon from years ago, foreign coins, reading glasses, distance glasses, my hairbrush, a battered lipstick with the lid missing –the lot. I bent down and started to shovel it all back in. Harry knelt down to help me, his face so close to mine that I could feel his breath. He smelt good. I hadn't been this close to a man for a long time, and it made my heart race even faster than Zumba. I told myself to stop being a bloody idiot. I was old enough to be his mother, or at the very least, a much, much older sister, for Christsakes.

'Thank you. That's very kind. I'm such an idiot,' I said, standing up and putting my bag over my shoulder.

'Not at all,' he replied.' We stood there. 'So can I interest you in that drink?'

'Well, it's very nice of you to ask, but I've really got to get back home to my son and my dog. They both need feeding, and Zac's revising, so I probably have to test him, and I'm working tomorrow and…'

Harry threw me a dazzling smile, which almost made me drop my bag again. 'Zac is the dog, or your son?' He laughed. 'Well, maybe next week, if you can manage it? I'll be at the class as usual. I'll look out for you.'

I pulled my hand through my tangled hair and my fingers got stuck. 'Oh, yes. Well, maybe, yes. That would be lovely. Thank you, yes.' I backed out of the door, tripping over my loose shoelace as I went.

Annie

Zac is here and he's asking me so many questions about the family. He says he wants to put together a family tree. We're sitting at the table in the conservatory overlooking the garden. The first of the crocuses and snowdrops are peeping their heads out of their leaves, trying to decide if they should come out yet or not. Zac has made us hot chocolate and the sweetness warms me. 'So Grandma, tell me more about Grandad's brothers and sisters. Did you ever meet any of them?'

'Well, yes of course, Zac, but there were an awful lot of them, so I get them a bit muddled up with who's who. There was Teddy and Peter, Grandad's older brothers. They ran the factory with Moishe. He was the youngest, but he died very young of a cerebral hemorrhage, like your great grandfather. Moishe was such a gentle soul – very kind to me – unlike the rest of them, who never really made me feel very welcome.'

'Why not?'

'Well, they never accepted me as a Jew, even after I converted. I was always an outsider, a shikse. I worked very hard to keep a Jewish home – even though your Grandad insisted on eating bacon butties on the sly– and

I made a Sedar dinner at Passover and everything. Well, I did until your mother left home. After that, it didn't seem worth it just for Joe and me.'

'It's funny, isn't it, Grandma, how you converted and that means Mum is Jewish, and then she married a non-Jew, but that still makes me Jewish.'

I frown. I never forgave Sasha for marrying out. Why couldn't she have found a nice Jewish boy? They were at least straight. It wasn't much to ask and there had been plenty of them to choose from. And she never even circumcised Zac, or the other unfortunate one. I sometimes wondered if that was why it had happened.

Sasha tells Joe and me that she's marrying Jeremy. Joe seems thrilled, even though Jeremy is not Jewish. He likes Jeremy, reassuring me that he considers Jeremy to be a stable sort of chap, who will look after his only daughter. Mind you, Sasha's never really been one for conforming to the religion. She's a real black sheep. I'm not pleased with her. We come from a strong Jewish family and yet, this doesn't seem to matter to her. Truthfully, I'm not so keen on Jeremy either. He seems quite uninteresting to me, rather bland. 'If you're getting married in a registry office, Natasha, then we will have to keep it very low key. None of our friends will be invited, and there can be no fripperies. Then we'll have a party in the evening, when you can change into a wedding dress, and we can invite everyone to that part. We'll just say it was a private family ceremony in the morning.'

Sasha explodes. 'The actual ceremony is the most important part to me, Mummy. I want Daddy to give me away and I will invite all my friends to it, even if you don't invite yours. I love Jeremy and that's what matters. I'm not ashamed of where we have the service.' She stomps off and out of the front door.

'Your father and I are the ones paying for this bloody expensive circus, you know,' I call after her.

The rows continue for months. We argue at the florist, when I say there's absolutely no need for a bouquet, as it's only a registry office wedding. We argue when I refuse to allow Sasha to have a photographer on the morning of the registry office service, informing her that he can come and take photos later on, when Sasha is in her proper wedding dress, not when she's wearing a boring, dowdy suit. I help her to choose her wedding dress, of course, as she'll be wearing that at the party, but she can choose the suit for the civil service herself. We argue about the number of people I'm inviting, most of whom Sasha has never even heard of, apparently. We argue about pretty much everything.

'Mummy, it's not my fault that we can't marry under the chuppah. We asked the Rabbi to bless us in synagogue, but he refused outright. You'd think, given the Jews' history of persecution, that they would be somewhat more welcoming, The registry office is our only option, so I want to make it as memorable as possible.'

But I don't want to draw attention to her treachery in marrying out, so only Joe and I, Jeremy's parents and siblings, and Sasha and Jeremy's friends attend the registry office. Their friends throw confetti and take photos with their small Kodak cameras and that's enough as far as I'm concerned. I want to get home as soon as possible to ensure all the arrangements are ready for the real celebration. We have official photos in the evening – just family obviously – and then we host a tremendous party in a marquee in our garden. The wedding is a great success, and I receive so many compliments. I watch Joe dancing with Sasha, the two of them having such a great time together, and I could not be more delighted that she's finally moving on.

I blow on my cocoa, take a small sip and stare out of the window. A black cat is tiptoeing through the shrubs in the garden. It leaps onto the fence and disappears. I wonder where he's going. If Joe was here, he'd set the dog on the cat. He hates cats.

'And Grandma, what about all my cousins?' asks Zac, biting into a chocolate digestive and spilling crumbs all over the table.

'What cousins?'

'You know, Peter and Teddy's kids and the rest of them. How come we never see them?'

'Oh, I don't know, Zac. They all just drifted apart, I suppose. You know how it is. Everyone has their own lives, Grandad got old and died, and I lost touch with them all, or rather they never kept in touch with me. I'm not really that bothered to tell you the truth. Now, shall I get more biscuits? Try to use the plate, darling.'

Joe is the last to die of all his brothers and sisters, except the one I never knew – the one in America who married the GI. Their offspring all attend the funeral – well, all those who are still with us – the cousins and the second cousins. The men file in wearing dark suits and black ties against stark white shirts, and the women cover their heads with patterned scarves. I listen to the rabbi drone on, but I don't understand the language. I stand there alone, amongst all these people, staring at the coffin draped in black velvet with gold Hebrew script woven into it. Joe is inside it, waiting to rest. Jeremy says a few words about Joe. I suppose it has to be Jeremy who speaks, as he's good at this sort of thing and does it for a living, but what does he really know about Joe? I should have asked the head of the BBC, but I can't quite remember his name. We traipse out to the grave, tiptoeing to avoid the mud splashing on our good shoes, and I stand there, swaying slightly, as they lower Joe down into the ground with the worms and the woodlice. Sasha holds my elbow as I walk over to the open grave and I shovel soil on top of my darling boy. Others follow, and soon Joe will be swallowed up completely.

I think back to that evening when I first met Joe in The Midland Bar in Manchester all those years ago when I was just twenty-one. How fortuitous it was that he just happened to be there that night and that we just happened to meet. I used to tell him it was fate which had brought us together and he'd smile. He was so charming and he wanted to talk to *me*. I couldn't believe that he wanted to talk to me then, and that he continued wanting to do so for the next for forty one years. I hope I don't have to wait too long before I join him in his box. Joe loves me and I love him. We need to be alone together and we don't need anybody else. I know he wasn't always truthful with me, but then I wasn't completely truthful with him. Joe is a good man and he is always there for me when I need him. I love him, it's that simple. I look down and despite my best efforts, my shoes are caked in thick, rust-coloured mud from the graveside. When I get home, I will throw them away.

'Zac, darling, shall I get some cake? I might just get myself a small glass of wine while I'm there, as it's almost dark.' I hoist myself out of my chair using both the arms and fumble for my stick. I look out again across the garden and the shadows are creeping around the trees and across the lawn, dimming the spring flowers. Soon it will be time to sleep.

Sasha

Jeremy and I were on better terms now. After he forced me to cease my internet terrorism by cutting off my supply of ammunition, I realised that I had to pull myself together and act more sensibly, even if most of the time, I still wanted to kill him. I often lay in bed at night wondering which was worse – to be abandoned for another woman, or for another man? Another woman implied that I had lost my sexual attraction and had effectively been part exchanged for a younger model, complete with new technology and far better road holding capabilities. This was undoubtedly devastating for one's self-esteem. So the fact that Jeremy had left me for a man must be preferable. Yet this outcome suggested long term duplicity, and it forced me to question whether Jeremy had ever loved me, or whether I had just been a convenient front for his life, until such time that he was able to confront his demons and be honest with himself. I didn't think either option was particularly preferable. It was desertion, whichever way you looked at it.

What I had decided, however, was that there was no point in making the divorce more acrimonious than it needed to be, particularly on account of Zac. Jeremy was being generous with regard to a potential settlement

– if only to assuage his guilt – allowing me to keep the house and providing me with an income and money for Zac's upkeep and education. In that regard, I couldn't complain. I could be careful with money, if I had to be, so I'd manage with whatever we agreed, within reason, and it would spur me on to keep working hard, which would be important once Zac had gone off to university. I wasn't so sure about Jeremy's new beau, though. He looked like a spender to me. The thought made me smile.

Zac was about to finish his A Levels and was then intending to take a gap year to travel, working his way around the world. He was planning his trip with a friend from school, so he wouldn't be alone, but even so, the thought of my young son braving foreign climes without me to watch out for him scared me senseless. This was the boy who lost his bus pass at least once a week, let money evaporate and who couldn't boil an egg. I'd be a nervous wreck by the time he got back, not to mention extremely lonely. 'It's going to seem like a long time when you're away,' I said to Zac one evening when we were on line searching for cheap accommodation.

'Oh, it'll fly by. Everybody says so,' he replied, flicking onto a hostel site. 'This looks like a good option for the hostel in Bangkok.'

'Hmm.' I didn't want to be critical, but it looked pretty grim in the photos, suggesting to me that it would look a great deal worse in the flesh. 'Look, there's plenty of time to look for place to stay, Zac. Let's sort the flights out first. How's the family tree coming along? Did you get anywhere with Grandma?'

Zac continues to flick through websites. 'Slowly. Grandma can't really remember much about anyone, and she keeps getting confused, or she wanders off onto another subject. I think I might see what I can find on one of the genealogy sites. But Grandma said that I could look through her filing cabinets. Once I've collated it all, I thought I might be able to add it onto whatever footage Sarah managed to get before we abandoned the film. '

'You are privileged if Grandma is letting you near her filing cabinets. She normally guards those like a Rottweiler. Let me know what you find out, Hercules! Right, I'm off to the gym. What time is your father picking you up?'

'He said he'd be here in about half an hour.'

'Great.' Not great, but anyway. 'Well, have a good time over there tonight, and I'll see you tomorrow after school.' I hated it when Zac stayed at Jeremy's, but I'd have to get used to it. I pulled on my trainers, which made me feel virtuous even before I stepped foot in the gym. I kissed Zac on the cheek – I felt the beginnings of stubble, which surprised me – and I headed out of the front door to do my warm up walk to the leisure centre.

I was late for Zumba, and when I got to the gym, I was saddled with the locker in the corner with no space to manoeuvre. I dumped my bag and coat and secured it with my padlock. I'd set it to four consecutive numbers this time, as I kept forgetting the combination, and the handyman was clearly fed up with braving the ladies changing rooms with his lock cutter on my account. I rushed off towards the studio, glimpsing my superfluous bulges in the mirror as I went. It was going to take more than Zumba to shift those. I felt even more self-conscious than usual going into tonight's class, in case Harry was there. He was, and as I entered, he waved at me from the other side of the studio. I gave him a half wave back, feeling my colour rising. The class was packed, which gave me an excuse to stay by the door and to make a quick exit if I wanted to avoid conversation when it finished. Then the music started up and my complete concentration was required. I stumbled my way through. I was absolutely hopeless at Zumba, but it was a laugh, and it made me feel more than justified in sharing an extra couple of biscuits with Stanley when I got home later.

The class ended and we stood there, collecting our breath. I began to join the file out of the door, keen to avoid another embarrassing encounter with Harry, when I heard, 'Hold on. You're not getting away from me that easily!' I looked over my shoulder and Harry was right behind me. 'Now about that drink? I'm not taking no for an answer tonight, young lady.' I wasn't sure if he was talking to me, or chatting up another woman in the sweaty queue, so I turned away again. 'Sasha, hold on, will you?'

I was out of the studio door now, just by the entrance to the changing rooms. A damp chlorinated smell seeped from under the doors. 'Oh, hi, how are you?' I tugged at my T-shirt, which had ridden up. 'Did you enjoy the class?'

'Yes, very much, actually. He definitely gets everyone moving, doesn't he?'

'That's an understatement,' I laughed. I could feel my legs stiffening up as I stood there.

'So, can I interest you in that glass of wine? There's a bar around the corner – that is if your dog, or son, or both, don't mind too much.'

'Well, I'm rather too sweaty to go for a drink and even if I do come, I really can't be long... but OK then, just a quick one. I'll go and grab my things.'

What was I doing? But then again, why shouldn't I go? I walked back into the changing room and headed for my locker, but it was surrounded by women in varying states of undress, or even total nudity, and I couldn't get to it for a few minutes. I never understood why some women chose to parade naked in changing rooms, and it was rarely the slimmer ones. When I finally got to my locker, I turned the padlock to 1234, which even I had managed to remember, and it opened, much for my relief. I threw on my sweatshirt– actually it was one of Zac's, and it enveloped me – then grabbed my coat and bag. I went over to the mirror, fighting for a tiny space to brush my hair and apply my lip gloss. I smiled at myself, and my wrinkles burst out all over my face. Whatever I did in the wine bar, I must not smile.

'I thought you'd disappeared,' Harry laughed as I emerged.

'Sorry, it's a scrum in there. You didn't have to wait.'

'Of course I did. Now, shall we go?' Harry smiled and my left knee buckled slightly. It must have been as a result of Zumba exertions.

Harry held open the door for me and the cold air rushed at my face, making me gasp. We turned down the street and Harry stopped outside a small wine bar just a few doors down. Inside, it was warm and welcoming. We found a table in the corner, which was lit with a candle, stuffed lopsidedly into a wine bottle, one of many which had melted its wax down the neck of the bottle. It would take the full force of my willpower not to pick at it while I was here. Harry went to the bar and ordered a bottle of red wine – he asked me what I'd prefer and I said I'd leave it up to him – and some nachos.

'So, Sasha, tell me what you do.'

'Well, nothing very interesting, I'm afraid. I'm a freelance copywriter, fulltime mother and regular dog walker. How about you?'

'I'm a writer just like you, but of software, not words.'

'Well that's the business to be in, for sure, although I wouldn't profess to understand the first thing about it.'

'That's just as well. It's only interesting for geeks. Anyone normal should steer well clear.'

'You don't seem geeky to me,' I told him and he didn't at all. I always imagined programmers to have oddly shaped heads and strange staring eyes, whereas Harry had a perfectly lovely head and eyes to match.

'And you don't seem copywriterly to me.' Harry smiled and I spilt my wine.

We chatted easily and I told him about Zac and showed him pictures of Stanley on my phone. He didn't ask whether there was a man in my life and I didn't proffer the information. It seemed too forward to discuss my divorce with a man I'd just met. We finished the bottle of wine – I hadn't drunk that much in a long time – and Harry asked if I'd like another.

'I'm so sorry, but I really must get home to Stanley. I don't like leaving him for too long if I can help it.'

'And Zac?'

'Oh, he's out staying with his father tonight.' As soon as I said that, I wondered why. I hoped he didn't think it was an invitation. Harry's monobrow lifted imperceptibly.

'Let me get the bill and then I'll walk you home.'

'Really there's no need,' I stammered, 'I only live down the road,' but as I got up, my head swam and I had to hold onto the back of the chair.

'Take it steady, Sasha. C'mon, let's get you home. It's no trouble, really.'

When we got to my front door, I felt it was only polite to ask Harry if he'd like a coffee. Surely that didn't still mean what it used to mean, did it? He accepted without hesitation and, as I opened the door, he was greeted by Stanley in full 'you've left me forever' mode, all sneezes and wagging tail, galloping in ever decreasing circles. Harry got down onto the floor and Stanley took immediate advantage of this by rolling over and making it clear that he was available to have his tummy tickled for some time. 'Would you like coffee or tea?' I asked, giggling as I watched the two of them.

'I'll have tea please, if you have it.'

'I have a whole selection, in fact. You can have green, mint, chamomile or builders?'

'Definitely builders please – milk, no sugar.'

'No problem.' I filled the kettle at the tap and set it down to boil. As I reached up to grab a couple of mugs from the shelf above, I felt Harry's breath on my neck and I froze for a moment, arms in mid-air with a 'I love my dog best' mug in each hand. He kissed the side of my neck and I brought the mugs down to the counter top with a clatter. I turned and as I did so, Harry encircled my waist and drew me in for a kiss. The kettle came to the boil, steaming the back of my neck. I pulled away. 'Did you say no sugar?'

'Never mind the tea, Sasha. Come here.' Harry led me by the hand over to one of the kitchen chairs. He sat down and pulled me onto his knee. He kissed me again, running his hands over my back. I was aware of a nose pushing between my legs.

'Stanley! Sorry, Harry, Stanley always likes to be part of any show of physical affection. He's just a great big hairy contraceptive, aren't you Stanley?' Stanley bowed to us and wagged his tail furiously, pleased with his intervention.

'Is Stanley allowed in the bedroom?' asked Harry.

'No, it's strictly off bounds. Well, most of the time'

'Well then, sorry, Stanley, old chap, but you must stay here while your mother and I discuss things further upstairs.' Stanley whined and pushed up against me.

'Let me just give him a few biscuits to settle him down.' I scattered some treats around Stanley's toys on his bed, which he bounded over to retrieve, and I led Harry upstairs to my room, shutting the kitchen door softly behind me.

Annie

I am going to the doctor's. Sasha drives, but I'm not letting her come in with me. She always has to take over with the doctor.

'But Mummy, if we go in together, we've got more chance of remembering the questions to ask.'

'You just keep your eyes on the road. I am quite capable of asking questions, thank you very much, Miss.' I am quite able, but sometimes I don't remember the answers – not by the time I get home, anyway. We park outside the surgery, using my disabled badge, and Sasha comes round to help me out of the car. 'Ow! Careful, Sasha. Don't pull at me!'

'I'm not pulling you, Mummy. I'm just trying to help you out.'

Sasha is looking tired. The break with Jeremy has taken its toll on her and she is really looking her age, although I must admit that she does at least look a bit smarter than usual today. She's got some makeup on and proper jeans, rather than the ones which make her bum look elephantine. It's good to make an effort, particularly for a woman of her age. She doesn't want to let herself go too much. We walk slowly up the ramp to the surgery. I am leaning on my stick and Sasha supports my other arm. I hate being so slow, so broken down. When we finally reach the reception area, Sasha helps me into a chair, before going to the desk to announce that we've arrived. She's muttering with the receptionist, and I can't hear what they're saying, but I know they're talking about me. Sasha comes over and grabs a battered magazine off the chair next to me, so that she can sit down. An old man opposite coughs and spits phlegm into his handkerchief. I hope we don't have to sit here too long. The waiting area is grubby and full of sick people, who probably never wash their hands. I've never liked doctor's surgeries – they remind me of when I came back from the war. They're never of much use, I find.

'Come on, Mummy. This is us,' says Sasha, standing and offering to help me up off the chair.

'No one said.'

'No, but it's on the information board, look. Mrs Stein to go to Room 5 to see Dr Chakrabati.'

I look up, and my name flashes on the message board in red lights. I am momentarily famous again. 'You stay here, Sasha. I'll go.'

'Mummy, you can't walk to the room by yourself. Come on, or we'll miss our slot.'

I hoist myself up with Sasha's help and we limp slowly to the back of the surgery, down a slope and through a set of swing doors. Room five is on the right. Sasha knocks.

'Come in.'

'Dr Chakrabati, hello. Good to see you. You remember my mother, Annie Stein.'

Sasha takes charge straight away, naturally. Of course the doctor remembers who I am. The doctor stands up and settles me in the chair next to her desk. She's Indian, of course. You never see English doctors these days. Her name is on her jacket, but it's a long foreign sounding one. I don't try to pronounce it. Sasha plonks herself down into the chair next to me. Why is she still here?

'So Mrs Stein, how are you feeling?'

'Oh, I'm fine, Doctor, really. I'm not sure why I'm here today. I'm sure I'm wasting your time, to be honest. I'm sorry about this. It's my daughter. She insisted that we come today'

'She was quite right. I needed to see you today, Mrs Stein, after the tests you had done recently at the hospital.' The doctor is peering at her computer screen, clicking buttons and not looking at me. Tests, what tests? I can't remember having any tests, but I don't say anything. Is the doctor confusing me with someone else?

'So we've had the test results back and I'd like to discuss them with you. Is that OK?' asks the doctor.

I need a wee, but I don't say anything. 'Yes, Doctor. Fire away,' I say, but I really don't want to listen. I want to go home.

'Well, as you know, you've been suffering from on-going urinary infections, so we did some further investigation to see what's causing them.'

'Oh, well, they're better now, thank you, Doctor. I

took the antibiotics and it's all gone.' I remember coming here now.

The doctor smiles at me. 'Well, that's good, but I'm afraid we have found out why they are recurring so often. I'm very sorry to tell you that the tests have shown that you have bladder cancer. I'm genuinely sorry to have to give you such distressing news.'

My heart beat quickens. 'Cancer? No, that can't be right. I'm fine, Doctor. I feel as fit as a fiddle... Are you sure?'

'Yes, we're sure.'

'So what is the treatment, Doctor Chakrabati?' asks Sasha, jumping straight in before I can speak again.

'Well, to be honest, treatment will be difficult. We could consider surgery, but I wouldn't recommend it. Your mother is rather frail, and I'm not sure she'd withstand it. So our main options are chemotherapy and radiation, but both of these will be very tough, and she will need a lot of help to get through it.'

'What's the prognosis?' Sasha is twisting a tissue round and round her finger.

'It's hard to tell, but it's not hugely optimistic. I'm afraid the cancer seems to be fairly advanced.'

'Sasha, Sasha.' I wave my hand at Sasha to beckon her over to me. Sasha rises from her chair. 'Sasha, we need to go now. I need the toilet,' I whisper in her ear. I've left it too late and my trousers feel wet. Sasha and the doctor exchange a look.

'Take your time, Mrs Stein. I'll get a nurse to help you.' The doctor lifts up her telephone receiver and a nurse appears with a wheelchair. The nurse and Sasha transfer me to the chair and wheel me to a cubicle outside doctor's office. Sasha produces a set of clean underwear and trousers from her bag and together, they help me to change. I don't know where Sasha got my dry clothes from. I thank the nurse profusely and then we go back to see the doctor.

I am back at home now and feel completely wrung out. I don't know why we had to go out when the weather is so cold. I'm sitting in my armchair with a blanket over my knees. Sasha has put the fire on and has made me a cup of coffee, but it's too hot to drink.

'Mummy, can I make you something to eat?'

'No, I'm not hungry, but you can fetch me a glass of white wine. There's some left in the fridge. Then you go home and leave me alone.'

'We need to talk first, Mummy, about what the doctor said.'

'What does that doctor know? I'm fine, Sasha. Stop worrying and go home.'

'I'll go soon, Mummy, but I think you're going to need some help here in the bungalow. If you're going to have the treatment, or even if you're not, you're not going to feel very well, and I can't be here the whole time. The doctor wants to send someone round to talk to you about finding someone who can come in to see you every day.'

'I'm not having any strangers in my house!' Why can't Sasha look after me? That's what daughters are supposed to do, but let's face it, I have never been able to rely on her. My own father died at home, and then my mother had to go into a home, but that was only because Joe wouldn't let me bring her to our house to look after her. She died there within the year, wilting before my eyes. Well, I'm not going into a home full of old, smelly people, and I'm not having anyone in my house either. I'm not a bloody geriatric. Where's my wine?

'Mummy, it's not a question of what you want at this point. We have to think about what you actually need. I know it's difficult, but when I'm not here, I worry about you falling, or getting to the toilet in time, or making food for yourself. It's not going to get any easier, so you have to be sensible.' Sasha is crying, feeling sorry for herself. She never was much of a coper, not like me.

'Sasha, pull yourself together, for goodness sake. I can manage on my own, thank you very much, and you're only round the corner if I need you. Let's not be over-dramatic, shall we?'

'I'm not exaggerating, Mum. I'm at least half an hour away by car, and when I'm out working, I am often much further away. You've just got to recognise that I will always do my best, but you also have to realise that you'll have to accept some help from other people as well.'

'Don't raise your voice to me, young lady. After everything I've done for you, is it too much to ask that it's you who looks after me in my old age?'

'After everything you've done for me?' Sasha reels away and smashes her hand down hard on the dining table. The candlesticks tinkle. 'What exactly have you done for me? You've never shown me any affection, even as a small child. You're critical and vindictive. I don't think I've ever had a compliment from you – or even a well done – at any point in my life. That's been hard enough to live with – to have a mother who fundamentally dislikes me – but I've learnt to live with it and to expect nothing from you. I can just about handle all of that, but you are forgetting something that I can never forgive. You're conveniently forgetting that I left you in charge of Sebastian and he died in your care. My poor innocent baby died when you were in charge, and I spend every day wishing it had been me in that cot, and not him. It's a miracle that I still see you, that I still speak to you at all. And you've never once said that you're sorry. Not once. Not ever.' Sasha crumples to the floor, sobbing and sniffing. I touch my face and it's wet too.

'Sasha, Sebastian is dead. I didn't kill him. It just happened.'

'But you were drinking when you were in charge of him. You didn't check on him during the night. He was all alone.'

'I looked after him just exactly the same way that I'd looked after you as a baby. If you'd have died in your sleep, I would have had to accept it, just as you have to accept that Sebastian died. It was just one of those things.' My head is thumping. I want her to leave.

'Just one of those things?' Sasha is whispering. I can barely hear her. 'Sebastian was just one of those things?'

'I didn't mean it like that.'

'So what exactly did you mean?'

'I mean that these things happen and there's nothing we can do to stop them. It's fate.'

'*These things happen? It's fate?*' Sasha is staring at me, her face contorted into an ugly smile.

'Sasha, it was a long time ago. There are worse things that can happen in life, believe me. You think I haven't been a good mother, but I've done the best I can. You have had a good life, by and large. You've lost a baby boy, but you have another beautiful son, who you love and he loves you. You've had a good life with Jeremy for many years, and even though that's over, and you're hurt and humiliated, your life will get better. You just can't see that at the moment. But you must appreciate what you have. At one point, I wasn't sure if you should have a life at all, but I decided to do my best by you. That's all I could do at the time. You can't ask me to give you much more than life itself.' I am so tired and I really need a drink. Sasha needs to go, so that I can drink my wine and go to bed.

'What are you talking about? You weren't sure if I should have a life? What the hell do you mean?' Sasha is screaming at me now, like she used to when she was a little girl. I start to heave myself up in my chair.

'I don't know what I mean, Sasha. I'm sorry. I'm sorry about Sebastian. He was a gorgeous baby and I was devastated when he died. Your father and I both were. I felt guilty, of course I did, but what could I say to you? What could I ever do to make it up to you? I'm sorry

I never apologised at the time, but it wasn't my fault. Sebastian just slipped away while he was sleeping, while we were all sleeping. What could I have done? Really? What else do you think I could have done?' I haul myself upright with my stick and shuffle over to where Sasha lies groaning on the floor. 'Can you help me get into bed? I'm tired.' Sasha unfurls and stands up. She takes me by the arm and leads me up the short corridor to my bedroom. She helps me undress in silence, pulling my nightdress over my head and placing panty liners into my knickers for me to step into. She brings me a glass of wine and one of water and places them on my bedside table. I'll swallow a sleeping pill with the wine when she leaves. I've never been able to sleep without one, not since they were prescribed to me after I came back from Carnforth as a child. I lay my head back on the soft pillows and sink into them as I hear the front door slam shut.

Sasha

My weekly dose of Zumba and sex – or Sexba night, as I'd call it in my head – was about the only thing keeping me going. I had suggested to Jeremy that it was less disruptive for Zac is we could arrange for him to stay over at Jeremy's place every Thursday, which coincidentally was the night I went to the gym. I followed the same pattern every week. Zac came home from school and I fed him in time for Jeremy to pick him up. Then I raced out of the door and down to the leisure centre for my evening dose of Sexba. Harry and I had dispensed with the wine bar after the first week, and now he came back to my place after the class, where we ate and made love, or made love and ate, or sometimes, we attempted both at the same time. I realised how totally inexperienced I was as a lover. I'd only slept with two men in my entire life, which meant that I was practically a virgin. I couldn't remember what the sex had been like with Neil – it was, after all, over thirty years ago – but I had a vague recollection that it was frequent and relatively short. With Jeremy, it had been very irregular – high days and holy days – and it was, well, perfunctory. I don't think either of us enjoyed it very much and, as a result, we didn't think about it that much either. Harry, on the other hand, had woken up parts of me which had lain dormant forever, and it was both exhilarating and exhausting.

We lay in bed, Harry tracing small post-coital circles around my spine. 'What are you doing with me?' I murmured.

'I would have thought that would be quite obvious, madam,' Harry laughed.

'No seriously. Why me? Why not choose someone nearer your own age, without the wrinkles and the stretch marks and the flab?'

'I have a fetish for wrinkles, stretch marks and most especially flab.' I picked up a pillow and hit him on the head with it. 'You're being ridiculous, Sasha.' He rolled me over and I pulled the duvet up to cover my breasts. 'I'm with you because I think you're gorgeous and sexy and funny and well, just lovely. Now where was I? Just about here, I think…'

'Harry!'

I knew that this thing with Harry, whatever it was, was temporary, but it was just what I needed. When I was with him, I could forget about Jeremy, and about the divorce, and about Zac's imminent round-the-world adventure and, of course, about my mother. I hadn't spoken to my mother for a couple of days after our trip to the hospital. I knew it was unkind of me, especially in light of the news she'd been given, but I was so wounded by our conversation that I needed some time to calm down. Maybe, when you get to be much older – the age my mother now was – you could rationalise life and say that things just happen. Maybe you could believe in fate. I also recognised that, when I was wearing my rational mind, some babies do just die in the night, and that Sebastian may have passed away in his sleep just as easily if I had been there, rather than my mother. But what I couldn't understand was her total lack of remorse. At least she has finally apologised, but it wasn't heartfelt. What had struck me to the core, however, was her unerring belief that it was enough to have brought me into this world and that beyond that, I was effectively on my own. And having never been able to rely on her, she now expected to be completely reliant on me. Life is like delicately balancing on a see saw. We spend the first part trying to climb up one side, aiming for the stability in the centre, but no sooner have we reached the middle, than we career back down the other side again. Zac was inching up the first half of the slope and, at some point soon, we would balance there momentarily, precariously, together, two adults able to have vaguely sane conversations. Yet before you knew it, I would be the one slipping down the other side and Zac would have to manage my fall.

It was plain that my mother was fading. I'd spoken to the doctor the day after our visit and it seemed obvious that little could be done for her now. The medical opinion seemed to be that surgery was impossible, and that chemotherapy and radiation would prove too much for her, so we had to let the cancer do its dastardly work. I wondered how much she really understood about her condition. She had already forgotten about the hospital and the doctor's visit and she did not appear to be in much pain. It was perhaps a blessing that her mind had deteriorated in step with her body. The worst thing was that I didn't know what I felt. I didn't know if I would be sad when she died, or if I would feel nothing at all. I sat Zac down and explained the situation to him. 'Zac, Grandma is very unwell.'

Zac was prone on the sofa in the lounge, watching football. It wasn't his team, so I felt permitted to speak. He glanced over to me. 'I'm sorry to hear that. Is it another infection?'

'No, I'm afraid not. We went to the hospital and the doctor said she had cancer of the bladder.'

Zac said nothing for a moment, and then put the game on pause. 'So what can they do?'

'Not very much, I'm afraid. She's too old, and it's too advanced for them to operate. She won't withstand the chemo. It's just a question now of managing the pain, I think.'

Zac put the remote down on the coffee table, and sitting himself up, shuffled across the sofa to me. He reached out and gave me an imperceptible hug. 'I'm really sorry, Mum. So, did they say how long she's got?' He looked very pale, suddenly younger and slightly disorientated, reminding me of when he used to wake me with his bad dreams in the middle of the night.

'No, they can't really say, but we need to be prepared, so I just thought you should know. Try not to worry about it too much.'

I kissed him on the cheek and gave him another hug. Then he turned back to the television and the game resumed.

I missed being able to talk to Jeremy. Despite the fact that our marriage had turned out to be spurious, we had been such good friends. He had always been a sympathetic listener and had generally given me good counsel. I needed him now more than ever. When Sebastian died, Jeremy held me together. I knew how much he was hurting too, but he took all my pain on himself, as well as his own, and absorbed it. He supported me through my neurotic pregnancy with Zac, when I was convinced that there was something wrong with the baby in the womb, and then, even worse, once he was born. I kept myself, Jeremy and Zac awake for the first two years after Zac's birth, because I was too paranoid to allow anyone of us to sleep through the night. Even after that, every childhood illness became a trauma. Zac's forthcoming travels would be no easier for me to manage. I thought of asking him not to go, given how ill his grandmother was, but I knew that wasn't fair and who knew how long she would be ill. My mother had the constitution of an ox, having withstood a lifetime of alcohol, which would have floored most mortals. I suspected she'd be with us for a long while yet.

Annie

I'm coming to see you soon, Joe. But before I do, there's something I've got to tell you. It happened a long time ago, so I hope that you can forgive me for lying to you about it. I think that if I'd told you the truth at the time, you would have walked away, and I would have just been another girl alone and in trouble.

I'm working late one Friday night in October in the atelier for Syd and Freda. The nights are drawing in and the weather has turned colder. We've had a hectic week, as all the main buyers have been in to place their orders for Spring/Summer. I've spent the last three weeks taking my clothes on and off to model the new range for the buyers – it's been no fun, as the gas heater has packed up – as well as helping Freda with the mountains of paperwork generated after each meeting. At the end of every day, we have to work through the order forms, so that we know how much of each garment every store wants, and then we place all the orders. I keep a file for each supplier, and I mark the quantities and order dates in red, so that I can keep track of them. We've finally got through to Friday and I'm really looking forward to seeing you on Sunday, if you can get up here after your show, Joe.

'Annie, well done on all your hard work this week, my love. We couldn't have done it without you. The orders are up massively on last year, and it's all down to you and that gorgeous figure of yours. You're irresistible, darling!' Syd flounces over, his red silk handkerchief bouncing in his top pocket, and plants a huge sloppy kiss on my cheek. 'This calls for a huge celebration. Let's all pop off to The Midland for a few sniftas before bed, shall we?' Syd pulls a wad of five pounds notes out of his pocket and thumbs through them, before putting them back and patting his trousers contentedly.

'Well, I'm definitely gasping for a very strong G&T, Syd,' says Freda, rising stiffly from the wooden table in the back room where we kept the garments and did all the accounting. She grabbed her coat off the umbrella stand and rammed her blue felt hat firmly onto her head. 'Coming, Annie?'

'Yes, absolutely, but I just want to finish tidying up in the back here. Some of the dresses aren't on their hangers properly. They're such pretty pastels, and I don't want them to get marked. And I need to put the files away.' The place is a tip and it will take me the best part of an hour to sort it out, but I know they'll be in the bar for hours, so there was no hurry.

'Such attention to detail, darling. You really are priceless. OK then, Freda, let's go. See you shortly, Annie. Will you lock up?'

'No problem. I'll follow you over there as soon as I've finished here.'

Syd wraps his paisley scarf around his neck with a theatrical flourish, places his black fedora firmly onto his head and holds out his arm to Freda. 'Shall we, my love?' They both wave and then I hear the faint thud of the front door.

I pick up a gown made from a pale pink silk with layers of chiffon under the skirt. When I wear it for the customers, I feel like Grace Kelly in *High Society*. I find a padded hanger and thread the sleeves onto it, using the dressmaking straps to secure them, while humming the tune to *Who Wants To Be A Millionaire* as I work. I am just about to hang it on the rail when the doorbell trills. It's very late for a delivery, but sometimes samples do arrive after hours. I lay the dress carefully over the battered chaise longue in the corner of the room by the garment rails, and walk through to the front to answer the door. The bell rings again as I hurry through the showroom, its mannequins dressed as if leaving for a debutante ball. 'I'm just coming,' I call out. As I open the heavy wooden door, a gust of cold air rushes in. I shudder and rub my arms with my hands. 'Oh, Mr Elliott. Hello again. How can I help you?' He is leaning casually on the door post, chewing a toothpick.

'Miss Brewer. Hello, I'm sorry to trouble you so late in the day, but I think I left my cigarette case behind when I was here earlier today.' He lifts his black felt trilby slightly, before replacing it low over his eyes, and smiles at me. A gold molar glints as his mouth moves over the toothpick.

'Oh, it's no problem at all. Do come in for a moment. I'm afraid Syd and Freda have just left and I must admit, I haven't seen your cigarette case, but then, I wasn't looking for it particularly. Have you any idea where you think you might have dropped it?'

'Well, I was sitting on the sofa here in the showroom for most of the time I was with you guys earlier – watching you parade up and down like a princess – but I also went out through the back to the gentleman's. So it might be anywhere. I'll help you to look.'

I lead the way through the dark hallway, which runs from the front door into the main showroom, and Mr Elliott follows me. I had not met him before today, as he had just taken over from the usual buyer. He is a burly, lumbering man, probably six foot two or three maybe, and he lurches slightly to the left as he walks. Maybe it's an old war wound or something, as I'm guessing that he must be in his late thirties, so he probably served. I can't quite place his accent either, but he sounds like he might be a Geordie, or something like that. I search around the sofa, bending down to feel under the cushions, and I look under the chairs and the coffee table, lifting up pattern books, rolls of ribbon and pin cushions, but I can't see a cigarette case. Mr Elliott does not appear to be helping, but I am aware of his eyes on me as I do the searching.

'Well, I'm afraid I can't see it anywhere, Mr Elliott. What exactly does it look like?'

'It's a silver case with my initials on it: T.E. for Thomas Elliott. Perhaps I did drop it in the back office after all?'

'Perhaps, but I have been in there for the past hour or so, and I've definitely not seen it. Wait here and I'll have a quick look for you.'

Mr Elliott now stands by the entrance to the back office and I have to squeeze past him to see if I can find his wretched silver case. I want him to leave. I'm tired, and Syd and Freda will be wondering where I've got to. I lift the dress, which I had laid over the chaise longue earlier when the bell rang, to see if it is underneath.

'Put it on.'

I jump, and my heart seems to stop momentarily. 'Mr Elliott, you gave me a fright. I'm afraid your case isn't here. I'll ask Syd and Freda on Monday if they remember spotting it and we'll call to let you know. I'm afraid I'll have to see you out now, as the others are expecting me for drinks.'

'I said, put it on.'

His face has darkened. I am standing at the end of the chaise longue with the wall of garment rails behind me. He moves towards me and grabs the top of my arm, pulling me towards him. His breath stinks of whisky and stale cigarettes.

'Mr Elliott, please let go of my arm. I must ask you to leave.'

He presses my arm tighter and seizes my other arm, driving me closer to his face, until his mouth is an inch away from mine. 'I want you to wear that dress for me again. The one you wore earlier. You looked like a film star.'

'I'm afraid I can't do that, Mr Elliott. We're closed now, and I'm not allowed to wear the stock when I'm alone. I really must ask you to let go of my arms and to leave now, please. You're hurting me.' My breathing is too fast and I need the toilet. I look around, thinking about a possible escape route, but the back door is hidden behind the garment rails, and it is bolted unless we are receiving deliveries. Mr Elliott is blocking the only other possible exit out to the showroom.

'I'll leave when I'm done, Annie.'

He tightens his grip, wrapping an arm around my waist and forcing his mouth onto mine, which I try to keep closed, but he's too strong and forces his tongue onto my teeth. His stubble scratches at my cheek. He releases one of my arms and tugs hard on the collar of my shirt. I hear a ripping sound and I feel cold air on my chest. He pushes against me and my knees touch the edge of the sofa. He shoves again, and I fall backwards onto the pale pink gown, which I have yet to hang. Mr Elliott somehow manages to grab both of my wrists at the same time and pins them above my head. He picks up a length of ribbon from the work table beside the chaise longue and wraps it around them tightly. He then ties my wrists to the arm of the chaise. I try to kick him, but his weight is on top of me now and I can't move my legs. His hands are free and he starts to rip again...my bra, my skirt, my panties. I scream, but no sound comes out of my mouth. He lifts his head away from mine and undoes his trousers, forcing my legs apart. I feel a searing pain as he enters. I don't know how long he stays there, pounding and pounding. I dig my nails into my hands until I cut the skin, trying to distract myself from the stabbing spasms. Suddenly, he strains and drops the whole of his weight on top of me for a few moments, before he stands, puts himself away and removes his cigarette case casually from his jacket pocket. 'Ah, I seem to have found what I was looking for. It was in my top pocket the whole time. Thanks for your help, kid.'

Mr Elliott extracts a cigarette, lights it and stands there, surveying me in my naked wretchedness. Then he bends towards me. I flinch, but he merely unties the ribbon before turning to leave, whistling as he waltzes away. I hear his thick footsteps as he carves through the showroom, and then the front door slams. I just lie there. I can't stop shaking. I'm so cold.

The chiffon gown is crushed and badly stained. I have no idea how I will explain it to Syd and Freda. My own shirt is ruined, as is my underwear. I find a bag to put them in. I'll throw them away on the way home, somewhere where no one will find them. I have a sweater over the chair by the work desk, which I usually wear as an extra layer of warmth when I'm working on the paperwork in the back, so I put that on and then throw my overcoat on top. I still can't stop shivering. The tops of my legs sting and burn, and I can feel bruises forming on my upper arms. I need to get this dress clean. I find a dishcloth and wet it slightly to blot the gown. The stain blooms more deeply pink, but I know that I can remove a silk stain this way with patience. I work on it for an hour so, alternately blotting the stain with water, and then with a dry cloth, and then I repeat the same process several times until it begins to fade. Eventually I hang the dress to air. I can come back over the weekend to do it again, and then press it. I hope by Monday there will be no trace of the stain, but it seems unlikely. This has to work, because it will take me weeks of wages to pay for the dress if it's ruined. I wash my face in the sink and dab it with a towel. Then I tie up the belt on my coat and pull on my shoes. I lock the heavy door behind me and step out onto the dark street to catch the bus home.

Sasha

We had to move my mother to a hospice. She had deteriorated faster than I had expected, shrinking into herself before my eyes. The harsh, unforgiving person I had always known had metamorphosed into a frail old lady, who acquiesced to whatever anyone said or did. It was unnerving. Going to the hospice wasn't like visiting someone in hospital, where there was hope that they would recover and you knew that you could take them home eventually. The hospice was like walking into the valley of death, yet bizarrely it wasn't a miserable valley. The nurses and doctors were cheery, positive, utterly amazing individuals, laughing and crying their way through the day and night with us. It was a strangely uplifting experience.

Mum was on morphine and not making much sense, babbling on about stains on a pink silk dress, silver cigarette cases and running away with a horse named Derek. Sometimes, she became angry, calling the nurses unforgiveable names and accusing them of stealing her furniture. They just smiled and assured her that they were too busy to rob her house at that moment in time. She wagged her finger at them and told me to go to speak to them, to ward them off. I sat with her and listened to her babble, nodding along, sometime cringing at what she said, and holding her head up so that she could take sips of water, or a teaspoonful of ice cream. I took Zac to see her on a couple of occasions, but he found it very hard to manage. Death for the young is so much more terrifying than for those of us in middle age, who have already experienced others passing on and are that bit closer to death ourselves.

When I visited on one occasion, my mother was very agitated. She was propped up on several pillows and her face was ashen. She said that she needed to speak to Joe.

'You want to speak to Daddy?'

'No, I don't want to speak to your father. I want to talk to Joe.'

'Joe is Daddy, isn't he, Mummy? I think you're getting a bit muddled up.'

'No, I'm not.' Mum frowned and tried to shout at me, but her voice lacked all strength and her vehemence faded into the air. She waved me away with her hand. 'Not your father. Joe. I want to speak to Joe. I need to tell him something important – something I didn't tell him before.'

'Mummy, Daddy's not here. You can't speak to him at the moment.' I didn't want to tell her that my father died so many years ago. I didn't want her to have to grieve all over again.

'I only let him in because of the cigarette case, you know. The dress was quite ruined. I never got the stain of it, no matter how hard I tried. I need to speak to Joe. I need tell him.'

My mother went on repeating herself, again and again. Finally, she exhausted herself and me, falling back asleep on her pillows with her mouth open. She must have been talking about some incident at a party or something. They used to have some pretty wild nights out together in the early days, before I was born, or so I understand. Dad used to tell me about how Mum would love going to parties and meeting people, but that once she had me, she withdrew and preferred to stay at home and host dinner parties there instead, until even these dwindled away. I watched her lying in her bed, swallowed up in the jaws of her pillows, snoring softly. She used to be such a tall, statuesque, beautiful woman, but now I towered over her. She seemed to be curling in on herself, preparing for death. I sat by her bed for hours, holding her hand and talking to her, or reading to her, even when I was fairly sure that she couldn't hear me. There was so much I wanted to ask her about her life, but I knew I couldn't. We hadn't spoke about so very much over the course of our lives and now it just seemed to be too late.

It was supposed to be Sexba night, but I was at the hospice. Harry and I were on the way to an amicable separation anyway. I had too much on my mind, and he needed someone closer to his own age, not so preoccupied with teenage sons, soon to be ex-husbands and dying mothers. I wasn't that much fun to be around. I was flicking through a copy of a gossip magazine, lying on a table in the deserted communal room. The room was ice cold, with six fraying red armchairs in sensible wipe down plastic, and a small television set on maximum volume in the corner. Inside the magazine, a variety of orange-skinned women with huge bosoms and even larger lips and hair smiled out of the pages shouting, 'Look at me! Look at my wonderful family! Behold my fabulous home!' I wondered whether my mother and father and even, heaven forbid, me as a child, might have adorned those pages, if such glossies had existed in those days:

At home with the sumptuous Steins. We meet them at their fabulous home in St Johns Wood, where they entertain the rich, famous and powerful. Come join us.

Mum's eyelids flickered and she opened her eyes, struggling to focus. 'Sasha, is that you?'

'Yes, Mum, it's me. Can I get you something?' I whispered.

'A little water, please.'

I put my hand under her head and helped her take a sip out of a plastic baby cup.

'Sasha, I've told Joe everything now, and I think he's alright about it. I did what I had to do, you see. I couldn't go to one of those backstreet places. I was too frightened and girls died in those days, you know. So I've told Joe that you are not his, and he is going to make it all OK.'

I tipped the cup too far and water spilt onto my mother's nightgown. I grabbed some tissues from the bedside table and mopped up the liquid with a shaking hand. I felt slightly nauseous and held onto the bottom of the chair, gripping it tightly.

'That awful man is part of you, but I've found you another father and he loves you. I gave you to Joe, and now he loves you more than he loves me. But I did my best, and I still try to do my best, you know that don't you, Sasha? But you must always be careful. He's waiting outside with his cigarette case.'

I suddenly felt icy cold and began to shiver. Tears fell slowly down my face and an unbidden noisy sob escaped from me. I stared at my mother, but she had closed her eyes. She looked relaxed, unburdened.

One of the nurses came over and patted me on the shoulder. 'How are you holding up? I don't think it will be long now, I'm afraid. Can I get you anything? You look a little pale. Would you like some water? A cup of tea, perhaps?'

I shook my head. 'No, thank you. I'm absolutely fine,' I answered in a strangulated voice. 'I'll be OK, thank you again. You're too kind.' The nurse smiled at me and walked away. Mum had fallen back to sleep and I watched her lying there through my net of tears.

Joe

There's a tipping point for all of us, beyond which we undergo an irreversible paradigm shift. I saw it in so many of my friends who waged war. They returned with altered personalities and shredded nerves to lead disconnected lives. If grown men cannot survive conflict unscathed, what chance is there for a child ripped from the bosom of their home and thrust into the arms of uncaring strangers? The damage done alters the course not only of one life, but of many. Those in their path must dodge and weave to avoid the flak, but inevitably shrapnel will hit you, and you must deal with the consequences. There is no point in apportioning blame, because in the end, it gets you nowhere. You must accept what life brings you, wipe your mouth, move forwards and walk on.

Sasha

Nine months after Mum died, I was still drowning in paperwork as I attempted to settle her affairs. It wasn't that they were particularly complicated, but rather that it was all down to me to manage and the process seemed interminable. Losing a parent was hard enough, but the accompanying administrative hell was truly intolerable. Tens of copies of death certificates were required by banks, insurers, solicitors, accountants, social security – virtually everyone. I even had to return her blue badge to the council. The bungalow was now on the market and I was painstakingly working my way through Mum's life, belonging by belonging.

She'd left everything to Zac. I'd suggested to her that she do so – he would need it more than I did – but it had still surprised me that she had followed my advice. Jeremy was helping me to set up a trust for Zac, which he could access when he was older. I was insistent that Zac did not receive the money now – even though he was eighteen – as I thought a young man in charge of reasonable fortune was a dangerous beast. Where would the incentive be to achieve a good degree, or to secure a decent job? Zac was blissfully unaware of his grandmother's bequest. He was currently on a beach in Thailand, engaging in various nefarious activities, which I tried not to think about. He skyped me whenever he came to a place with an internet connection, and my heart leapt when I saw his tanned, stubbled face. He had, as I had feared, lost various possessions on his travels, including his phone and at one point, his wallet, but I managed to wire him additional funds, so that he could carry on his adventures, and I could continue to fret. I missed him profoundly, but I found that it went in waves. Some days, it was a dull, manageable ache, yet at other times, it was a searing pain. Just three more months to go.

I was emptying the contents of my mother's wardrobe. She had hundreds of pairs of identical trousers and thousands of the same sweater in a variety of shades. Some clothes lay unopened, still encased in their packaging, Maybe I could sell them online. I'd arranged for an auction house to come to assess the furniture, as I had nowhere to store it, and Zac certainly wouldn't ever want a damson three piece suite with a matching poof. Before they arrived, I needed to clear out the cupboards and drawers. On the bed were organized piles of clothing: one for the charity shop, one for possible resale and a final one for the tip. Having emptied the rails, I started on the shoes and created the same pattern of piles for distribution. Mum's shoes were so different from the ones I remembered her wearing when I was a child. There were no precarious stiletto heels here; merely multifarious pairs of flats with decent grip. She had been forced into practicality.

As I reached to the back of the wardrobe, I felt a large cardboard box with a lid, the kind you might find in an office for storage. It was heavy and I had to use both hands to drag it out and onto the carpet. The lid was dusty and I wiped it with my sleeve before wiggling it off the box. Inside was a bundle of letters, piles of photographs, as well as a strange assortment of artifacts. Each item had a parcel label attached to it, or a sticker placed on the back, denoting its origin.

Red button:
First date with Joe.
Menu from the Midland Hotel:
Dinner Joe, Syd and Freda, December 1962
A flower pressed in cellophane:
Flower, Honeymoon, Nassau
An envelope containing a lock of hair:
Sasha's first haircut
A plastic bag of baby teeth:
Sasha's milk teeth
A large manila envelope:
Sasha's school reports

I squatted on the carpet until the light faded, unravelling the treasured highlights of my mother's life. There were so many memories mashed together. Old sepia photographs of her confirmation aged fourteen, glamorous polaroids of her modelling gorgeous gowns and hundreds of photographs of Mum and Dad posing with celebrities. But what shocked me most, what made me weep as I turned over photo after photo, item after item, was that the majority of memorabilia related to me. There I was smiling out at the camera, sporting silly hats and starchy dresses with ridiculous bows. I was cuddling my father, I was pulling funny faces, I was laughing. I was cradling Sebastian. Mum was kissing Sebastian, Mum had Zac on her knee, Zac and I were making a cake. It had all been buried.

My phone rang and woke me from my reverie. I retrieved my handbag from under a pile of tip-bound shoes and fumbled to answer. It was Zac. I pressed the button to accept the Skype call and he faced me.

'Hi, Mum. How are you? Hey, are you OK? You look sort of puffy.'

I sniffed loudly and wiped my eyes with the back of my hand. 'I'm OK, Zac. Don't worry about me. I was just clearing up at Grandma's and I found a box of old photos. I suppose they just made me feel a bit sad, that's all.'

'Oh, I'm sorry, Mum. 'Fraid I can't give you a proper hug, but here's a virtual one,' Zac laughed, as he wrapped his arms around himself.

I smiled and blew my nose loudly on a scrofulous tissue I'd found stuffed up my sleeve. 'Thanks, darling. I really miss you, you know that.'

'I miss you too, Mum, and I miss Grandma. It's seems so weird that she's not here anymore.'

'I miss her too, Zac, I really do.'

Joe

Just because you cannot say I love you does not mean
that you do not love.